A Few Dead Men

A Hellbound Western

Van Holt

King of the Hellbound Westerns

CHAPTER 1

The two men met on the trail, strangers with only one thing in common—they happened to be going in the same direction.

They did have one other thing in common, a deadly skill with firearms, but they did not discuss that at the time, though each was curious about the other.

Ben Cobbett would never see thirty again. Joe Deegan would never see thirty at all.

Cobbett was a tall lean man with pale hair, bleak gray eyes and a weathered brown face that might have been carved from solid rock. He wore a dust-colored hat, a faded corduroy coat, gray trousers, and a walnut-butted Colt .45 on his right hip.

Joe Deegan was about two inches shorter, five ten or a little better. He had rich dark chestnut hair, laughing blue eyes and a smooth round baby face that made him look younger than his actual age of twenty-five. He wore a black hat, black leather vest, blue shirt, black trousers and a black gun belt, with the holster and ivory-handled Colt .44 on the left side. He also rode a beautiful black horse that Cobbett suspected was stolen. Cobbett's own gelding was a rangy sorrel, and he had a bill of sale in his saddlebag.

As it was getting late, the two men decided to camp for the night beside a little stream near the trail. They took care of the horses first, then boiled coffee, cooked bacon and beans and pan bread. It was fall in the high desert country, warm days, cold nights, and the fire felt good. The hot coffee was fine also, and Cobbett sipped a second cup while Deegan finished the beans and bacon.

Deegan studied Cobbett with his smiling blue eyes. The younger man, not yet saddened by age or experience, seemed to find everything mildly amusing—even the bleak humorless face of Ben Cobbett and the high-peaked Montana hat he wore. Or perhaps it was Cobbett's neatly trimmed mustache that was a lot darker than his hair.

"You from Montana?" Deegan asked.

"I was there a few years," Cobbett said quietly. In keeping with western tradition he had not asked any questions himself, would not ask any.

Joe Deegan laughed quietly at the older man's taciturnity, his blank-faced disapproval of the question. Deegan was a young man and he did not have much regard for customs he considered out-of-date, especially as lawmen had never hesitated to break tradition and question him. He had little doubt that Cobbett had worn a badge at one time or another. He looked like the type—Deegan often bragged that he could spot a lawman a mile away.

Deegan drank his coffee thoughtfully, a hint of malice in his grin. He reflected that many ex-lawmen, without their badge to shield them, became sensitive and secretive about their former occupation. And well they might, for there were a lot of men around who would jump at a chance to fill them full of holes. Deep down nobody had much use for a lawman. Outlaws were a lot more popular.

"What were you back in Montana?" Deegan asked finally. "Lawman?"

"For a while," Cobbett answered shortly.

"I figgered you were," Deegan said. "I can always spot a lawman. Something different about them."

"I'm not a lawman anymore."

Deegan showed his white teeth in a hard grin. "They'll try to pin a badge as you the minute you ride into Rockville. The last marshal has prob'ly been shot by now. They bury one about once a month."

Cobbett finished his coffee and laid the tin cup aside. His face seemed even harder in the flickering firelight. "I'm through wearing a badge," he said. "I figure it's time I tried something else."

"If you ever aim to, it is," Deegan agreed. He glanced at the pale hair under Cobbett's hat. "That hair gray, or has it always been like that?"

"Might be a little gray in it. Seems to be getting lighter anyway."

Deegan chuckled. "Well, I guess everybody gets old sometime."

Cobbett's cold gray eyes narrowed a little. "Yeah, if they live long enough."

"How old are you anyway, Cobbett?" Deegan asked.

"Thirty-four."

Deegan's surprise showed. "Hell, I figgered you were closer to forty."

"Lot of people figgered that," Cobbett grunted. "I believe I'll turn in. Old man like me needs his rest."

"I think I'll ride on to Rockville," Joe Deegan decided. "It's only a couple more hours, and the boys are more likely to be in town at night. I ain't seen them for a while.

"Suit yourself." Cobbett was already spreading his blankets.

Deegan looked at him for a moment, then shivered and glanced at the sky. "You gonna get wet," he said. "I think it's gonna rain."

"I've been wet before."

Rockville was a one-street town of false-fronted frame buildings, surrounded on three sides by boulder-strewn hills and sagebrush. Just east of the town there was a stream in wet weather, a dry wash at other times. Once a few cottonwood trees had grown along the wash, but there were none left near the town. They had been used for lumber and firewood.

To Joe Deegan the place looked as if it had shriveled up and died. He had only been gone a few weeks, but evidently his memory had already started playing tricks on him. He had remembered a wide street filled with people on foot scrambling to get out of the way of wild riders galloping into town and firing their guns into the air. And on either side bigger buildings, mostly saloons and gambling halls, brightly lit with chandeliers and glowing in the dark, and noisy with the clink of chips, the tinkle of glass, the jingle of spurs, and the laughter of girls in gaudy low-cut dresses. But there was none of that. At ten o'clock the town was dark and quiet and almost deserted, with dim lights showing in only a few buildings and half a dozen horses tied in front of a saloon.

Toward the saloon Joe Deegan drifted, his face lighting up when he recognized the horses. He swung down at the rail, tied the black, and went in through the swing doors, spurs jingling, a reckless carefree smile on his round baby face. It was good to be back, even better when he saw the five men at the bar turn and start grinning from ear to ear. They were his pals, the fun-loving, work-hating boys he rode and rustled with. Even the bartender's bulldog face cracked in a grin. Even old Duffy Shaw, who had a heart like stone, was glad to see him back, and it was always good to see a friendly face, even one like Duffy's.

"I'll be a suck-egg mule!" Barney Nash roared. "If it ain't Joe Deegan, in the livin' flesh!"

The others greeted Deegan as he stepped up to the bar beside Nash and ordered a whiskey. Nash was a rock-hard heavyset bruiser wearing a small derby on his huge head, a tacky green coat and a red shirt that hung outside his striped trousers. By now he had killed at least a bottle by himself and his dark-stubbled red face had a bloated look. His mean little eyes were bloodshot and bleary and there was a kind of challenge in them, in spite of his show of friendliness. He had long suspected Deegan of trying to take his gang away from him, replace him as the leader, and he probably wasn't as happy to see the baby-faced killer back as he pretended.

"How was Cheyenne?" Barney asked, his voice a natural roar.

Deegan rolled and licked and lit a cigarette. "I didn't go to Cheyenne."

"You didn't?" Barney asked. "You said you was!"

Deegan glanced at the heavyset man, his blue eyes cold under slightly raised dark brows. "I changed my mind."

"Where the hell did you go?"

"Salt Lake."

"Salt Lake!" Barney Nash exclaimed. "What the hell did you go there for? Ain't nothin' there but a bunch of wife-beatin' Mormons."

Joe Deegan chuckled. "Then they must do a lot of beating, 'cause they sure got lots of wives."

Some of the boys laughed at that, and Chuck Moser, a big-toothed, pop-eyed young man, asked, "What was it like in Salt Lake, Joe?"

"Dead," Joe Deegan said. "Dead as this place." Then he squinted through his cigarette smoke and asked, "You boys been up to anything while I was gone?"

"Nothin' 'cept the usual," Barney Nash said, and a couple of the others chuckled. "Pickin's is gettin' slim and the competition tougher."

"The Pasco boys still acting tough?"

"'Bout like usual," Barney Nash said. Then he looked at Joe Deegan with a malicious grin. "They said if you ever come back around here they was gonna have you for breakfast."

Joe Deegan's blue eyes were narrow and cold under raised brows. "They better bring plenty of help."

Barney Nash spread his hamlike hands, watching Deegan with his mean little eyes. "Leave me and the boys out of it," he said. "It ain't our fight. It's between you and them. You got them sore foolin' around with Molly."

"They still better bring plenty of help," Joe Deegan said.

It was raining the next morning when Ben Cobbett rode into town. He left his horse at the livery stable, tramped through the mud with his saddlebags, blanket roll and Winchester and turned into the town's only hotel, brushing rain from his slicker and cleaning his boots as best he could before entering. At the desk he signed the register, climbed the stairs and cleaned up in his room.

He cleaned his guns, the Colt and the Winchester.

When the rain slacked off to a slow drizzle he left the hotel and crossed the mud to a restaurant for a late breakfast.

Just as he was finishing his bacon and eggs Joe Deegan came in with a cheerful grin. He sat down opposite Cobbett and laid his wet black hat on the table, running his fingers back through his wavy dark hair. "Saw you ride in," he said. "How you like our little town?"

Just then the waitress, who had barely spoken to Cobbett, came from the kitchen with a big smile and said, "Joe! When did you get back?"

"Last night," Deegan said, laughing quietly at her surprise.

"And you ain't even been in to say hello!" the waitress said. She was a rather pretty but tired-faced woman who appeared to be in her late twenties. She might have been either younger or older, for the dry climate had already gone to work on her face, making it hard to guess at her exact age.

Joe Deegan was still chuckling, pleased with the world, but pleased most of all with Joe Deegan. "It was raining too hard," he said. "Jane, this here is Ben Cobbett. He used to be a lawman back in Montana. Jane Keller, Ben."

Jane Keller glanced sharply at Cobbett, then looked at Joe Deegan in surprise. "He's a friend of yours?"

Deegan glanced at Cobbett and showed his white teeth in a generous smile. "Sure," he said and shrugged. "Everybody's my friend, Jane. You know that."

Jane Keller's sun-cured face was serious and her green eyes were worried. "I don't know," she said. "George and Dave Pasco say they ran you out of town and you better not ever come back."

Joe Deegan's laughing baby blue eyes suddenly narrowed and turned cold. But he quickly erased that expression and said easily, "Them boys just enjoy hearing theirselves talk. They didn't mean no harm."

"You're only saying that, Joe. Everybody knows they've got it in for you." Then she said, "Molly Hicks was in town the other day."

Joe Deegan's eyes brightened with interest. "She pretty as ever?"

The waitress pursed her lips. "She's pretty all right," she said in a way that seemed to leave a lot unsaid. "What can I bring you, Joe?"

"A big platter of steak and potatoes and about a gallon of black coffee," Deegan said cheerfully.

She glanced at Cobbett's cup. "Can I get you anything else? How about some more coffee?"

"You could fill it back up."

Joe Deegan chuckled and winked at the waitress. "A man of few words."

About to turn away, the waitress raised her brows as if she thought even those few would be better left unsaid. She looked suspiciously at the former lawman, then smiled at Joe Deegan, a known rustler and horse thief. Cobbett had heard about the baby-faced outlaw even before meeting him on the trail yesterday.

The waitress went into the kitchen and returned with the coffee-pot and a cup for Deegan. She filled both cups, then paused beside Deegan's chair, glancing down at him. "Are your friends still in town? I heard them making noise down at Duffy Shaw's saloon last night."

Deegan grinned. "I left them sleeping it off on the saloon floor. That's where I spent the night myself, as a matter of fact."

"I wish you wouldn't hang around with that bunch, Joe," Jane Keller said. "They're going to get you in bad trouble one of these days. I know you ride with them just for the fun and excitement, but they're no good, Joe. A bad lot, all of them, and Barney Nash is worse than the others. He'd cut his own mother's throat just for the fun of it." Then she glanced uneasily at Cobbett, as if worried that she might have said too much.

Joe Deegan also looked at the ex-lawman, but he did not seem in the least worried. Rather he seemed to be enjoying himself. "They won't get me in no trouble," he said. "I'm more likely to get them in trouble."

"You shouldn't say things like that, Joe," Jane Keller said, again glancing at Cobbett. "I know you don't mean it, but others might get the wrong impression."

Deegan grinned. "You don't have to worry about Cobbett. He claims he's through being a lawman. But I figure somebody will try to pin a badge on him if he stays around here long."

The waitress gave Cobbett a guarded look. "Do you plan to stay in Rockville long, Mr. Cobbett?"

Cobbett was sitting back in his chair with his coffee, looking through the window with bleak eyes. It had started raining again. "Not long," he said.

The waitress looked relieved. She shifted her glanced back to Deegan and said with a smile, "I'll be right out with your breakfast, Joe. Would you settle for some bacon and eggs, like Mr. Cobbett had?"

Deegan shrugged, grinning his indifference. "Sure," he said, "If you'll throw in the hen."

Jane Keller smiled and went into the kitchen.

"Raining again," Joe Deegan said. "Looks like I'm gonna get wet yet." He smiled at Cobbett. "I can't stay in here long, or that girl would try to have me up before a preacher."

"You might do worse."

"She's more your type, Cobbett," Deegan said. "She'd start trying to reform me the first thing. She'd tell that preacher we'd be back in church on Sunday."

Cobbett did not say anything. His long weathered face was blank as if he had not been listening.

Joe Deegan regarded him with mild amusement. "You met the marshal yet? You two might hit it off."

"Not yet," Cobbett said.

"He don't leave his office much when it's rainy like this," Deegan said. "I was surprised we didn't have a new one by now, but one of the boys said it was still the same one, Tobe Langley. Maybe you've heard of him. Around here he's known as a bad man with a gun."

"The name doesn't ring a bell."

Deegan shrugged. "Well, Montana's a long ways from here. What brought you out this way anyhow, Cobbett?"

"Just riding," Cobbett said. "I've always had the feeling that if I kept on going, sooner or later I'd find what I'm looking for. It comes on me every two or three years and I quit whatever I'm doing and hit the trail again."

"What are you looking for?"

"Maybe that's the trouble," Cobbett said. "I don't know."

Joe Deegan chuckled. He seemed to find the tall quiet man more and more amusing. Perhaps not wanting Cobbett to leave and deprive him of entertainment, he said, "Maybe you should hang around here a while. You might find whatever you're looking for."

"I doubt that," Cobbett said. "I guess I'll push on when it quits raining and my horse gets a few days' rest."

Chapter 2

As Cobbett was leaving the restaurant, a huge man in a wide hat and a yellow slicker pulled up in a buckboard. The man gaped at him and yelled as he started back across the muddy street, "Ben Corbett! I'll be a son of a gun, if it ain't Ben Corbett, here in Rockville!"

Cobbett turned and peered through the drizzling rain at the huge figure in the slicker. Under the wide-brimmed hat the man's face was round and strong, set off by a great beak of a nose and muttonchop whiskers. Cobbett had never seen him before. He would hardly forget a face like that.

He shook his head. "Afraid you've got the wrong man."

"I've got the right man! I was in Miles City a couple of years back when you was the law there! They told me what a fine job you was doin'. I was goin' to introduce myself, but somethin' come up, I forget what, and then you rode out with a posse to round up some cow thieves! It wasn't even yore job, you only bein' the town marshal, but you went anyway!" The big man on the buckboard bared yellow teeth and cackled. For so huge a fellow he had a high, almost shrill voice. He seemed a little cracked. "Now that's the kind of law I like!" he cried, obviously wanting the whole town to hear him. "I always wished I'd gone along with you boys and talked you into comin' back here to Rockville with me! You're the kind of lawman we need around here! Not what we've got now!"

The big man turned on the seat and rolled his eyes angrily. Glancing in the same direction, Cobbett saw a bulky figure standing in the door of the marshal's office.

Then the man on the buckboard looked back at Cobbett and displayed his yellow teeth in a smile, suddenly all charm. His tone became persuasive, gentle as a kindly old grandmother. "I'm Mac McCabe. I own the Big M, biggest spread in these here parts, and that general store just down the street there. I got tired of getting cheated every time I come into town to buy something, so I opened my own store. Then old Snively came down on his prices—he had to if he wanted to stay in business. Now he tries to undersell me all the time, the old scamp. He'll take a loss rather than let anyone buy stuff at my store. What folks don't seem to realize, he's just tryin' to drive me out of business so he can go back up on his prices!"

Starting out quiet and soft, McCabe's voice had again risen to a howl. Evidently he wanted everyone in Rockville to know what a scoundrel old Snively was, including Snively himself. For he was glaring at a doorway where stood a small stooped old man with a bristling mustache and angry black eyes under overhanging gray brows.

All along the street people had come to windows and doorways to peer out. Two men stood grinning in front of a saloon, one of them a heavyset fellow wearing a small derby, a green coat and striped trousers.

Ben Cobbett glanced at the dripping gray sky with bleak eyes. He had come out without his slicker and was slowly getting soaked while Mac McCabe, protected by his wide hat and slicker, ranted and raved about matters that in no way concerned Cobbett.

"But it ain't that old rascal I wanted to talk to you about, Corbett," McCabe added in a somewhat calmer tone, though his eyes still rolled with anger at all the wrongs done him. He had noticed the two men in front of the saloon, and a third that had appeared at the entrance behind them, holding a whiskey bottle by its neck. "It's all this stock stealin' that's been goin' on around here! Everybody knows who's doin' it! Yet they ride into town bold as brass and spend money they never earned! Money they got out of stock they stole from me and a few other honest ranchers! And ain't nothin' bein' done about it! But somethin's gonna be done about it, I can tell you that!"

He was getting excited again, his voice rising back to a howl of righteous rage and indignation. But he got hold of himself and smiled toothily at Cobbett to show what a sweet old man he could be, in spite of unbearable afflictions. Cobbett did not return the smile. He stood stiffly in the rain with his wet clothes clinging to his long frame and stared back at the old man with hard eyes.

"How'd you like to go to work for me, Corbett?" McCabe asked. "That no-account marshal says he can't do nothin' outside of town, and he won't do nothin' when they're in town! I've tried to get the county sheriff to send a deputy over here or come hisself, but he won't do nothin' either."

Just then Joe Deegan came out of the restaurant and stood on the boardwalk picking his teeth with a match stem and grinning. "Morning, Mac," he said easily.

McCabe raised his whip and pointed the stock at Deegan. "He's one of them! Him and Barney Nash and that other scum hangs out at Duffy Shaw's saloon! They steal my beef and run off my horses and then ride into town bold as brass and that marshal won't even say nothin' to them about it! He acts mighty tough till they show up, then he goes back in his office and won't even come out again till they leave town!"

"There's nothing I can do about it," Ben Cobbett said in a quiet, patient tone. "I've got no authority here. I've quit wearing badge anyhow."

"Who said anything about a badge?" Mac McCabe asked impatiently. "What we need around here is a man who's good with a gun, and I understand you're one of the best."

"It comes down to the same thing," Cobbett said, "except I wouldn't have any legal backing. I couldn't do anything even if I did, without proof. And it sounds like you haven't got any."

"Proof!" McCabe cried. "Everybody knows who they are!" He bent forward on the seat, peering at Cobbett. "What if it was your stock they were stealin'? Put yourself in my place, Corbett. You tellin' me if somebody stole your horse, you wouldn't go after him?"

"I guess I would," Cobbett admitted, aware that Joe Deegan was watching him with an amused grin. "But I'd do it myself," he added. "I wouldn't try to hire someone else to do it for me."

"Of course you'd do it yourself!" McCabe cried in an angry, impatient tone. "That's what you're good at, and you ain't got nobody but yourself to worry about. But I ain't got a bunch of gun hands workin' for me, just ordinary cowhands who try to stay out of trouble. And would you like to know what happen every time we try to go after a stolen herd ourselves? They ambush us, that's what happens! Then they don't give us no peace day or night, runnin' off stock and takin' shots at my men to let us know what will happen if we try to stop them!"

Joe Deegan chuckled, idly rolling a cigarette. He seemed as happy as a mean kid who had just put a tack in his grandpa's chair. "I wonder who'd do a thing like that," he said.

"You know who's doin' it!" Mac McCabe cried, trembling with anger. Then he turned his bitter eyes back to Cobbett. "You see what I'm up against? They run off my stock and then laugh in my face, because they know nothin' won't be done about it!"

"If the law won't do anything about it, there are other men you could hire," Cobbett told him. "They're not very hard to find."

"Men no better than they are!" McCabe cried. He turned and shook his whip at the marshal's office and jail, at Tobe Langley standing broad and powerful in the doorway. "Men like him! Everybody knows he used to be a outlaw! But in this country we don't believe in holdin' a man's past agin him. It's what he is now that counts. And we figgered because Langley was a outlaw hisself once, he'd know how they operate and how to handle them. But he don't do nothin' but set on his big rump and draw his pay! And everybody in this town's scared to fire him or say anything!"

"I don't know what to tell you," Cobbett said quietly.

"That's just what that lazy sheriff over at the county seat told me!" McCabe said savagely. "The exact same words. I expected more than that from a gunslingin' lawman like you. What's a few dead men to a feller like you, Corbett? Them sons of bitches is overdue in hell."

"I already told you, I'm not a lawman anymore."

"Do what you gotta do, Corbett," McCabe said bitterly. He gathered the lines, then glared at Joe Deegan, pointed the whip at him. "You keep away from my daughter!"

Deegan smiled and said, "Better tell your daughter to keep away from me."

Trembling in a fury, McCabe raised his whip to lash at the impudent young man.

Deegan was suddenly holding a cocked gun in his left hand, and there was a cold deadly look in his blue eyes. "Don't make me kill you, old man," he said quietly.

McCabe groaned in bitter frustration and lashed the horses with his whip, racing away down the muddy street in the rain, leaving the hateful town behind him.

"Old fool," Joe Deegan said, chuckling again. He twirled his ivory-handled gun on his finger and let it drop back in the holster. He grinned at Cobbett. "You see what I mean, Cobbett? You ain't been in town no time and already somebody wants you to be the new marshal. They just ain't got around to plantin' the old one yet. But even that might be arranged, if you're interested."

"I'm not," Cobbett snapped.

Deegan shrugged. "The offer stands, in case you change your mind. Anything to oblige."

Cobbett gave the baby-faced outlaw a cold hard look, then turned away without a word and tramped back across the muddy street to the hotel.

The desk clerk, a colorless middle-aged man with thinning hair, looked sadly at Cobbett's muddy boots.

Cobbett stopped at the desk. "You got any cigars?"

The clerk shook his head. "We used to keep them here, but we don't anymore. Why don't you try the store across the street, or one of the saloons. I'm sure they're all open by now."

Cobbett looked through the window at the drizzling rain and sighed. "Well, I can't get much wetter," he said, and went back outside. Joe Deegan had apparently gone back into the restaurant, for Cobbett did not see him. But the stout marshal, Tobe Langley, still stood at the jail door, scowling when he saw Cobbett.

Cobbett decided he could use a drink. He was wet and cold and he needed something to warm him inside, where he felt the coldest. So he headed for the nearest saloon and pushed in through the swing doors. The place was empty except for a fat bartender with a bald head and a jutting chin. He did not look very friendly.

"Whiskey," Cobbett said.

The bartender silently uncorked a bottle and filled a glass, watching Cobbett with hard eyes.

"Got any cigars?"

"Sorry. Fresh out."

"So am I."

The batwings creaked and Tobe Langley, the town marshal, came in, his badge conspicuous on his heavy coat. He had a strong dark face and unpleasant eyes. Stepping up to the bar he crooked his finger for a drink and said to Cobbett, "I wouldn't pay no attention to what that old fool said if I was you, Corbett. Everybody around here knows he's half crazy."

"Cobbett. Ben Cobbett."

"That's what I said. Corbett."

"That's what I though you said."

The marshal gave him a hard look. "You figger on bein' here long?"

"Just till it quits raining."

"That's a good idea. I was gonna advise you not to hang around here long. After what old McCabe said out there, yellin' his fool head off, somebody might get the wrong idea."

Cobbett motioned for another drink. "That's their problem."

"It could be yores," the marshal said. "And mine, if you get yoreself killed in my town."

"Your town?"

Langley's jaw hardened. "That's what I said. I'm the marshal here."

Cobbett shrugged. "You can keep it for all I care."

"I aim to." The marshal drained his glass and set it back down, his face hard and ugly. "If I was you I wouldn't get no ideas about becomin' the marshal here. I like this job and I aim to keep it."

"So I gathered."

"And another thing," Langley added. "Don't let old McCabe talk you into goin' to work for him. I don't want no trouble in my town."

Cobbett turned his head and looked at the marshal with cold eyes. "You don't intend to do anything yourself and you don't want anyone else to, is that it?"

"What's that supposed to mean?"

"I think you know what it means."

"If you're talkin' about the rustlin', that ain't no concern of mine," Langley said. "What happens outside of this town ain't none of my business and I don't stick my nose in it. As long as Barney Nash and his boys don't cause no trouble inside this town, I let them alone."

"I gather they've already caused quite a bit of trouble," Cobbett said. "Yet I'm the one you're trying to run out of town. What trouble have I caused?"

"None yet," Langley admitted grudgingly. "But I know there'll be trouble if you stay here. Barney Nash and them heard what that old fool told you and they won't like it if you stay here. They'll start wonderin' if you aim to cause them trouble, and they may decide not to wait for you to start it. That means trouble in my town, and I can't have that."

Cobbett set his empty glass down and studied it for a moment with narrow eyes. "You keep talking about Barney Nash—what about Joe Deegan?"

Langley rubbed the back of his heavy neck. "Don't nobody know what Joe Deegan might decide to do. He lets on like he's everybody's friend, but all the time he may be plottin' mischief behind yore back. Tell you the truth, I was hopin' he wouldn't come back. But I guess he couldn't stay away from his pals, Barney Nash and Dill Stringer and them. Now it's anybody's guess what will happen when the Pasco boys hear he's back in town. They swore they'd kill him if he ever come back."

"Maybe you should run him out of town before they get here," Cobbett suggested.

Tobe Langley gave him a mean look. "You tryin' to be funny, Corbett?"

"I thought that was how you operated," Cobbett said. "You've just been trying to get me to leave before Barney Nash and his pals come after me."

"I thought you might listen to reason, since you was a marshal yoreself," Langley said. "But if I asked Joe Deegan to leave town, he'd prob'ly call me out."

Cobbett shrugged. "Far as I know now, I'll be riding on when it quits raining."

"If I was you, Corbett, I wouldn't even wait that long," the marshal said. "A little rain won't hurt you. But if you stay around here Barney Nash and them are liable to use you for target practice."

"Barney Nash and them are liable to find the target shooting back at them."

Chapter 3

Back in his room, Cobbett decided to remain there until the rain let up enough for him to leave Rockville behind him. He had no intention of becoming involved in the trouble brewing around here, for once involved he knew he would never leave until it was over. That was the kind of man he was.

If the rain did not let up by tonight, he would ride out anyway as soon as it got dark.

In the meantime it would be a good time to try to get some sleep. At the least he could get out of these wet clothes.

He took off his coat and hung it on a nail in the wall, then sat down in the only chair to pull off his boots. He got one boot off and started on the other, but at that moment there was an urgent knock at the door and a hoarse voice said, "Hey, Corbett, you in there?"

Cobbett drew his gun and aimed it at the door. "I'm here."

"Well, I'm Mort Crumby, the hostler down to the stable. Afraid I got some bad news for you. Somebody just rode off on yore horse."

For a long moment Cobbett sat in the chair without moving or speaking. His face looked as if it had turned to stone.

"You hear me?" Mort Crumby asked in a worried tone. "I said somebody just stole yore horse."

"I heard you," Cobbett said, tugging his boot back on. "Saddle the best horse you've got and put some grain in a gunny sack."

"You goin' after him?"

Cobbett made an unpleasant sound in his throat that the old hostler took to be an affirmative. He clumped back down the stairs and trudged back to the stable to do as he had been told. When he passed Duffy Shaw's saloon he pretended not to notice Joe Deegan and Barney Nash grinning at him over the batwings.

It took Cobbett only a few minutes to get ready, although he did not hurry. In his time he had been a Texas Ranger, a deputy marshal for Judge Isaac Parker in the Indian Territory, a deputy sheriff in Colorado, a stock detective in Wyoming and a town marshal in Montana, and now his hands did everything from habit, leaving his mind free to speculate about the crime itself, and the criminal.

He found himself remembering the way Joe Deegan had grinned when he, Cobbett, told Mac McCabe that he would go after his horse if it was stolen, and he had a hunch that Deegan was behind it. Deegan probably had not stolen the horse himself, but he might have put one of his friends up to it, just to see what Cobbett would do. To call his bluff.

Cobbett did not know when he would get back, and he decided not to leave anything in his room. He always traveled light, and he did not have anything that would encumber him or slow him down. He did not have anything he did not need.

When he came down the stairs in his slicker, carrying his saddlebags, canvas-wrapped blanket roll and rifle, the desk clerk looked up at him in surprise.

"You checking out?"

Cobbett dropped his key on the desk. "I expect I'll be back. If I'm not back by tomorrow, you can rent the room to someone else."

"We can hold it longer than that if you like."

"Suit yourself. I figure I'll be back. And I may decide to stay longer than I expected. Certain parties seem to think it would be fun to have me around, and I hate to disappoint them."

His face grim and hard, Cobbett left the hotel and went along the muddy street to the marshal's office and jail. He opened the door and found the big lawman sitting in a swivel chair behind the desk with his hands clasped behind his head and his boots up on the desk. The marshal looked pleased when he saw the saddlebags and blanket roll. He assumed that Cobbett had decided to take his advice and leave town.

"My horse was just stolen out of the livery stable," Cobbett told him.

A look of worry and irritation crossed the marshal's face. Evidently this was the first he had heard about it. Mort Crumby had not bothered to tell him, knowing it would do no good. "I was afraid something like this would happen," Langley said, frowning.

"The horse was stolen in your town," Cobbett said. "You intend to do anything about it?"

Langley shrugged his heavy shoulders, his muddy boots still up on the desk. "What can I do? He's miles away by now, and like I said, I got no jurisdiction outside of Rockville."

Cobbett nodded, showing no surprise, just a hard dislike. "I figured you'd say that. I only told you because you're the marshal here. I didn't figure it would do any good."

He turned to leave, but paused with his hand on the doorknob, watching the marshal through cold eyes. "I'm going after my horse and the man who stole him. I guess it would be a waste of time to bring the thief back here. You'd let him go as soon as I leave town."

"Hell, I'd have to," Langley said. "There wouldn't be nobody to bring charges against him, and no witnesses. It'd just be yore word against his anyhow. My advice to you is to forget it. You'd never live long enough to testify against him in court. His friends would see to that. It's happened before around here, more than once."

"I'm beginning to see why McCabe was so mad," Cobbett said. "The law around here doesn't do anything to protect honest people and their property. It just does everything it can to keep them from protecting themselves. Well, if you don't intend to do anything, I am, and you better keep out of my way. That's my advice to you."

His dark eyes glinting with anger, the marshal jerked his muddy boots down off the desk and straightened to his feet. He pointed his finger at Cobbett and said, "Now don't you go blamin' me, mister. I warned you to get out of town before anything happened. Now if you cause any trouble I'll throw you in jail just like I would anyone else."

"You might if I let you," Cobbett told him.

The marshal stared hard at Cobbett through his glinting dark eyes. But he did not say anything else, and after a moment Cobbett opened the door and went back out into the rain.

Joe Deegan stepped out through the batwings of Duffy Shaw's saloon, grinning as the tall man in the yellow slicker came down the muddy street. "You leavin' already?" Deegan asked.

Cobbett's cool gray glance touched the young outlaw. "Just going for a ride," he said evenly, moving on down the street in long unhurried strides.

Joe Deegan lifted his smooth face and squinted at the dark sky, at the steadily falling rain, and his grin became skeptical. "In this weather?"

Cobbett's hard face remained expressionless. He did not want Deegan to think he was upset about the horse, Deegan or any of his pals, whose sneering faces showed at the saloon windows and above the batwings.

"Fellow could catch his death in this weather," Deegan added, still grinning.

"Depends on which fellow you have in mind," Cobbett said, and continued on down the street to the livery stable at the lower end.

The short gray-bearded hostler had a horse saddled and ready. Cobbett ran a sharp eye over the animal. It was a mahogany bay, a rangy gelding built for speed and stamina. Cobbett had no doubt that it was the best horse the old man had, and he rammed his Winchester into the scabbard and threw his saddlebags and blanket roll on behind the cantle, tying them down.

"Which way did he go," he asked.

The old man pointed. "I saw him headin' south along the wash."

"What's in that direction?"

"McCabe's ranch, and a few smaller outfits back up in the hills away from the river."

Cobbett looked the old hostler in the eye. "Barney Nash and his pals got a place out there somewhere?"

Mort Crumby gave him a startled look. His bearded lips trembled a little when he spoke and so did his voice. "Mister, I wish you wouldn't ask me no more questions. If you find him too quick they gonna know I tipped you off, and then they'll make it hard for me."

"You've already told me what I needed to know," Cobbett said as he stepped into the saddle. "I just wanted to make sure my hunch was right."

From the saddle he looked along the puddled street and saw Joe Deegan and four other men standing in the rain outside the saloon, watching him. For a moment he returned their attention from under the wide dripping brim of his hat. Then he reined the dark horse away and followed the tracks of his sorrel south through the gray rain.

The tracks, still visible but no longer clearly defined, kept to the wagon road along the rim of the wash, at the bottom of which there was already a little stream of muddy water winding through the rocks and sand. The rider had galloped the sorrel for about a half mile and then had slowed the pace to a steady distance-eating lope, which Cobbett knew the sorrel could maintain for hours if need be. In the past the sorrel's speed and endurance had often proved handy, but now it worried him. If the thief pushed the gelding to the limit, Cobbett doubted if he would be able to overtake him on the bay. But he did not believe the man would go far in this weather. He would head for a dry place to hole up, thinking the rain would soon wash out his tracks.

When Cobbett had gone about five miles, two riders appeared on the road ahead, coming toward him at a leisurely trot. When the distance between them narrowed he saw that they were unmistakably brothers, two chunky young men with sandy hair and hazel eyes. In spite of the cold rain they wore neither coats nor slickers. But both wore gunbelts, and the bigger of the two, who appeared also to be the older, was packing an extra gun in his waistband. In the walnut handle of this gun were carved the initials "G.P." The owner, then, was probably George Pasco, and the other one would be his brother Dave.

Cobbett halted in the road facing them and nodded his head about an inch in greeting. They also halted and returned the spare nod, sizing him up with hard eyes.

"You boys meet a fellow on a sorrel back down the road a piece?" Cobbett asked.

A cold grin twisted George Pasco's mouth. "We shore did. It was Chuck Moser and he was ridin' like a posse from hell was atter him."

"Just me," Cobbett said. "He borrowed my horse without telling me."

The two men chuckled, and George Pasco said, "Chuck's bad about that. When he saw us he cut off through the sage. I guess he decided to take a shortcut to the old shack up in the hills where they stay a lot, him and Barney Nash and them."

"In case I lose his trail in the rain, how will I find it?"

George Pasco hooked his thumb over his shoulder. "It ain't hard to find. A few miles back down this here wash, there's a fork in the trail. Take the fork that leads up into the hills and it'll take you right to it." The chunky man's eyes suddenly hardened and he gave Cobbett a sharper, almost suspicious look. "It ain't the first house, though, the one you can see from the wash, settin' up in a notch in the hills. Just foller the road on past there and it'll be the next old shack you see, at the end of the trail. Moser and them don't usually go by the first house, unless they're lookin' for trouble."

Cobbett nodded his thanks, preparing to ride on.

"We could ride along with you, if you think you might need some help," George Pasco said suddenly. "We got some business to take care of in town, but it can wait."

"Obliged," Cobbett said. "But I don't think I'll need any help."

The younger brother spoke up. "Something maybe you should know, mister. That probably wasn't Chuck Moser's idea, to steal your horse. He don't usually think of things all by hisself. I figger Joe Deegan or Barney Nash put him up to it."

"That wouldn't surprise me," Cobbett admitted.

"They all in town?" George Pasco asked. "Joe Deegan and Nash and all of them, besides Chuck Moser?"

Cobbett hesitated, studying the two hard-eyed young men. From old habit he did not want to say anything that might cause trouble. "I'm a stranger around here," he said. "I'm not acquainted with those men."

George Pasco scratched under one eye, raising the opposite brow. "We saw Mac McCabe earlier and he said Joe Deegan was back in town."

"You boys work for McCabe?" Cobbett asked.

The two brothers looked at each other and grinned, and George Pasco said, "You might say that. We work his cows anyhow. Mac knows about it, but he ain't said much. He ain't got no use for us, but he hates Joe Deegan even worse, and he keeps hopin' we'll kill Deegan or he'll kill us. Either way Mac will come out ahead and he knows it."

"I see," Cobbett said, his face blank.

George Pasco's grin got bigger on one side. "Mac didn't much like it when he found me and Dave up at his girl's place. He come up to tell her Joe Deegan was back and to warn her to keep away from him. While he was at it he told us to keep away from there too, but we didn't make him no promises. Did we, Dave?"

Dave, the quieter and more cautious of the two brothers, was watching Cobbett with uneasy eyes. "This stranger ain't interested in our troubles, George," he said.

But George was in a talking mood. It might have been nerves—the thought of facing Joe Deegan and all. "It won't hurt to tell him," he said. "Like you say, he's a stranger. And he just said he was goin' after Chuck Moser, one of Deegan's friends."

"That don't mean he's got time to listen to the story of our life," Dave said. "He's probably in a hurry, ain't you, stranger?"

"I should be getting on," Cobbett said. "I'd like to get that sorrel back."

"I don't blame you," Dave Pasco said. "That was a fine looking horse, best I could tell. Me and George have got that business in town to take care of anyway, ain't we, George?"

"Ain't no rush," George said in a worried tone. "It's waited this long. It can wait a while longer."

"No, it can't neither," Dave said, a stubborn set to his jaw. "You told everyone we were gonna kill Joe Deegan if he ever showed his face around here again. Now I reckon we'll have to back up your big talk. That big mouth of yours will get us both killed before it's over."

"You shut up," George Pasco said, scowling. "You been sayin' how you'd like to kill the bastard, same as me."

"That was private talk between ourselves," Dave said. "I never told everybody we saw about it, and you shouldn't have neither. Now if we don't back it up everyone will say we're yellow."

"Just let 'em say that around me," George Pasco said. "I'll show 'em who's yeller."

The two brothers rode on toward Rockville, quietly arguing, and Cobbett continued south, following the tracks of the stolen horse.

CHAPTER 4

Where the tracks left the road Cobbett drew rein, undecided whether to keep to the road or stay with the sorrel's tracks. If the rain continued the tracks would soon be washed out, but on the other hand Chuck Moser might decide not to go on to the shack where Cobbett assumed he would go. With this in mind Cobbett decided to follow the tracks as long as he could, and if he lost the trail, then he would look for the shack.

So he left the road and followed Moser's trail through the sage and up a rocky slope to the crest of a bald hill. Beyond was a jumble of higher hills rising toward mountains obscured by the rain and the clouds. Just ahead there was a narrow valley that wound up through those hills, and that was the way the trail went. There was a little stream of runoff water coming down the valley, and after a short distance the tracks disappeared in the water. Cobbett also entered the shallow stream and rode at a walk, watching on either side for fresh tracks.

On the slopes above him stunted cedars began to appear among the rocks. These gave way to piñon and juniper, and finally he saw a tall pine on the shoulder of a hill. Beyond the pine there were others, shading a dreary log shack and a pole corral. In the corral stood Cobbett's sorrel, looking over the top pole at him as he climbed into view.

Cobbett halted at once, got down from the saddle and tied the bay to a pine limb behind some big rocks. He drew his Colt and went forward on foot until he could see the shack. Crouching in some brush, he watched the shack door for a short time, then retreated to lower ground where he would not be seen and worked his way around behind the shack.

There was no door at the back, only a small high window, not much larger than a loophole, and it was covered by a shutter on the inside. But with little doubt there was a peephole in the shutter or a crack in the log wall that served the same purpose. So he was not much better off back here. Chuck Moser might see him coming toward the shack and poke a gun barrel through the hole, blast him at close range.

Cobbett noticed that the rain had slacked off to a slow drizzle, the pines dripping water on his hat and slicker. As he was trying to decide what to do now, he heard his sorrel whinny in the corral and the sound of another horse coming up the muddy road to the front of the shack. The shack door creaked open and a drawling voice said, "You shore are a sight for sore eyes. Better git down and come in 'fore you git any wetter. But I'm the only one here in case you was lookin' for—say, did you hear old Joe come back? Rode into town last night while we was in the saloon."

"That's why I rode up here, Chuck," Cobbett heard a woman say, as he moved toward the rear of the shack. "Mac came by and told me about it. George and Dave Pasco were there, and they headed for town right after Mac left. You better ride in and warn him to watch out for them, Chuck. I think they mean to do more than just talk this time. I'd go myself, but I know it would just cause trouble instead of preventing it."

"Shucks, I can't do that."

"Why can't you?" the woman asked in an impatient tone.

"You see that sorrel in the corral there?"

"What about it?"

"Well, it's stole."

"That's not very unusual, is it? I mean, don't you steal all the horses you get?"

"This is different, though. That horse belonged to a stranger in town, a feller from Montana. He was a marshal there, and he may come atter me."

"Then why did you take his horse?"

"It was a prank, like. Joe Deegan put me up to it. He thought it would be funny, and I did too at the time. But now I don't know. What if that feller comes atter me?"

"He probably will come after you," the woman said. "You better turn that horse loose and maybe it will go back to town. If Joe says anything I'll tell him I told you to."

"I don't know," Chuck Moser said. "Tell you the truth, I was thinkin' about throwin' the saddle back on that horse and goin' on back to town my own self, by a different route. I can turn it loose outside of town and maybe that stranger will just think it got out of the livery corral somehow and strayed off. I don't want to be here by myself if he comes lookin' for me."

"That might be a good idea," the woman agreed. "But what if you run into him on the way back to town? There ain't that many routes you can take, especially in this weather."

"Yeah, I thought about that," Moser said.

"Turn the horse loose," the woman said. "You can ride down to my place behind me and stay there till it's safe."

Chuck Moser gulped. "You mean that?"

"Of course. Why shouldn't I?"

"You don't think old Joe'll mind, do you?"

"I don't care whether he minds or not."

"No, I reckon you don't, or you wouldn't fool around with them Pasco boys."

"What!" the woman said sharply.

"Nothin'. I'll go ahead and turn that sorrel loose and start it back towards town," Moser said and slammed the door, tramping across the yard.

Cobbett stepped around the corner of the house with his gun leveled at Moser's back and said, "Hold it."

The horse thief stopped in his tracks and his arms shot up as if he were reaching for the sky.

Cobbett glanced at the girl, who was still in the saddle and seemed to be unarmed. She was a lot prettier than he had expected. Almost beautiful, even with her hair wet. It was some hair, red-gold, and lots of it. She was some woman. But just now she had a cold look in her eyes that Cobbett did not like.

He said to Moser, "Unbuckle your gunbelt and toss it away. Left hand."

Moser obeyed, groaning softly to himself. "I just knowed somethin' would happen to spoil it. Why couldn't you of waited a few more minutes. We'd of been plumb gone."

"So I gathered," Cobbett said, glancing again at the young woman.

She returned his glance defiantly, even scornfully, as if she did not care in the least what he thought of her. Cobbett had seen people like that before, who had passed some point in their thinking, where the opinions of others no longer mattered and were merely to be ignored or sneered at. He had found that it was a waste of time to talk to such people. But then he had never been much at talking anyway.

"You can stay or go," he told her. "It's up to you."

Her long lips slowly parted. "What do you intend to do with him?"

"I haven't decided," Cobbett said, looking hard at Moser as the latter turned to look at him. Moser had a pop-eyed startled expression that did not fit his drawling voice.

"It was just a prank," the young woman said. "Some of his friends put him up to it."

Cobbett kept his eyes on Moser. "Joe Deegan?"

Moser bobbed his head, looking both scared and embarrassed. "It was just a prank, like she said. I never meant to keep the horse."

"Horse stealing is not a joking matter," Cobbett said. "It's a hanging offense. But I guess Deegan forgot to mention that."

Chuck Moser's face paled behind the rusty tan. He did not say anything.

Cobbett's eyes got colder and colder. "But I guess he knew nothing would be done about it," he added. "I understand you boys make a living that way, running off people's stock, and everyone's afraid to do anything about it. If I took you back to town, the marshal would just let you go, because he's scared, too."

"It was just a prank," the girl said impatiently. "You don't want a man to hang for that, do you?"

Ignoring her as if she was not there, Cobbett said to Moser, "You got any horses around here, besides the one you stole from me?"

"Some back in the timber somewhere. But they don't never come in when you need them. Somebody has to go out and drive them in."

"How many of them are stolen?" Cobbett asked.

"What business is that of yours?" the girl asked. "Maybe you were a sheriff or something back in Montana or someplace, but you ain't nothing here. And I'd advise you not to make a big thing out of this. The people around here don't bother Joe Deegan and Barney Nash and them because they know better. If you'd lived around here very long, you'd be glad to get your horse back and let it go at that."

"I can handle this without your assistance, Miss McCabe," Cobbett told her.

"My name ain't Miss McCabe," she retorted. "It's Molly Hicks."

"She used to be Molly McCabe," Chuck Moser said. "But that was before she married Roper Hicks. Somebody shot old Roper one night, but Molly still stays down there at his shack."

"I see," Cobbett said softly.

"You don't see nothing," Molly Hicks told him. "And my advice to you is to take that sorrel and get out of here before Barney Nash and them get back. If they catch you messing around here they'll fill you full of holes."

Then she turned her bitter eyes on Moser and her voice lashed him like a whip. "As for you, Chuck Moser, you can walk back to town for all I care, for running your big mouth."

Moser flinched. "Sorry, Molly. I just didn't think we should git him mad."

"What happens to you is no concern of mine," she said, reining her chestnut around and riding back down the muddy road.

"I never meant to make her mad," Chuck Moser sighed. "It's beginnin' to look like this here ain't my day."

"You're in with the wrong bunch," Cobbett told him.

"Yeah, I reckon I am," Moser admitted, with a varied grin.

Cobbett saw that he was wasting his time. Moser would agree with everything he said, but it would not change anything. He would be back with his pals the first chance he got, and when he got over his scare he would be joking with them about stealing Cobbett's horse. He would not admit how scared he had been, or how ridiculous he had looked. He would make it seem like the joke had been on Cobbett from start to finish.

But Cobbett believed in giving men like Moser enough rope to hang themselves.

"What do you think would happen if I let you go?" he asked. "How long do you think it would be before you're stealing horses again, or running off somebody's cows?"

Moser looked at him with the startled expression on his face that seemed completely natural and gave no clue to his actual thoughts. "I wouldn't bother yores no more or cause you no more trouble, I can tell you that," he said.

"Uh-huh," Cobbett said, watching Moser with cold eyes. "Was that your saddle you took, or did you grab the first one you saw?"

"No, that was my own saddle. I got it in the shack there. That's where we always keep them when we're here. We use them for pill-ers. There ain't no beds, so we bunk on the floor."

"All right, Moser," Cobbett said. "I'm going to let you go this time. But if anything like this happens again, there won't be another next time."

The rain started coming down harder again as Cobbett rode back down out of the hills, with the sorrel on a lead rope. There was no thunder or lightning, but wind tugged at his hat and slicker and blew the cold rain in his face. Familiar with flash floods, he kept to high ground, avoiding the narrow valley he had used on his way up, and the wind was stronger on the ridge tops.

From the top of one of the lower foothills he saw a rider moving along the river road toward town. He thought it was Molly Hicks, but he could not be sure at that distance, in the rain. By the time he got down to the road the rider was no longer in sight. He glanced at the ground and saw fresh tracks in the mud, but could not tell if they were the tracks of her chestnut. For that matter she might have changed horses at her place, if it was her.

He noticed that there was not much more water at the bottom of the wash, and no danger of it overflowing the high banks anytime soon, unless a sudden wall of water rushed down one of the narrow valleys or ravines out of the hills. But he thought that unlikely. For the most part it had been a slow gradual rain, the kind that soaked into the earth instead of running off to lower ground. Yet he was not a man who took anything for granted, or took unnecessary chances. That was the reason he had kept to high ground when possible, and now kept a watchful eye on the mouths of arroyos and ravines he passed on his way back to town.

And that was the reason why he circled around and entered the town from the west end, riding down the muddy street past people who were watching for him in the other direction. Among them were Joe Deegan and some of the Nash gang, peering through the foggy windows of Duffy Shaw's saloon. Joe Deegan merely grinned, but the others looked surprised when they saw Cobbett trotting down the street on the mahogany bay, leading the blaze-faced sorrel Chuck Moser had stolen. Cobbett barely glanced at the saloon in passing, his long poker face like granite.

He saw Molly Hicks's chestnut tied in front of the restaurant, and Molly herself sitting at a table, watching him through the window as he rode by.

Then he noticed the horses of George and Dave Pasco tied at the rail in front of the Silver Dollar Saloon. That meant trouble. But it was not his problem. He was not the marshal here, and that should have been a big relief. But somehow it wasn't. He had worn a badge too long to shrug his shoulders when people broke the law. It bothered him to see them get away with it. Come to think about it, it had always bothered him. Maybe that was why he had pinned on a badge in the first place.

Mort Crumby, the old hostler, limped from the stable as Cobbett rode up and dismounted. Cobbett had not noticed the limp before, and he had the feeling that Crumby had developed it quite suddenly, for no apparent reason, while he was gone. Crumby had rotten teeth and behind the reek of whisky his breath smelled like something that had died. Cobbett had not noticed the whiskey on the old man's breath before either, and suspected he had downed a few drinks to settle his nerves.

"Well, it looks like you got him back," Crumby said, with a worried look up the street toward Duffy Shaw's saloon. "Tell you the truth, I was hopin' you wouldn't find him. Them boys will think I told you who took him."

Cobbett gave the old man a cold glance. "What do you do, hide every time somebody steals a horse out of your stable?"

Crumby fingered his gray whiskers nervously. "Mister, I got to live in this town. I'm too old to pull up stakes and start over someplace else, and it ain't much different anyplace you go. There's people like them everywhere. I've found it's better not to cause them no trouble and hope they won't cause you none."

"Most people seem to feel that way," Cobbett said. "That's what makes it possible for people like them to go on causing trouble. They pick towns like this, where everyone's scared. There are towns where they wouldn't last a week and they know it. They'd either be run out of town, thrown in jail, or strung up."

"That what happened where you was the law?" Crumbly asked.

"No," Cobbett said, slinging his saddlebags over his shoulder and pulling the Winchester from the scabbard. "Where I was the law people like that were usually shot."

CHAPTER 5

The old hostler gave Cobbett a shocked look. "Them ain't bad boys," he protested. "Sure, they steal a few horses and run off a batch of cows time to time when they're short of spendin' money, and they like to have their fun. But they don't mean no harm."

Cobbett stood in the archway of the stable, looking along the rainy street. "That's another thing they've got going for them," he said. "About half of the people are always convinced that they're just high-spirited, fun-loving boys who'll settle down after a while and quit causing trouble. I won't deny that's been known to happen, but it doesn't happen very often. Most of them don't stop until somebody stops them."

"Well, I don't know who's gonna stop them around here," Crumby said. "But it won't be Tobe Langley, I can tell you that. They made him the marshal because he was supposed to be a tough man with a gun and they thought he could keep them in line. But so far he's kept out of their way. Mac McCabe was right about that."

Then the old hostler combed his beard with his fingers and said, "I saw Mac's girl ride in not long ago. That's her horse at the restaurant. She shore is a mighty fine lookin' girl. Lots of folks around here find it hard to believe she's really his daughter, him bein' such a ugly old rascal and all, and I've heard Mac has had some doubts about it his own self. Specially after she took up with that no-account rustler, Roper Hicks. Mac as good as disowned her when she went and married Roper. Then after Roper got shot, Mac went over there and tried to get her to come back home. But she wouldn't do it. She seemed to think Mac was behind Roper's death, and then it was her who disowned him. Ain't set foot back in the house at the Big M. Mac told me he was glad her ma was dead or it would of broke her heart. He swore he never had nothin' to do with Roper gettin' shot. Said he figgered it was one of them rustlers who was always hangin' around there, somebody who wanted to take Roper's place with Molly, like Joe Deegan or one of the Pasco boys. He told Molly that, but she wouldn't believe him. Said she just seemed to get madder and more set against him."

Cobbett turned his head and regarded the old hostler with something like bleak amusement in his gray eyes. "I bet McCabe doesn't share your opinion that those aren't really bad boys."

"No, he'd like to see them all shot or hung," Crumby said. "You heard what he said out there. The whole town must of heard him."

Cobbett nodded. "Well, don't let me keep you from your work. Both of those horses need some attention. Whatever I owe you for using the bay, you can add to my bill."

"That's all right," Crumby said, sheepishly rubbing his mouth. "I'll just forget about that because of the trouble you went to, gettin' your horse back.

Cobbett nodded and stepped out into the rain, going along the muddy street toward the hotel. The desk clerk, he thought, would be awful glad to see his boots.

George Pasco swaggered out of the Silver Dollar, wearing a lopsided grin and not quite steady on his feet. Evidently he was already a little drunk, and Dave Pasco was close behind him, almost imperceptibly shaking his head, a worried look in his eyes. Perhaps Dave was more convinced than ever that George would get them both killed.

"Hey, Cobbett," George called, having learned Cobbett's name from someone. "Looks like you got yore horse back."

"Looks like it," Cobbett agreed, without slackening his pace. He had no wish to carry on another conversation today in the rain, and he had no wish to carry on a conversation with George Pasco anytime, not even in good weather.

"Hold on a minute," George Pasco said. "If them bastards cause you any trouble, me and Dave will be glad to help you out."

"Thanks, but I don't believe I'll need any help."

He walked on up the street and behind him he heard the batwings flap shut behind the Pasco brothers.

A moment later Joe Deegan came out of Duffy Shaw's saloon, followed by Barney Nash and the rest of the gang. Deegan showed his usual grin, but Barney Nash was scowling. Cobbett did not pay much attention to the others. If anything started, Deegan or Nash would start it.

"You get your horse back?" Deegan asked.

"That's right."

"I sure was surprised when I heard it was my old pal Chuck Moser who took it," Deegan said, grinning happily, convinced that no one and nothing could spoil his fun.

"He said you put him up to it," Cobbett said, stopping in the rain to face Deegan and the others. His Colt was under the slicker, but the Winchester was in his hand and he knew how to use it.

"Don't pay no attention to what old Chuck told you," Deegan said easily. "He's the biggest liar I ever saw. That was his own idea. But he was just having a little fun. He didn't mean no harm."

"He wouldn't mean no harm if he cut someone's throat," Cobbett said. "There's something you should know about me, Deegan. I've never been known for having much of a sense of humor. And the next time I have to go out in the rain to bring my horse back, the one who stole him will come back with me—across the saddle."

Deegan's smile glittered like sunlight on ice. "That sounds almost like a challenge."

"You take it however you like," Cobbett said flatly. "I don't play games."

Ignoring the murderous scowls of Barney Nash and the others, he went on up the street. Molly Hicks was standing at the door of the restaurant, watching, perhaps also wanting to be seen—by Joe Deegan. Cobbett did not try to fool himself that she might have developed a sudden interest in *him*.

Tobe Langley, the marshal, was keeping out of sight in his office, the door closed.

Cobbett turned into the hotel, and the clerk winced at sight of his muddy boots, but handed him his key without comment.

"Any chance of getting anything to eat in the dining room? Cobbett asked.

The clerk shook his head. "Not till six. Afraid you missed lunch. Why don't you try the restaurant."

Cobbett went on up to his room. He had hoped to avoid Molly

Hicks—that was why he had not gone to the restaurant. But he was hungry and in no mood to wait until she took a notion to leave. She might be waiting for the rain to stop, although that seemed unlikely, since she had ridden to town in the rain.

He left his stuff in his room and came back down the stairs, unbuttoning his slicker. Without his Winchester he wanted to be able to get to his .45 in case it was needed.

He left his key at the desk, although he expected to be right back. He had always done what was expected or, failing that, what seemed best to him. Some rules and customs seemed pointless, but there was a sound reason for most of them; they grew out of necessity.

He stepped out on the veranda and looked both ways along the street from old habit. Joe Deegan, Barney Nash and the other four men still stood in front of Duffy Shaw's saloon, their heads close together, ignoring the rain. When Cobbett stepped down off the veranda, Barney Nash left the others and came toward him, tramping through the mud. Nash had his head down and from under his brows his mean bloodshot little eyes watched Cobbett like gun muzzles. He looked somewhat ridiculous in his small derby, green coat and striped trousers, but that did keep him from being a tough, dangerous man.

Cobbett stopped and waited, watching the heavyset man approach. He noticed that Nash's dark face looked as if it had several layers of skin, with hard lumps between the layers, and the surface had been scarred by both smallpox and fistfights. Most cowboys and gunfighters did their fighting with guns and avoided fistfights, which they called dogfighting. But Barney Nash was not a typical cowboy and he looked more like a brawler than a gunfighter. As a lawman, Cobbett had found himself in a few fistfights, for he hated to shoot everyone who wanted to fight.

When Nash was still twenty feet away he asked, "You want to fight, Cobbett?"

"Not unless I have to," Cobbett said bleakly. "Nobody but a fool likes to fight?"

A look of malicious satisfaction crept into Nash's little eyes. He stopped in the mud and asked loudly, wanting everyone to hear him, "You callin' me a fool, Cobbett?"

"I said anyone who likes to fight is a fool," Cobbett said in the same quiet tone.

"Well, I like to fight," Nash said, taking off his green coat and folding it over the hitchrail in front of the hotel veranda. He did not remove his little derby, however. "I reckon that means you callin' me a fool. And nobody but a damn fool would do that." He bared his yellow teeth suddenly and laughed at his own joke.

Cobbett saw Joe Deegan and the other four men moving slowly this way, grinning broadly. "Deegan put you up to this?" he asked.

Barney Nash's mouth fell open in surprise. Then he scowled. "What gave you that idea?"

"Just a guess."

Out of the corner of his eye he saw Molly Hicks standing in the door of the restaurant. But she did not look at him. She kept her eyes on the grinning Joe Deegan who with the other four had halted back out of the way and stood watching. She did not seem to be aware that Cobbett was even standing there. It should not have mattered. He had never seen her before today, and after he left he would never see her again. She did not mean anything to him. Yet the sight of her standing there, tall and slender, with her womanly curves, looking at another man, made him feel bleak and lonely inside.

He scarcely noticed the slighter, plainer woman, Jane Keller, standing at Molly's elbow, with a look of tense dread on her face.

"Naw, didn't nobody put me up to it," Barney Nash was saying loudly. Then he suddenly lowered his voice, wanting only Cobbett to hear him, "But I can tell you this. When you cause one of us trouble you got us all to worry about. All I aim to do now is bust you up good and maybe kick in a few ribs. But if you done anything to Chuck Moser, we'll kill you, mister."

"You'll need a gun for that."

"No, I won't neither," Nash said. "My bare hands is enough—and you can see I ain't armed."

"I am," Cobbett said pointedly, pulling back his slicker so he could get at his gun.

Barney Nash had started toward him, big hands fisted. But he stopped in his tracks, looking worriedly at the holstered gun. "What's wrong, Cobbett? Ain't you got the guts to fight a man with yore hands?"

"A man?" Cobbett asked. "What man? All I see is an animal that looks a little like a cross between an ape and a grizzly bear. A man would be a fool to use his hands on a critter like that."

Barney Nash's lumpy face slowly congested with red anger. "Don't you call me no animal," he said.

"You were looking for an excuse to fight," Cobbett said. "Now you've got one."

As he spoke he ran his eyes over the stocky man, searching for vulnerable spots. Nash looked rock-hard all over, except for his belly, which looked soft, pampered. Of course, there would be other vulnerable spots. His throat, for example, if a man could get to it between his bearded chin and barrel chest. And there were the mean little eyes, if a man really wanted to fight dirty. And the ears. A good clap with the open palms on both ears at the same time and the pain would stun Barney Nash for a moment, long enough to work on other areas.

Barney scratched his head under the little derby, studying Cobbett's gun with his bloodshot eyes. The gun had him stumped. He did not know what to do about it. He was a very tough man and he could take a lot of punishment and a lot of pain, but a well-placed bullet would stop him dead in his tracks. It might even kill him.

Then Joe Deegan said, grinning maliciously at Cobbett, "He won't shoot you, Barney. Not while you're unarmed. He knows they hang people for that."

"They also hang people for stealing horses," Cobbett retorted.

"Not around here they don't," Deegan said, still grinning.

"Exactly. Around here they don't hang people for anything. So I haven't got anything to worry about."

"You got us to worry about," said one of the men, a tall bony young man with large blinking dark eyes and a growth of black beard on his lantern jaw. "Go ahead, Barney. If he goes for his gun we'll plug him for you."

"That's right, Barney," Cobbett said. "You haven't got a thing to worry about with those boys to back you up—except maybe getting shot in the back by someone trying to hit me."

"You boys hold yore fire," Nash said. "Like Joe said, he knows not to shoot a unarmed man."

Then without warning the heavyset man charged Cobbett in a crouch.

Cobbett brought the sharp toe of his muddy boot up into the pit of Nash's soft belly. As Nash doubled over with a grunt of pain, holding his belly with both hands, Cobbett kicked him in the face. As Nash's head jerked back, the edge of Cobbett's left hand sliced him in the throat. Then in a swift blur Cobbett's open palms clapped like thunder on Barney's ears.

Nash howled and bent over sideways, holding his hands over his ears. Cobbett lifted his gun from the holster and brought the long barrel down on Nash's head, dropping him like an axed steer into the mud.

Tap Grodin, the black-stubbled bony fellow who had offered to back Barney's play, had his hand on the butt of his gun, his dark eyes blinking angrily.

Cobbett cocked his gun and leveled it at the man. "Go ahead. Try it."

Grodin stood in a crouch, his hand gripping his gun butt, his dark eyes flashing. But after a moment he let his breath out and his hand eased away from his gun.

Cobbett ran his glance over the others. "Anybody else feel lucky?" His eyes settled on Joe Deegan, whose grin had become a little strained. "How about you, Deegan?"

Deegan glanced at the cocked gun, rock steady in Cobbett's hand. "Not that lucky," he said. "Maybe some other time."

"Let me know when," Cobbett said idly. Then he asked, "You going to leave your fat friend there in the mud?"

Deegan gestured at the other men and they came forward, watching Cobbett's gun uneasily. Two of them picked Barney Nash up out of the mud and carried him down the street and into Duffy Shaw's saloon. The other man, a tall sandy-haired fellow with hazel eyes, followed them with Nash's coat and derby, looking back at Cobbett.

Cobbett noticed George and Dave Pasco standing in front of the Silver Dollar, silently watching.

Joe Deegan stood with his back to the Pascos and did not see them. He squinted a look of mild reproach at Cobbett and said, "You sure fight dirty for a ex-lawman."

"Where do you think I learned how?" Cobbett asked.

Deegan chuckled. "Old Barney's gonna wonder what happened when he wakes up. Them boys won't ever let him live this down."

"He may be sore for a while," Cobbett said, his eyes cold. "Sore at you for talking him into it. Pretty soon those boys are going to start telling you to pull your own stunts."

"You think so?" Deegan asked easily.

"I wouldn't be surprised." Cobbett saw George and Dave Pasco coming up the street through the slackening rain, walking abreast, their hands brushing the butts of their holstered guns. Cobbett holstered his own gun and said, "I don't think I'll need this. Looks like you're going to have your hands full."

Deegan looked over his shoulder and his smile began to resemble a grimace. But he said carelessly, "Ain't nothing to worry about. Them boys are old friends of mine."

"So I heard," Cobbett grunted. "But I hope for your sake you haven't got many old friends like them."

Molly Hicks suddenly called from the door of the restaurant, "Joe! Come over here, please!"

Deegan flashed a big smile at her and said, "Sure thing, Molly." Then he looked at Cobbett and asked, "You hungry?"

"Not that hungry," Cobbett said. "I don't think I want to be too close to you just now. You go ahead. I'll just stand here and see what happens."

Deegan shrugged and started across the muddy street toward the restaurant.

"Hey, Deegan!" George Pasco called. "You keep away from my girl!"

"I'm not your girl!" Molly Hicks said angrily.

"That ain't the way you talked when he was gone!" George Pasco said.

"Oh, shut up!" she said, blushing furiously.

Joe Deegan stopped and turned his head sideways to look at George Pasco with icy blue eyes. Cobbett noticed that he kept his left shoulder turned toward the two brothers, making as small a target as possible. He also noticed that Deegan was no longer smiling.

"You ain't been messing around my girl while I was gone, have you, George?" Deegan asked.

"Your girl!" George Pasco echoed.

"That's right," Deegan said. "If I ever hear you been around her place again, I'll put a bullet in your fat gut."

"Just try it!" George Pasco cried, going into a crouch with his hand near his gun. Dave Pasco shook his head sadly and got set to go for his own gun. George was his brother and right or wrong, Dave would stick by him.

"Hey, Joe!" Tap Grodin called from the entrance of Duffy Shaw's saloon. He was already holding a big pistol in his hand. "Don't worry about Dave. If he goes for his gun I'll let him have it!"

"Keep out of it!" Joe Deegan snapped. "Put that gun away! This is my fight. And George needs all the help he can get."

"Like hell!" George Pasco cried, and grabbed for his gun.

Joe Deegan's gun left the holster in one smooth effortless movement and seemed to cock itself. The gun roared and jumped in Deegan's hand and George Pasco fell to his knees, dropping his own gun and grabbing his chest.

By then Dave Pasco had his gun out but before he could get off a shot Joe Deegan's second bullet tore through his heart and Dave's own bullet went wide.

George Pasco, on his hands and knees, saw his brother pitch to the muddy ground on his face. George fumbled blindly for his own gun and his bloody hand lifted it out of the mud.

Deegan, talking deliberate aim this time, shot the chunky man in the head and George Pasco slumped into the mud beside his dead brother.

For a moment Deegan stared at them with cold eyes, ready to fire again if necessary. Then he holstered his gun and glanced at Ben Cobbett in an odd way, with one eye half closed and the other brow slightly raised. Cobbett stared back impassively. Neither said anything. A moment later Deegan turned and looked toward the restaurant doorway where Molly Hicks stood poised and cool, if a little pale behind her light tan. He did not seem to notice Jane Keller who stood trembling in the taller girl's shadow, clutching her throat as if trying to choke herself.

Then Marshal Tobe Langley came out of his office and called, "Deegan."

Everyone turned to look at the big swarthy marshal. He looked scared and sounded scared, but he left his office and stepped out into the street, started across it. "I can't allow no killin' in my town, Deegan," he said. "I don't mind you boys havin' a little fun, if you don't go too far with it, or havin' a little fistfight now and then. But I can't allow no killin' inside this town. I'll have to take yore gun."

Deegan's eyes had that cold narrow look Cobbett had noticed before. "You'll have to take it, is right," he said.

The marshal stopped at the edge of the street and stood there with his big feet spread apart in the mud, his dark eyes staring resentfully at the baby-faced killer. But there was also fear in his eyes and he did not move or speak for so long that it became apparent to everyone present that he was not going to do anything. But that surprised no one. He never had done anything about the rough element since becoming the marshal of Rockville.

"What did you have in mind, Marshal?" Joe Deegan taunted. "I shot them two in self-defense, so there's nothing you could do but run me out of town. If you had the guts. Was that what you were gonna try to do, run me out of town?"

Tobe Langley did not say anything. His heavy shoulders seemed to sag. No doubt he would have felt more at ease back in his little office, with his feet up on the desk.

"Get out of my sight," Joe Deegan said in disgust, contemptuously turning his back on the marshal. "You're through in this town," he added over his shoulder. "If you ain't gone by tomorrow I'll come after you. Do yourself a favor and sneak out tonight while it's dark. That's about your style."

Deegan went on into the restaurant and closed the door, taking Molly Hicks's arm and guiding her to a table.

Marshal Tobe Langley stood in the rain and watched the restaurant for a few minutes, ignoring the people who had gathered on the street near the two dead men, staring at him with accusing eyes. Then he turned and went back into the marshal's office, carefully avoiding Ben Cobbett's eyes.

Cobbett glanced toward the restaurant, then turned and went back into the hotel. He no longer felt very hungry.

CHAPTER 6

Cobbett cleaned up in his room and ate supper in the hotel dining room. He sat at a table where he could watch the street through the window. While he ate, several men rode past through the rain, cowhands from local ranches, he supposed. He did not see anything of Barney Nash and the others, but Joe Deegan and Molly Hicks were eating supper in the restaurant across the street. Her chestnut and Deegan's black were tied at the hitchrail.

When the rain slacked up for a few minutes Deegan and the girl left the restaurant, mounted up and rode slowly out of town. Jane Keller stood at the door hugging herself and watched them ride down the street.

While darkness settled Cobbett had a second cup of coffee, paid for his meal and went back up to his room. He had intended to go to bed early and get a good night's sleep. But he was restless and in no mood to remain in the small room with its peeling gray wallpaper and few sticks of plain furniture.

Stepping over to the window, he parted the curtain and looked at the restaurant across the street, where dim yellow lights glowed through the rain and Jane Keller could be seen moving about near the windows. She would make some man a good wife, he thought. But he knew he was not the man, and he was not interested in Jane Keller. It was Molly Hicks he kept thinking about with an odd little ache of loneliness inside him.

But deep down he knew Molly Hicks was not the right kind of woman for him either. A woman whose shack was apparently a hangout for rustlers and horse thieves, three of whom had already fallen out over her and shot it out on the street this afternoon while she watched with no sign of guilt or remorse on her face—no, she was not the sort of woman for an ex-lawman like Ben Cobbett. He knew that, and still he thought about her. He could find no comfort in his small dry room while she rode off into the rainy night with Joe Deegan.

He looked at his bleak hard face in the bureau mirror, then put on his slicker and went downstairs, leaving the hotel. He crossed the muddy street in the rain to a store, where he bought a half dozen small cigars. Lighting one up, he stood on the boardwalk under the awning for a few minutes and studied the town.

It was not much of a town. Just this one muddy street, lined on either side by a row of frame buildings with false fronts. The hotel was the only two-story building, and the only hotel. There was only one restaurant, one small barbershop, the livery stable, two stores and three saloons, a few dwellings. It was just like a hundred other towns he had seen. It had the same kind of people. And the next town he saw would be about the same. There were men like Joe Deegan and Barney Nash everywhere, and others who just wanted to live out their lives in peace, without having to worry about being run down by a galloping horse or cut down by a stray bullet every time they stepped into the street.

Cobbett saw Barney Nash stagger out of Duffy Shaw's saloon and shoulder a cowhand out of his way. The cowhand slipped and fell into the mud, got up and stared after Nash for a moment, then went on into the saloon. Meanwhile Nash staggered on along the street, head down, hunting trouble.

Cobbett started back across the street toward the hotel, his cigar hissing in the rain. Barney Nash saw him but did not recognize him. Or perhaps he did. In any case he altered his route so as to intercept the tall man in the slicker.

Cobbett did not change his even stride or his direction, merely shifted his eyes to watch the heavyset man lurching toward him. It was obvious what Nash had in mind. He meant to bump into Cobbett hard enough to knock him down, as he had knocked the cowhand down. Cobbett saw him crouch and tense his heavy body for the lunge, but he waited until Nash was almost against him, then stepped to one side and Nash fell into the mud with a grunt and began cussing.

"Trip me, will you?" Nash cried, pulling himself up out of the mud. "Well, if it's a fight you want, bucko, you picked the right man."

Cobbett stepped back and waited with his boot ready.

Nash, now on his hands and knees, looked at the boot, then peered up at Cobbett. "You!" he roared. He pointed his finger at Cobbett and said angrily, "You didn't fight fair!"

"That's right," Cobbett agreed. "I won't fight you with my fists any more than you'd fight me with a gun. Not unless you were hiding behind something or my back was turned."

Barney Nash climbed to his feet and looked down at his muddy clothes. "I'll be damned!" he said. "Took me two hours to get the mud off my clothes and now look at them! This is the second time today you've ruined my clothes!"

Three men came out of Duffy Shaw's saloon and one of them called "Hey, Barney! Where the hell did he get off to?"

"Over here!" Barney Nash roared, and the three men slogged through the mud toward him and Cobbett.

Cobbett watched the three with cold eyes, his unbuttoned slicker flapping around his legs. The wind had picked up, blowing rain in his face.

"You think you can whup all four of us?" Barney Nash asked.

"I don't intend to try," Cobbett said.

"You don't? What if you ain't got no choice in the matter?"

Cobbett stepped off a little to one side where he could watch Barney Nash and his pals at the same time. They came up and halted when they recognized Cobbett.

"You two fixin' to go at it again?" one of them asked.

"Hell no," Barney Nash said. "He won't fight fair." Then he said, "Cobbett, meet my friends. That there's Ned Ribble, that tall skinny one is Dill Stringer, and that other one is Tap Grodin."

Cobbett and the three men stared at each other in silence, not acknowledging the introduction by so much as a nod.

Barney Nash added maliciously, "I just wanted you to meet the boys who're just shore to fill you full of lead if you stay around here long."

"I hadn't planned to be here long," Cobbett said. "But if you boys keep trying to make my stay so pleasant I may change my mind."

"I hope you do stay," Barney Nash said. "Me and you has got a few things to settle."

"Then let's settle them here and now," Cobbett said impatiently.

"I'd as soon get it over with. Then I can ride on without you telling everyone you ran me out of town."

Nash stepped back shaking his head. "Oh no you don't, Cobbett. You ain't gonna trick me into drawin' on you. I've had a few drinks, but I ain't that drunk. Besides, Joe Deegan does most of our gun work."

Cobbett glanced at the other three, who stood there on the dark windy street in the rain watching him silently.

"Ain't none of them boy scared of you," Barney Nash said. "They're just waitin' to give Joe Deegan the first crack at you."

"I thought Deegan was my friend," Cobbett said.

Barney Nash let out a snort of laughter and the other three chuckled. "When he starts talkin' that way you better watch out," Nash said. "He's told a lot of fellers he was their friend one day and shot them the next."

"What about you boys?" Cobbett asked. "He told me you were his friends."

"We are his friends," Dill Stringer, the tall thin one, said. But he looked uneasy and so did the others.

Cobbett glanced at his cigar, which had gone out in the rain. He had been holding it in his left hand. "Better watch out then," he said. "Like you say, his friends don't last very long."

He put the dead cigar back between his teeth and went on toward the hotel, walking slowly as if he was in no hurry. He did not look around but his back was tensed for the shock of a bullet. Behind him he heard Dill Stringer say, "The bastard's trying to trick us. Joe wouldn't turn on his friends. Not if they're really his friends?"

"Wouldn't he?" Barney Nash snorted. "George and Dave Pasco used to be his friends, didn't they?"

"That was different. They shouldn't of started fooling around with his girl."

"Hell, they were foolin' around with her first, you knothead!"

The four men stood there in the rain, none of them wearing slickers, and watched Cobbett enter the hotel. Through the window they saw him start across the lobby toward the desk at the foot of the stairs. But from where they stood on the dark street they could not see the desk, and after a moment they could no longer see Cobbett, except in their minds. In their minds they could see his hard arrogant face—a face they were all beginning to hate.

Tap Grodin stood with his head tilted back slightly, blinking his angry dark eyes. He bared his yellow teeth and said, "Who the hell does he think he is?"

Dill Stringer, who had done his talking to Cobbett, now said nothing. He stood watching the hotel in silence, his long narrow face and hazel eyes expressionless in the dark.

Ned Ribble, a stout young man who bore a noticeable resemblance to the late George Pasco, shifted his feet uncomfortably. He too was silent, thinking about what Cobbett had said, and about the face of the dead George Pasco. That face haunted him, because it looked so much like his own. He was sure Joe Deegan had noticed it also. Would his face begin to haunt Joe Deegan, because it reminded him of a man he had killed? If it did, then Ned Ribble was afraid his days were numbered. Joe Deegan might be haunted by the dead but he would not be haunted by the living for very long.

The cold rain and another dip in the mud had apparently sobered Barney Nash up quite a bit. "It ain't no fit night to be standin' out here in the rain," he said, his mean little eyes on the hotel. "I'd stay in Duffy's saloon again tonight if I had any dry clothes to sleep in. But that bastard tripped me and I'm all wet and muddy again."

"You gonna let him get away with that?" Tab Grodin asked.

"Hell no, I ain't gonna let him get away with it," Barney Nash said. "Come on. I got me a idea. We're goin' home, and we're gonna take his horse with us—part of the way. He'll know it was us, but there won't be a thing he can do. He won't have no proof, and by mornin' the tracks will be washed out."

Late that cold rainy night Tobe Langley left the dark marshal's office wearing a slicker and carrying a worn carpetbag and a double barrel shotgun. He went down the dark deserted street to the livery stable and saddled his horse while the old hostler, Mort Crumby, snored in the hayloft. Langley tied his carpetbag on behind the saddle and rammed the shotgun in the boot, then mounted up and rode quietly away from the sleeping town of Rockville. As soon as everyone believed he had left for good, he intended to sneak back and kill Joe Deegan, when Deegan least expected it. No baby-faced punk was going to run him out of town and get away with it.

Ben Cobbett was eating breakfast in the hotel dining room the next morning when Mort Crumby came in. The old hostler looked at his hard face with dread and limped over to his table, bringing with him the odors of the barnyard and the stale reek of whiskey.

"I don't know how to tell you this," Crumby said in an unsteady voice, "but yore horse is gone again."

Cobbett looked up at the old man with no sympathy in his cold gray eyes. "What time was he stolen?"

Crumby shook his head, holding his grizzled chin as he spoke. "I ain't got no idear. The rain made me sleepy and I hit the hay early last night. That's where I sleep, up in the hay. I never heard a sound till I woke up this mornin' and found yore horse missin'."

"Barney Nash and his pals still in town?"

"No, their horses was gone too. And they took Chuck Moser's roan with them. Tobe Langley's mouse dun was gone also. Looks like he took Joe Deegan's advice and pulled out last night. So many horses gone I thought at first they'd been a raid on my stable during the night. But I reckon yore sorrel was the only one that was actually stolen."

Cobbett glanced down at his plate, finishing his breakfast. "And you slept through all that?"

Crumby covered his mouth with his hand, scratching his dirty gray beard with his fingers. "Yeah, I reckon. I shore didn't hear nothin'. Barney Nash and them usually wake me up when they leave town. But they was mighty quiet last night."

Cobbett looked through the window at the street. It had quit raining during the night, but it was cloudy and cold and windy.

"Saddle the bay," he said. "I'll be down there in a few minutes."

"Whatever you say," Crumby muttered and headed for the door.

Just then the elderly waitress came from the kitchen and her face lit up in a smile when she saw the old hostler. "Good morning, Mort," she said. "How about some coffee?"

Crumby looked at the waitress and forgot everything else. "Love to, Hettie." He pulled a chair back from a table, then saw Cobbett watching him and cleared his throat. "Be back later for the coffee, Hettie," he said sheepishly. "I just remembered somthin' I got to do right now."

"Why, you're limping, Mort," the gray-haired waitress cried. "Did you hurt your foot?"

Crumby looked around in surprise. "Huh? Oh, no. Just my old rheumatism actin' up on me." His wrinkled leathery face creased in a smile. "I ain't as young as I used to be."

"None of us are," the waitress replied. "Don't you forget about the coffee, now."

"I won't, Hettie. You can count on that." Crumby glanced again at Cobbett, coughed and went on out.

The waitress brought the coffeepot over to Cobbett's table and refilled his half-empty cup. "How are you this morning, Mr. Corbett?" she asked.

"Cobbett."

She looked at him in surprise. "I thought I heard Mr. McCabe call you Corbett."

"The whole town heard him, and now everyone thinks that's my name. But it happens to be Cobbett."

"I don't believe I've heard that one before."

"There are not many of us left. One here and there. How much do I owe you?"

"Fifty cents, the same as supper. But we can put it on your hotel bill if you like."

"That will be fine. Thank you."

"How long do you expect to be with us, Mr. Corbett? Mr. Cobbett, I mean."

"I'd planned to leave this morning. But it seems my horse has been stolen again."

"Oh, no!" the old lady said, her face expressing both horror and sympathy. "Well, I hope you get it back again. But be careful. There are some very bad men around here. If you get them mad at you, they'll stop at nothing to get even. Mr. McCabe tried to put a stop to the rustling, and now they concentrate on his stock. Never give the poor man any peace. And to make it worse, his own daughter is in with them. Or at least she knows about it, and she still lets them hang around the old shack where she lives. The good Lord only knows what all goes on around there. Something should be done about it."

Cobbett silently drank his hot coffee in scalding gulps while the waitress talked, and then he pushed back from the table.

"Would you like some more coffee?" she asked.

"No, I've got to go."

"You be careful now, if you mean to go after your horse."

Cobbett nodded, already heading for the door. He went up to his room, got his rifle and saddlebags and came back down.

"You leaving?" the clerk asked.

"I'll be back," Cobbett said. He handed the clerk his key and left the hotel, going down the still muddy street to the livery stable. Crumby had the mahogany bay ready and he stepped into the saddle and headed south without wasting time. The rain last night had washed the tracks out but there was not much doubt in his mind as to the direction that the horse thief, or thieves had gone.

Cobbett had not gone more than a mile and a half when he found the horse, lying dead beside the road. The sorrel had been shot several times and its throat had been cut, just to make sure.

CHAPTER 7

Cobbett returned to town, his face like stone, a slow rage building inside him. He left the bay at the livery stable without a word to the old hostler and walked up the street to the hotel. He left the rifle and saddlebags in his room, then went to the small barbershop. While the barber trimmed his hair and shaved his face he watched Duffy Shaw, in a soiled white apron, sweep off the boardwalk in front of his saloon across the street.

"Want me to do anything to the mustache?" the barber asked.

"Get rid of it."

"Yes, sir."

The barber, a middle-aged man with curly black hair and friendly brown eyes, kept studying Cobbett's face as he worked on his hair. "I guess you know by now the marshal left town last night?" he finally said.

"So I heard."

"I understand you were a marshal back in Montana. Miles City, was it?"

Cobbett grunted an affirmative.

"There's already talk about making you the marshal here, in case you're interested."

"I'm not."

"Everyone saw what you did to Barney Nash out there yesterday. I never thought I'd live to see that happen. He's had it coming a long time. A lot of people in this town feel the same way."

Cobbett was silent, watching Duffy Shaw through the window. Shaw had finished sweeping off the boardwalk and he stood for a moment looking along the empty street, then went back into his saloon, the batwings flapping behind him.

"I'm Hank Gilbert," the barber said. "Sheb Snively and some of us ate breakfast at the hotel. We were sort of hoping to see you, but you hadn't come down. Of course, by then everyone knew Tobe Langley had left, just like Joe Deegan told him to. Say, isn't that Joe Deegan riding up the street now? Yes, that's him. I guess he rode in to see if Langley had left or not."

To Cobbett's surprise, Deegan reined in before the hotel, got down and went inside. Moments later he came back out and crossed the street to the barbershop, having no doubt been told that was where Cobbett was. Deegan stopped in the door and studied Cobbett uncertainly. He was not smiling, but his eyes were not cold the way they usually were when he did not smile.

"I saw your horse as I was riding in," he said. "Couple miles outside of town. Somebody shot it. Did you know about it?"

Cobbett silently nodded, watching Deegan. Cobbett's own eyes looked frozen and not likely to thaw anytime soon.

"I didn't have nothin' to do with that," Deegan said. "Playing a little prank is one thing, but I can't see shooting a man's horse. It made me mad as hell when I saw that sorrel. If Barney and them had anything to do with it, they're gonna get a piece of my mind." He hesitated. "I ain't talked to them since I left town late yesterday."

That meant he'd spent the night at Molly Hick's shack. Cobbett sat in the barber's chair looking through the window. The bleakness in him grew.

Joe Deegan tried a grin. "If that was them did that, I'll see that they get you another horse just as good," he said. "How's that?"

Cobbett's cold eyes returned to Deegan's face. "If you didn't have anything to do with it," he said, "just stay out of it. I appreciate the offer, but I know any horse they brought me would be stolen."

Deegan shrugged, holding onto a fragment of his grin. "I tried," he said and turned to leave. Then he paused, looking around at Cobbett. "They'll prob'ly pin Langley's badge on you, now that he's left. That's the main reason I ran him out. I figgered it would be interesting, having you for a marshal."

"It might be more interesting than you think," Cobbett said quietly.

"It might be," Deegan agreed, with a broader grin, and went on out. He mounted his black and walked it across the mud to Duffy Shaw's saloon.

"You mean they killed your horse?" Hank Gilbert asked, in a tone of quiet outrage.

"Somebody did."

"Who else would have done it?" Gilbert asked. "It was some of that bunch. They probably did it to get even with you for what you did to Barney Nash out there yesterday."

Cobbett was silent, watching Joe Deegan dismount in front of the saloon, wrap the reins and go in through the batwings.

"You ain't going to let them get away with that, are you?" Gilbert asked.

"Why not?" Cobbett grunted. "Haven't they got away with everything else they've done around here?"

"Yes, and they'll get away with that too, if you leave now," the barber said, removing the apron from around Cobbett's neck and brushing off a few loose hairs. "Won't a thing be done about it unless you do it yourself."

"That's the way it's usually been," Cobbett said, rising from the chair and reaching for his hat. When he stood up, the barber, a much shorter man, appeared to sit down, although he remained on his stunted bowlegs. "How much do I owe you?"

"On me," the barber said. "I always did Tobe Langley's barbering free of charge, and I'm still hoping you'll decide to take the marshal's job."

"I'll pay," Cobbett said.

Gilbert shrugged. "Four bits, then. But I still say you should think it over. You look to me like a man who believes in getting even, and I don't blame you, after what they did to your horse. But why not be smart and get paid while you're at it? Langley was getting a hundred a month for doing nothing. That's what it amounted to. I believe the people of this town would be willing to pay a man like you a hundred twenty-five a month, at least till things quiet down. But the job would be yours for as long as you wanted it. We need a good man here that we can rely on, but above all we need someone who can handle men like Barney Nash and that bunch. I'm sure you've already heard how Langley let us down. From what we'd heard about him we figgered he was just the man for the job, but he never did anything. I don't believe he ever arrested anyone the whole time he was here. And the county sheriff"—Gilbert shook his head—"he's just as bad. He hardly ever sets foot out of New Hope."

Cobbett stood at the door looking out at the street. "How far is it to New Hope?"

"About a day's ride west of here. But if you're thinking about riding over there to see the sheriff about what happened to your horse, it would just be a waste of time. He's scared to death of Barney Nash and them. Just like everyone else around here."

"He sounds a lot like some lawmen I've known," Cobbett said, and went out pulling his hat low over his eyes. The sun had come out and seemed unnaturally bright after a day of rain and dark cloudy skies. It seemed like a lot longer than a day.

He angled across the street to the hotel. On the veranda he hesitated, then sat down in one of the barrel chairs, putting his boots up on the rail that ran along the edge of the veranda. He took out a cigar and lit it.

Out of the tail of his eye he saw Joe Deegan leave the saloon and untie his black horse, but he did not turn his head to look at Deegan. Deegan mounted up, sat his saddle looking toward the hotel veranda for a moment, then turned the black and came along the street until he was abreast of the veranda. There he halted and sat his saddle grinning cheerfully at Cobbett's hard impassive face. It had not taken him very long to get over any regret he might have felt about Cobbett's horse, and he seemed to think that Cobbett, who showed no anger, felt none.

"You looked better with the mustache," Deegan said.

"I thought you'd approve."

Deegan chuckled. "Why shouldn't I? When it comes to women I don't need no competition. It leads to trouble."

"I don't think you've got any," Cobbett said. "Now that the Pasco boys are dead."

Deegan shrugged. "I never figgered you'd be as crazy as them two." Then he glanced toward the restaurant and said, "But I wouldn't mind letting you take Jane Keller off my hands."

"No, thanks."

Deegan laughed quietly, then grew sober as he studied Cobbett's face. "What you plan to do now? Get another horse and ride on? Or let them pin that badge on you?"

"I haven't decided anything definite yet."

Deegan shifted in his saddle. "What I said earlier about that being Barney and them—I don't know who it was. It wouldn't surprise me if it was someone in this town who done it so Barney and them would be blamed."

"You know damn well who did it," Cobbett said quietly.

Deegan frowned and his eyes became even colder than Cobbett's, if that was possible. "You're beginning to sound just like everybody else around here," he said. "Every time anything happens, everybody says it was me or Barney and them that did it. They don't need no proof, they just take for granted it was us. Seems you're just like them after all. But I've noticed lawmen are worse than anyone else about suspecting the wrong people. How long have you worn a badge anyway, Cobbett?"

"Too long, I guess," Cobbett said. "I hate to see people get away with anything they take a notion to do."

"I had that feeling when I first saw you," Deegan said. His eyes brightened with malice and his voice became low and deadly. "That's why I said it might be fun having your around. I really get a kick out of breaking the law around ex-lawmen who can't do a thing about it. Even if they make you the town marshal, you still won't be able to do anything about all the rustling. You'll know who's doing it, just like you know who shot your horse, but there won't be a damn thing you can do about it."

"Don't be too sure," Cobbett said.

"I'm plenty sure," Deegan said, and reining the black horse away he loped out of town, turning south along the river road.

Cobbett sat in the chair on the hotel veranda and finished smoking his cigar, his eyes narrowed in thought.

Then he got to his feet and entered the hotel. He went up to his room and came back down a few minutes later with his blanket roll, saddlebags and Winchester. At the desk he paid his bill, then left the hotel and walked down the street to the livery stable.

Mort Crumby had seen him coming and stood in the wide doorway waiting for him. "You want the bay again?" Crumby asked.

"I'd like to buy him," Cobbett said, "if the price is right."

Crumby removed his battered old hat, scratched his thinning gray hair and thought for a moment. "Well, I don't know. I'd sort of planned to keep that bay. That's the best horse I got. But seein's yore horse was stole out of my stable, I guess I can let you have him for fifty dollars. He's worth a hundred."

"Fifty sounds more like it," Cobbett said, counting out the money.

Crumby stuffed the money in his pocket. "I'll saddle him up for you. I don't think you'll regret buyin' him."

West of Rockville the road crossed a spur of barren rocky mountains. To the north were real mountains, with trees on them, and high peaks above the trees. But the road skirted to the south and Cobbett followed the road, maintaining a steady trot most of the time.

The bay was a good horse, but he was not used to Cobbett and Cobbett was not used to him. Cobbett missed the sleek sorrel and was gripped by anger every time he thought about the senseless killing of the horse. He knew who had done it and he knew he would never be satisfied if he let them get away with it.

He rode steadily throughout the long day, pausing only twice to give the bay a breather. After the mountain spur there was a monotonous stretch of gray sage rolling away into the distance seemingly without end. But late in the day he entered the foothills of more mountains and noticed dark clouds massing overhead. Shortly before dark it started raining again and was still raining when he rode into New Hope, a smaller town then he had expected, although it was somewhat larger than Rockville, with a small square at the center around which most of the buildings were clustered.

Cobbett left his horse at a stable and walked to a hotel where they were still serving supper. He went directly into the dining room, hanging his slicker on a nail in the wall and depositing his gear, including the rifle, in the corner near his table. It was not unusual behavior for the time and place, and no one paid much attention to him as he silently attacked his food.

At the next table sat four men whom Cobbett took to be townsmen or possibly retired cattlemen who lived in town. One of them was a large fat man with a huge belly and a deep loud voice, who reeked of expensive cigars and soft living. This one was in the midst of a long story, supposed to be funny, about a train trip he had once made to Chicago, Illinois.

When he slacked off for a minute to catch up on his eating and also no doubt to rehearse in his mind what he would say next, Cobbett asked, "Anybody know where I can find the sheriff?"

The fat man looked up from his plate with sudden interest. "It important?" he asked.

"It is to me. It might not be to him."

The fat man laughed and pulled back the lapel on his overcoat to reveal a badge pinned to his vest. "You just found him, son. What's on yore mind?"

Cobbett glanced at the other men, who were watching him with interest. Then he said to the sheriff, "You might prefer to hear about it in private."

"These boys are old friends of mine, son," the sheriff said. "Whatever you got to say, you can say in front of them."

Cobbett shrugged. "Somebody shot my horse. Since it happened in your county I thought I'd ride over and tell you."

"If you come on the same horse, they must not of been very good shots," the sheriff said, with a loud laugh that caused his huge belly to shake.

"I had to get another horse," Cobbett said.

The sheriff winked at his friends. "Somebody must have been awful mad at you to go and kill yore horse. What did you do to get them so hot under the collar, son?"

That "son" was beginning to annoy Cobbett. He was thirty-four years old and unless he got himself killed pretty quick he would soon be thirty-five. He could not put it off much longer. And he certainly was not the "son" of this fat lazy sheriff, who was scarcely old enough to be his father.

"I had a little fight with one of them," he said.

"I figgered something like that," the sheriff said, spooning more sugar into his coffee. "Where did you say this happened?"

"Over at Rockville."

The sheriff's mouth fell open and a look of irritation came into his eyes. Up to now he had treated the matter like a joke, a source of mild amusement on a dull rainy night. But at the mention of Rockville he immediately lost his sense of humor. "You mean you rode way over here just to tell me that?" he asked. "That sounds like a job for the town marshal."

"He quit," Cobbett said. "Left town already."

There was a look of increasing gloom on the sheriff's face, which seemed to sag with the weight of worries and afflictions. He scarcely resembled the jolly clown of a few minutes before. "That don't surprise me," he said. "I been expecting to hear he's been shot or run out of town. They can't keep a marshal over there, and then they pester me about little squabbles they should settle among theirselves." The sheriff's eyes darkened with anger and he attacked his beef as if it still needed killing. "I don't know why they expect any help from me.

Ain't nobody in that town voted for me in the last four elections. But just let any little thing happen and they come running to me about it."

Cobbett finished his food and sat sipping his coffee, a look of weary boredom on his long hard face. "I was told it would be a waste of time to come over here and see you," he said. "But since you're the sheriff of this county I thought I should report the matter to you before I do anything about it myself."

The sheriff glanced at the other three men at his table, then scowled at Cobbett. "What's yore name anyhow? I don't believe I've seen you around here before."

"The name's Cobbett and I haven't been around here before."

"I knew a Cobbett back in Kansas," the sheriff said. He looked down at his empty plate in surprise, then began sopping the plate with a little piece of bread, hunting for any speck of food he had overlooked. "Everybody called him Corbett."

"I know what he was up against," Cobbett said.

"Well, I don't know why you're so hot under the collar," the sheriff said, looking sadly at his empty plate. "Strangers has to expect a little razzin'. Who shot yore horse anyway?"

"I'm not sure. Or at least I didn't see them do it."

The sheriff's mouth fell open in a look of baffled rage. "You mean you rode all the way over here in the rain, busted in here and ruined my supper, and you don't even know who done it?"

"I know who did it all right," Cobbett said. "But there weren't any witnesses."

"Then there ain't anything I can do about it. I can't go over there and arrest somebody on yore say-so. Not unless you've got some proof that will stand up in court."

"I'm not getting paid to do your job," Cobbett said.

"You have any idea how big this county is?" the sheriff howled, picking up his fork to begin eating again, then putting it back down when he noticed his empty plate. "It's bigger than some of them states back East. Even bigger than some countries, from what I've heard. And all I got is one deppity who's laid up from a fall he took last Sunday when he was racing his horse. I ain't about to go over there myself in this weather. I been wet so much already I think I'm coming down with the flu." He suddenly pounded his chest and coughed loudly, startling those around him.

Cobbett alone showed no change of expression. What people did no longer surprised him. He had got over his surprise long ago. But he had not got over his anger, although it rarely showed on his rock-like face.

He glanced through the rain-fogged window and saw the reflection of the fat sheriff bent over his empty plate, dwarfing those around him. Beyond the lamplit reflection, the shadows of men flitted across the square, bent over and hurrying through the rain. Cobbett shifted his eyes and saw his own long face staring back at him, looking strangely naked and exposed without the mustache.

"You need a deputy over there, and somebody who knows what he's doing," he said. "All hell is about ready to break loose."

With that he laid a dollar on the table, picked up his stuff and left the dining room.

CHAPTER 8

In the lobby Cobbett paused. There had been a man at the desk earlier, but no one was there now. As Cobbett was trying to decide what to do, the fat sheriff, Gordon Bailey, lumbered out of the dining room after him, calling his name.

"What did you mean in there when you said all hell was about to break loose?" the sheriff asked.

Cobbett looked around at the sheriff with cold eyes. "Aren't you aware of what's going on over there?"

The sheriff glanced about the lobby, saw that it was empty, then slowly nodded. "It ain't like I don't care, Cobbett," he said in a low tone. "But there ain't nothing I can do. There've been threats made on my life, and the last time I went over there I was warned not to come back again. Joe Deegan come up to me in the street and smiled like we were old friends, and then he told me if I ever tried to put a stop to the rustling or caused him and his friends any trouble, he'd get me personally. He said he'd put a bullet in my fat gut. Everyone was watching us and he kept his voice down so they wouldn't hear what he said to me and he kept smiling just like we were old friends. Made it seem like I was on his side or that he'd bought me off or something. I was so mad I couldn't see straight, but I knew better than to do anything but just nod my head. That damn boy would have killed me, and prob'ly got away with it. Nobody in Rockville would dare testify against him. And nobody over there likes me anyhow."

The sheriff took out a soiled handkerchief and mopped his heavy round face, which was beaded with sweat although it was damp and chilly in the lobby. "You can call me a coward if you want to," he said. "But I ain't going over there and get myself killed for a few people who don't give a damn about me and vote against me every time there's an election. They don't just vote against me theirselves, they come over here and try to get the people here in New Hope to vote against me too! And there ain't a thing I can do about it, not legally."

"Then make me a deputy," Cobbett said suddenly. "I'll do something about the rustling."

The sheriff promptly shook his head. "That would be the same as me going myself. Joe Deegan warned me not to send any deppities snooping around, while he was at it. Besides, it sounds to me like you want to use the law to settle a personal grudge with them. If you've got a grudge, then settle it yoreself, but leave me and my office out of it."

"In that case," Cobbett said, "I'll tell you what I told Tobe Langley before Deegan ran him out of town. If you're not going to do anything, then keep out of my way."

The sheriff nodded, showing no anger. "I'll make a deal with you," he said. "You keep out of New Hope and I'll keep out of Rockville. For all I care, you people over there can kill each other till there ain't a one of you left. It would save me a lot of worry and headaches."

Just then the three men who had dined with the sheriff came out of the dining room putting on their hats and raincoats. They had heard the last of what the sheriff told Cobbett and there was a look of shock and astonishment in their eyes. But the sheriff turned to them and smiled as if nothing was wrong.

"You boys about ready? It don't look like this rain is going to let up, so we might as well head for that poker game at the Comstock."

As he talked, the sheriff put on a yellow slicker that one of the men handed him, and then he went out with them, his arms over the shoulders of two of them, still talking. The third man looked around curiously at Cobbett, but the sheriff had finished with him and let on like he was not there.

The desk clerk came out of the dining room picking his teeth and gave Cobbett a questioning look. He did not even glance at the mud on his boots or his wet slicker dripping water on the carpet. That was the way it usually was in the West. You did not stare at a man's outfit, no matter what shape it was in. The clerk at the Rockville hotel was an exception, and out of place on the frontier. He belonged back East where the streets were paved.

"You need a room?" the clerk at the New Hope hotel asked.

Cobbett silently nodded, his thoughts still on the fat sheriff, and followed the clerk to the desk in the corner. The clerk indicated the register and moved around behind the desk to get a key while Cobbett signed his name. For an address he gave Miles City, Montana. There had been towns before Miles City, too many towns, but he had made no friends in those towns and no one in them cared what happened to him. He knew everyone in Miles, and had even made a few friends there.

He carried his stuff up to his room overlooking the square. It was a larger room than the one in the Rockville hotel, a much nicer room, with a double bed, a bureau in the corner, a clothes closet, two chairs and a washstand with a pitcher of water and a basin. There was even a towel and a small bar of soap.

Cobbett was tired from the long ride, but he was not sleepy, and the talk with Sheriff Bailey had left him restless and filled with discontent. It bothered him to see a man like Bailey, doing an incompetent job and ignoring the demands of people whose rights and property he was supposed to be protecting. Men like Bailey and Tobe Langley gave all lawmen a bad name. What bothered him even more was the knowledge that he could not do anything about it. At least he could not think of anything at the moment.

He stood at the window and looked down at the dark square for a short time, then decided he needed a drink. There was not a saloon in the hotel, but a little more rain would not hurt him, and he had his slicker which would turn most of it. He put the slicker back on, then went downstairs and left the hotel, heading for the first saloon he saw.

It turned out to be the Comstock, and it was noisy and crowded, filled with smoke and whiskey fumes and the smell of wet clothing and unwashed bodies. At a rear table the sheriff and his friends sat playing poker and smoking fat cigars. All care had vanished from the sheriff's plump round face and once more he seemed jovial and thoroughly at his ease, doing most of the talking and smiling at his cards like he had a winning hand. Cobbett got the impression however that it was just a friendly game and no one cared much who won or lost.

It annoyed him to see the sheriff enjoying himself at the taxpayers' expense and gambling with money he had not really earned. But

the annoyance did not show on his poker face. He had gambled quite
a bit himself from time to time, losing more often than he won.

Passing on around the smoke-filled room, his glance came to rest
on a rather small man standing about ten feet down the bar from him.
He had not noticed the man when he first came in because two burly
fellows had been standing between them who had since left. The slight
fellow's hat was shoved back on curly reddish hair and his small face
had a curiously twisted, evil look that was merely emphasized by the
smile it wore as he watched Cobbett with bright little eyes.

It was a face with which Cobbett was altogether too familiar. He
had seen it many times before. The man's name was Archie Beebe
and Cobbett had killed his whiskey-peddling partner in Indian Territory years before. Archie himself had served a stretch in prison. After
his release he had dogged Cobbett's trail, following him from place
to place and doing everything he could, short of getting arrested, to
make Cobbett's life miserable. Usually he encouraged Cobbett's enemies to cause trouble, then stood back himself and watched, smiling
his vindictive smile and waiting for the moment when he would see
Cobbett brought down. But he was in no hurry. He had developed
his little game of revenge into an art, and it was a game that never
ceased to amuse him. To get even with Cobbett, and to do it in a way
that would enable him to escape the consequences, had become the
only purpose of his empty, twisted life. For almost ten years Cobbett
had been looking over his shoulder, expecting to see Archie Beebe's
grinning, evil face behind him, and he knew Archie was not here in
New Hope by accident.

It suddenly occurred to Cobbett that in some ways Archie Beebe
and Joe Deegan were a lot alike, although in most ways they were
completely different. Archie Beebe was a ridiculous little man who
did everything in his power to make Cobbett seem even more ridiculous or, failing that, to make him seethe with silent, helpless, bitter
rage. After his term in prison, Beebe had been very careful not to
get himself thrown in jail, but he had learned that there were many,
seemingly innocent little ways to provoke a man and make it seem
that the man himself was in the wrong if he did anything about it.
Cobbett had learned that it was best simply to ignore the little man—
when he could.

"I was beginning to think I'd lost track of you," Beebe said. "But I
just kept going the way you was headed, and somehow I got ahead of
you without seeing you anywhere on the trail. I come through Rock-

ville a few days back and then stopped here when the rain started. Then just a minute ago I heard that fat sheriff over there mention your name, and I found out you'd been having some trouble in Rockville. Seems somebody shot your horse—is that right?"

Cobbett stared at Beebe's grinning face with cold gray eyes, stared through him as if he was not there, then turned his attention to his drink.

Just then Sheriff Bailey saw him and called, loud enough for everyone in the saloon to hear him, "Hey, Cobbett, why didn't you tell me you were a lawman back in Montana?"

Cobbett deliberately finished his drink, then turned his back to the bar and stood looking at the sheriff's smiling round face. This, he decided, was how the sheriff liked to appear in public, agreeable, good-natured, everybody's friend. And everyone in the saloon was smiling and listening to catch Cobbett's answer. They all liked the sheriff and they were ready to like him too if he was the sheriff's friend and he knew he would feel tainted if he let anyone think he was.

"I didn't figure it was any of your business," he said.

There was a moment of shocked silence. Then an angry murmur ran through the saloon. Everyone was offended for the sheriff's sake. Some of the men shook their heads sadly. Others glared at Cobbett, wanting to punch him in his hard unfeeling face. How could anyone talk that way to a nice man like Sheriff Bailey, who only wanted to be everyone's friend? They could overlook anything except bad manners. Stab a man in the back, but don't insult him to his face.

The sheriff's face turned red. "You shouldn't talk like that in my town," he said. "It ain't healthy. You remind me of a fellow who tried to choke a bear to death by jumping down his throat."

The men in the saloon howled with laughter, cheering the sheriff and jeering at Cobbett—and no one enjoyed it more than Archie Beebe. His twisted little face lit up like a lopsided jack-o'-lantern and he gazed about in gleeful amazement at the people laughing at Cobbett. It was the first time he had ever seen anything of the sort unless he himself had instigated it.

He sidled along the bar toward Cobbett and yelled to make himself heard above the racket in the saloon. "It never fails. Cobbett! You make enemies quicker'n anybody I ever saw! And this time you can't blame it on me!"

"That must make you feel awful bad," Cobbett retorted, and turned his attention back to the sheriff, dismissing Archie Beebe.

Bailey glanced about at his supporters, laughing louder than any of them at his joke. He was in his element—surrounded by a cheering audience. He was part politician, part actor, part clown, all hot air. It was easy to see how he did an incompetent job as sheriff and still got reelected time after time, for people loved an entertainer. He would probably go far, Cobbett thought. He might even become governor someday, if somebody didn't kill him first.

Then Cobbett noticed that one of the men at the sheriff's table was not laughing with the rest. He was watching Cobbett thoughtfully through the cigar smoke and seemed oblivious to the mindless cheering and jeering. He was the one who had looked around at Cobbett as the sheriff's party was leaving the hotel.

When the laughter abated somewhat, the sheriff tried to enlarge upon his little joke, but it had gone stale by then and got him only a few more strained laughs and some coughs.

"I'm the big daddy bear around here, Cobbett. You don't want to jump down my throat, do you?"

Cobbett watched the huge fat sheriff for a moment in silence, despising him and everything he stood for. But he knew now that anything he said would be held against him, not against the sheriff. So he turned and paid for his drink and headed for the door.

"You ain't the law around here, Cobbett, I am," the sheriff called after him. "You better remember that."

Cobbett went on out, ignoring the sheriff's empty threat. It was what Archie Beebe called quietly after him that gave him a moment of uneasiness. "I'll see you in Rockville." Knowing Cobbett, Beebe knew he would go back to Rockville, and Beebe meant to follow him and make things as uncomfortable for him there as he had done in Miles City and other places.

Cobbett walked back across the muddy square in the pouring rain, his long face bleak and still with weariness and fading hope. It looked like he could not escape his past any more than he could escape himself.

He entered the hotel, went up to his room and washed up. He was almost ready to get into bed when there was a knock on the door. He had heard no footsteps in the carpeted hall, nor any other sound, just that sudden knock, which surprised him a little and annoyed him a great deal.

Half expecting it to be Archie Beebe playing one if his little games, Cobbett silently pulled his pants back on and jerked the door open. If

Beebe was still there he meant to grab him by the collar, march him to the head of the stairs and give him a good kick back down them.

But it was not Beebe. It was the man Cobbett had seen studying him in the saloon. The man glanced along the hall, then said quietly, "Good evening. I'm Lot Tidings. I wonder if I might come in and talk to you a minute? It's rather important."

Puzzled, Cobbett stepped back and the man came in, softly closing the door behind him and standing with his back to it, studying Cobbett silently.

He saw a tall man with pale hair and a lean, leathery face, wearing only his pants—a man with stronger arms and shoulders than would be apparent when he had on a shirt.

Meanwhile, Cobbett was studying his strange visitor just as carefully. Tidings was still wearing his raincoat, a well preserved mackintosh, and rain beaded his stiff gray hat that looked like a derby with a wide brim. He was a man of fifty or a little better, with an erect, almost military bearing and the air of a world-weary gentleman a little tarnished by experience. His face was rather large and round, with a look of ripe firmness that was on the point of going soft. But his eyes were small and deep-set; they were pale, bleak eyes, with a guarded look in them. Cobbett had the feeling that Tidings was not what he seemed to be, and the man made him uneasy.

"I was watching you tonight in the dining room and the saloon," Tidings said.

"So I noticed," Cobbett grunted.

"There was a reason for it. I believe you're the sort of man I've been wanting to meet. You must be the Cobbett that Mac McCabe has been talking about ever since he came back from Montana?"

"You know McCabe?"

"Everyone around here knows McCabe," Tidings said. "He comes over here all along, trying to get Sheriff Bailey to do something about the rustling around Rockville. As a matter of fact, that's what I wanted to talk to you about."

"Oh?"

Tidings nodded. "I own a ranch near here. I don't spend much time there. My wife prefers to live in town. We came out here not long after the war. My father left me a small fortune and I decided to invest part of it in a cattle ranch. I don't think of it as a money-making venture. It's more like a sport or a hobby. But if something belongs to me I don't like somebody trying to steal it. That's what I wanted to see you about."

Cobbett put on his shirt, watching Tidings silently.

Tidings took off his damp hat, looked at it blankly and put it back on. He walked over to the window, parted the curtain to look out, then immediately turned and regarded Cobbett thoughtfully with his bleak eyes. Trying to make up his mind about something.

"I'd like to hire you to clean out those rustlers around Rockville," he said finally. "Joe Deegan in particular. It's worth five thousand dollars to me."

Cobbett, who was not easily surprised, stared at the man in astonishment.

"They've just about cleaned McCabe out," Tidings went on, "and he's the only big rancher around there. He told me he soon wouldn't have a cow or a horse left if it kept up. He's already had to let most of his hands go because he can't afford to pay them. How long do you think it will be before those rustlers start stealing stock from me and the other ranchers around New Hope?"

"I can understand your concern," Cobbett said. "But I'm afraid you've misjudged me. I'm not a hired killer."

"No offense, but any man who wears a badge in this country is a hired killer. He has to be if he does his job. Sheriff Bailey never kills anyone, but he doesn't do much of a job."

"That's why I quit wearing a badge," Cobbett said. "I got tired of killing."

Tidings looked at him carefully. "That's strange," he said. "When you told the sheriff about your horse, I got the feeling you'd like to do some more killing."

Cobbett did not say anything, and after a moment Tidings asked, "Who was it? Some of those troublemakers around Rockville, who're also doing most of the rustling?"

"Probably."

"That's what I figured. That's why I thought you were just the man I need. You've had some experience dealing with people like Joe Deegan and his friends, and you have reason for wanting to see them punished."

"Punished?"

Tidings hesitated for just a moment, his round face and bleak eyes showing no change. Then he said calmly, "I want them dead. My wife and I are planning a trip back East to see her folks before long, and when I return I don't want to find all my stock run off."

"Shouldn't you talk to your friend the sheriff about it?"

"I have talked to him," Tidings said. "He told me about what he told you. He was just more polite about it. Everyone knows he's afraid to go near Rockville. But even if those men were arrested, it would be hard to get them convicted in this county. They'd be out in no time and rustling stock again, bolder than ever."

Cobbett studied Tidings for a moment with hard eyes, then asked with a note of impatience in his tone, "How many men have you got?"

"Seven regular hands and a manager. Why?"

"Then you don't need me," Cobbett said. "Take your men and do you own dirty work."

Tidings looked embarrassed. "I can't do that."

"Why can't you?"

"In the first place, I couldn't ask my men to do it, until those boys start stealing my stock," Tidings said quietly. "And I don't want to sound like a hypocrite, but I don't want my name mixed up in it. My wife would never hear of it, and my friends here and back East would be appalled. I was a colonel in the war and we did what we had to do, and got medals for doing it. This is a kind of war also, but a great many people wouldn't see it that way. My wife's folks are what you might call the upper crust of society and I don't want to do anything they wouldn't approve of. One of her brothers is thinking about running for Congress and they'd never forgive me if I did anything to hurt his chances. In fact, they've never forgiven me for bringing Julie out here to what they call this godforsaken country. She was just a girl when I married her—a very beautiful girl—and I was close to forty. Her folks thought she could have done better, even though I was something of a war hero and the son of a rich businessman."

"It sounds to me like you're taking an awful chance just talking this way to a stranger," Cobbett said. "And you'd stand to lose more than you cold hope to gain by hiring me. You may not ever have any trouble with those rustlers."

"*That* is a chance I can't take," Tidings said, his eyes even bleaker than before. He thought for a moment. "You see, her folks thought it was crazy for me to invest so much money in a ranch out here. They said all my stock would be run off by white trash or wild Indians. So far that hasn't happened and I intend to see that it doesn't."

"Then I suggest you hire more men and put them to guarding your stock around the clock," Cobbett said. "No one could blame you for that."

Tidings looked at him bleakly. "Perhaps I did misjudge you, Cobbett. Do you have any idea how many men that would take in a country like this, where stock runs loose and spreads out all over creation, mixing in with other people's stock?" Not waiting for an answer, Tidings shook his head. "No, that just wouldn't be feasible. I was considered something of a strategist during the war, and believe me, my plan makes a lot more sense. Clean out the rustlers and there's an end to the problem."

Cobbett shrugged. "Then clean them out. But you'll have to get someone else to do it."

Tidings studied him thoughtfully. "If you're worried about getting in trouble with the law, I think I can safely assure you that you have nothing to worry about on that score. The governor is a personal friend of mine and he wants this rustling stopped as bad as I do. He has assured me, in the strictest confidence of course, that he would sanction any steps I wished to take to put an end to it."

Seeing the skeptical look on Cobbett's face, Tidings added, "As a matter of fact, I'm leaving on the morning stage to see the governor, and I intend to come back through Rockville. I should be passing through there in about a week, and there's a good chance I'll have something in writing from the governor to prove what I say."

"That won't change anything," Cobbett said. "Not as far as I'm concerned."

"I want you to give it some thought," Tidings told him. "A lot of thought. Think about how long it will take you to earn five thousand dollars wearing a badge, and doing the very same work on a deputy sheriff's pay. After all, wasn't that the real reason you came to see the sheriff—to try and get him to give you a deputy's badge?"

Chapter 9

After Lot Tidings left his room, Cobbett went to bed, but he did not go to sleep. He lay awake listening to the rain on the roof and thinking about what Tidings had said. And, in spite of himself, he thought about the five thousand dollars Tidings had offered him to clean out the rustlers around Rockville.

Five thousand dollars was a lot of money, more than Cobbett had managed to save in fifteen years of wearing a badge and risking his neck almost every day.

And there had been a certain logic in Tidings's argument. If Cobbett pinned on a badge, he might end up killing some of the rustlers—he might end up killing some of them even if he didn't pin on a badge. But there was a difference, even if Tidings could not see it and Cobbett could not explain it. To kill in the line of duty or in self-defense or in the heat of an argument was one thing; to kill for money was something else entirely.

Beyond this, there was something about Tidings that did not strike him right. It was more a feeling then anything he could put his finger on, but Tidings did not seem like the sort of man who would hire several men killed just on the chance that they might start stealing his stock. Cobbett had a hunch there was more to it than that. A lot more. And until he found out what it was, he decided it would be a good idea to have as little as possible to do the Mr. Lot Tidings.

He finally went to sleep, and woke up later than he had intended.

It had quit raining and the sun shed a diluted glow on the window curtains. When he got down to the dining room everyone else had finished eating and had gone out to see the stage off. In the small crowd on the boardwalk he saw Lot Tidings waiting to board the stage. Beside Tidings stood a slender young woman with honey-blond hair. When she turned her head to look at someone behind her, Cobbett stared through the window at her in surprise. She was the most beautiful woman he had ever seen. Even more beautiful then Molly Hicks.

Her eyes were sky-blue and she had a small, perfectly shaped face, with a cute little nose and pouting lips that looked like they wanted to be kissed. Her clothes had been tailored to fit and there were firm curves below and above her slender waist.

A moment later she turned her attention back to the stage without seeing Cobbett and he sat down with a sigh, feeling the old pang of loneliness inside him. Feeling the morning stubble on his hard face, he reflected that he had never paid much attention to ugly girls, and the pretty ones had never paid much attention to him. But if he could not have what he wanted, he did not want anything. He would rather live out his days alone—and it was beginning to look like that was just what he would have to do.

Not that he minded, most of the time. It was just when he saw someone like Julie Tidings or Molly Hicks that his loneliness bothered him.

When he saw someone like her husband, or Gordon Bailey, or Archie Beebe, then he did not mind being alone. He preferred it.

Not that women were necessarily any better than men. They just looked better. Even the ugly ones looked better than men, with a few notable exceptions like the double-chinned fat waitress bearing down on him and frowning like she was debating whether to throw him out by herself or call for assistance.

"Am I too late to get anything to eat?" he asked, ready to get back up.

The scowl left her dark warty face, to be replaced by a sympathetic look. A big eater herself to judge by her size, she probably hated to send anyone away hungry. "We might still find something for you," she said. "What would you like?"

"Whatever's left. Coffee's the main thing, and I like it straight."

The fat waitress let out a raucous laugh that made Cobbett wince, then she turned and bawled at the kitchen, "Another mouth to feed!"

Cobbett sat a little lower in his chair as several people out front turned to peer through the window. Lot Tidings saw him and nodded his head slightly, his face expressionless, then turned and gave his young wife a hand into the coach, following her and closing the door. They seemed to be the only ones leaving on the stage.

The fat waitress still stood at Cobbett's elbow. She bent down slightly, the better to see through the window, and lowered her voice like a true gossip. "That Julie Tidings! Always puttin' on airs and showin' off her fine clothes. But if you ask me, she ain't a bit better than them girls what works at Mama Jo's place. She just got back from Salt Lake two days ago. At least that's where she said she was. Didn't nobody even know where she was till she got back. I'm surprised she come back at all. Now she's goin' off again with Mr. Tidings, but I don't think she's goin' all the way back to Salt Lake with him. He let on like he was goin' there on business, but if you ask me, he's goin' to check up on what she was doin' there for three whole weeks and he didn't even know where she was. I heard them arguin' when they was eatin' breakfast, over there in that corner where they didn't think nobody would hear them. I don't think she wanted him to go, and she said she wasn't goin' to stay here by herself while he was gone, with the whole town gossipin' about her and all. She said if he was goin' to Salt Lake, then she was goin' with him as far as Rockville and stay there while he was gone.

Cobbett looked up in surprise and said softly, "Rockville?"

The waitress nodded. "The stage goes through Rockville and then at the next way station east of there it swings north toward the railroad." Her tone dropped even lower, to a conspiratorial whisper. "But if you ask me, the real reason she's goin' to Rockville is to see that rustler, Joe Deegan. She's been over there several times before and they were seen together two or three times."

"I see," Cobbett said. He was beginning to see a good deal.

He glanced through the window, but the stage had already left, and the crowd was beginning to disperse. Sheriff Bailey wobbled up from somewhere, but was too late to do more than wave at the departing stage. No doubt he had overslept, being fat and lazy, and having no actual work to do, none that he ever did anyway. He saw Cobbett through the window, started to lift his hand, then turned and waddled across the square toward a restaurant on the other side.

The waitress, thinking the sheriff had lifted his hand to her—which after all was possible—started to wave back, then slowly lowered her hand when he turned away. "That was Sheriff Bailey," she said in a puzzled tone. "He usually comes in here to eat. I wonder why he didn't this mornin'."

"I wouldn't know," Cobbett said. "Maybe he thought it was too late."

"That ain't ever stopped him before," she said. "Oh, I almost forgot! Your breakfast is prob'ly ready by now."

"I was hoping you'd think of it."

The waitress frowned and was framing an angry retort. But then she changed her mind and shattered his ears with her raucous laugh, which was far worse than anything she might have said.

On his way to the livery stable, Cobbett glanced about carefully and once looked quickly back over his shoulder, half expecting to see Archie Beebe creeping along behind him or just ducking around the corner of a building. But he did not see anything of the little man.

At the stable, while the hostler saddled his horse, he asked, "You seen anything of a little fellow named Archie Beebe?"

The hostler nodded. "He had his horse here for a coupla days, but he come for it late last night, right after it quit rainin'. I was half a mind to charge him extra, roustin' me out at that time o' night."

"You see which way he headed?"

"East, I believe."

Cobbett stepped into the saddle and headed east himself, soon leaving New Hope behind him. The sun was bright in his eyes and the bleak rocky hills before him seemed shrouded in mist and haze. This, he thought, would be a good place for Archie Beebe to hide behind a rock and even his old score. But that was not Archie Beebe's way. He was too clever and cautious, too conscious of the fact that something might go wrong at the last minute, as it had for his grinning yellow-toothed pal, Whiskey Grogan, whose old Henry had jammed on him. Beebe had contrived to be elsewhere at the time, with witnesses to prove it, and he would no doubt manage to be elsewhere the next time someone tried to ambush Cobbett, just in case. His revenge would be spoiled if he got punished for it, or if he had to spend the rest of his days on the run.

After a night's rest the bay seemed fresh and ready for the long ride back to Rockville. Cobbett kept him at a fast trot, uneasily watching some clouds gathering over the mountains that formed the northern horizon. The same thing happened as on the day before.

The rain held off until late afternoon, when Cobbett was no more than five miles from Rockville. Then, as he was nearing a rocky ridge, the first drops fell.

And at that moment, without any warning whatever, the bay screamed and dropped to its knees. From the rocks on the ridge a rifle roared and Cobbett saw the white puff of smoke as he left the saddle, jerking out his long-barreled Colt. He hit the ground and rolled into a shallow brush-lined gully, peering up at the ridge with his gun cocked and ready, coldly watching for a target.

Then he heard a snort of harsh laughter that sounded vaguely familiar. A moment later at least two horses galloped away, hidden by the ridge.

Cobbett got to his feet, looked at the dying horse with his jaws clenched in cold rage and put a bullet in the animal's head to end its suffering. He stripped the gear from the horse, hid the saddle and walked on toward Rockville carrying his rifle, saddlebags and blanket roll. By then it was almost dark and pouring rain, but his slicker kept him reasonably dry down to his boots, which hurt his feet less than they would have if they had been dry.

He felt certain that Archie Beebe was behind this. Beebe probably had not fired the shot himself but it had been his idea. He would know that killing this horse also would make Cobbett madder than anything else, and a word to Barney Nash and his friends would have been sufficient.

Cobbett had bought the horse only to make it seem like he was leaving Rockville for good, so the Nash gang would not have any sort of surprise waiting for him on his return. But Archie Beebe had left New Hope last night, had ridden hard and warned them that he would be coming back and had suggested that if they really wanted to annoy him, all they had to do was kill the horse he had bought to replace the dead sorrel. With little doubt, they had not needed much persuading, and might have done it even if Beebe had not suggested it.

But Beebe would not have left it to chance. He knew Cobbett pretty well by now and felt certain he would not do anything about it without proof, even if there was virtually no doubt in his mind who had done it. He had worn a badge too long and was handicapped by a lawman's code, by his own personal code as well. Beebe would know that. He would also know, from personal experience, the corrosive, self-punishing quality of helpless rage and hatred.

One day, Cobbett thought grimly, that little bastard will go too

far. And on that long walk in the cold rain he thought of all the ways
he would enjoy killing Archie Beebe.

By the time he reached Rockville he had his anger under perfect control. Those who knew him would have said his studied calm
was a bad sign, like the calm before the storm. But no one in Rockville knew him well enough to recognize the danger signals. Yet old
Mort Crumby, when he crawled down out of the hayloft where he had
taken refuge, sensed that there was something deadly in the quiet,
casual tone of the tall man standing there in the rain looking off up
the dark street of the town.

"You afoot again?" Crumby asked in amazement.

"Afraid so," Cobbett said, watching the rain slanting through dim
lanes of light from windows along the street. "A little red-haired fellow rode in sometime around noon. Was he packing a rifle?"

"Crumby thought for a moment, holding his chin, then shook his
head. "No, he didn't have no rifle."

"Did he leave again later?"

"Not unless he went on foot, without me seein' him. He never
come back for his horse. It's still there in the stall, a pretty little
paint horse. If you like paints."

"I don't. Barney Nash and his friends in town?"

Crumby hesitated. His tone became guarded and uneasy. "At
Duffy Shaw's saloon, I reckon."

"How long have they been in town?"

The question sounded idle and casual enough, but it made Mort
Crumby still more uneasy. "Rode in about midafternoon, I believe,"
he said cautiously.

"Two of them left again later and didn't get back till after dark,"
Cobbett said. "Which two was it?"

"Why ask me?" The old hostler said, sounding frightened and re-
sentful. "Anyone in town could tell you that."

"So could you."

"And I could get myself killed for runnin' my big mouth too,"
Crumby said hoarsely. "I'm off down here by myself. Them next two
buildings is empty, except for some hay I got in one of them. They
could kill me and nobody might not even know about it, if they used
a knife. Tap Grodin's got him a big bowie and he'd cut my throat just
for the fun of it. That boy's mean as a snake."

"Forget it," Cobbett said shortly. "Go on back to your hayloft. I'd
like to borrow one of your horses for a while, but I can get it myself."

"You mean you goin' out again in this weather?" Crumby exclaimed.

"I'm getting used to it."

"Well, I better get the horse for you," Crumby said. "In the dark you're liable to take one of theirs by mistake, and then I'd be in real trouble."

"Don't worry about it," Cobbett said. "Go on back to sleep."

He said it quietly, but something in his tone warned the old hostler to do as he had been told, and after watching Cobbett uncertainly for a moment he climbed the ladder and felt in the hay for his bottle. Cobbett heard him uncork it.

Cobbett hid his saddlebags and blanket roll in a dark corner and took the first horse he came to. He did not put a saddle on the horse, but led it out into the rain and swung up onto its bare back with his rifle in one hand. He circled around town, as he had coming in, and struck the road beyond the first rocky hill to the west. He followed the road back to the site of the ambush, threw his own wet saddle on the borrowed horse and looped his rope around the hind feet of the dead horse. With the other end wrapped around the horn he dragged the dead horse out of the road. Then he recoiled his rope, hung it on the horn and rode back to Rockville.

He was tempted to ride boldly down the street on the borrowed horse, which probably belonged to one of the Nash gang. But at the last minute he circled around again and came around the corner of the dark stable without having been seen by anyone.

"That you, Cobbett?" Mort Crumby called worriedly from the hayloft.

"Yeah. Go on back to sleep."

Cobbett unsaddled the horse and rubbed it down carefully. He put his saddle in the tack room and carried his saddlebags, blanket roll and Winchester up the street to the hotel. The clerk did not look too happy to see him in his dripping slicker and muddy boots.

When Cobbett picked up the pen to sign the register he noticed Julie Tidings's name written in a neat feminine hand.

It was dark and pouring rain when the stage reached the Crooked Creek Station fifteen miles east of Rockville. Lot Tidings, the only passenger, made a dash for the door of the station and entered the large room brushing rain from his overcoat. The rambling log building housed station, crossroads store and a hotel of sorts under one leaky roof. The main room contained a half dozen plank tables and a plank bar along one wall. Through an open door on the left was the store; to the rear, the kitchen and sleeping quarters. The station man was outside helping the profane driver with the horses and there was no one in the room but a big man in a shabby dark overcoat standing alone at the bar with a bottle and glass before him. There was a yellow slicker on the bar near him.

Lot Tidings took a closer look at the man's swarthy face under the low brim of his hat and saw that it was Tobe Langley, the former marshal of Rockville. On a sudden impulse Tidings crossed the room and stepped up to the bar not far from the heavyset man. He looked at Langley out of his bleak eyes and shook his head. "It's raining cats and dogs out there, and me without a raincoat."

Langley's only response was to turn a little more away from him and lower his head so that the wide brim of his hat hid more of his face.

"I let my wife have mine," Tidings added. "She stopped off in Rockville and it was raining there too. I didn't even get out of the coach. The driver never stops there any longer than he has to because of the Nash gang. They never carry anything of value on this run. That's why there's no shotgun guard."

Tobe Langley turned and gave Tidings a hard stare. "Why you telling me all this?"

Lot Tidings's face did not change, but his pale eyes got a little bleaker, then flickered faintly with sardonic amusement. "I guess you know it better than me. I understand Joe Deegan ran you out of Rockville."

Langley grunted and started to turn away, then suddenly gave Tidings an even harder stare and said flatly, "You ain't got much room to talk. He just spent three weeks with your wife in Salt Lake."

"I heard a rumor to that effect," Tidings admitted. "That's where I'm going now. I've got some other business to attend to in Salt Lake, but that's the main reason. I want to find out what she did there and who she saw. Not that it really matters. I'm well aware that they've seen each other before and will do so again." He looked directly at Langley. "That's what I wanted to talk to you about. It seems we've got something in common. We'd both like to see Joe Deegan dead."

CHAPTER 10

It was too late to get anything to eat in the hotel dining room. Cobbett carried his stuff up to his room—the same room he had had before, overlooking the street—and was on the point of leaving again, when the door of the room next to his opened and Julie Tidings stepped out. In the dimly lit hall her face seemed both pale and flushed and her blue eyes were strangely clouded. Cobbett got the feeling that behind her ladylike poise, her rigid composure, she was furious about something.

"Excuse me," she said. "I heard you come in. Are you going out again? Leaving the hotel, I mean?"

He nodded. "I was thinking about it."

"I wonder if you'd to me a favor?" she asked. "There's a man in the restaurant just across the street. Joe Deegan. Would you please tell him there's a lady at the hotel who would like to see him, if he can spare the time? I'd go myself, if it wasn't raining so hard."

Cobbett watched her silently for a moment and saw her blush deepen and her fine brows knit in a frown. She stood motionless and held on to her careful poise, returning his glance with an icy chill in her own. Her attitude suggested that, although she was asking a favor, it was none of his business and a lady did not explain herself to a dirty, unshaved stranger with mud on his boots. She had not seen Cobbett staring at her through the window of the New Hope Hotel, but that would hardly have been a mark in his favor if she had.

He felt bleak and empty inside. He had felt that way for a long time, but at that moment the feeling seemed worse than usual. "I was on my way to the restaurant," he said. "It won't be any trouble to tell him."

"I thought you might be going there," Julie Tidings said. The frown had left her face but she did not smile. She nodded her blond head, dropped her blue glance and stepped back into her room, closing the door.

As he went down the stairs and left the hotel, Cobbett reflected that she had not bothered to thank him, unless that little nod had been meant as thanks. Perhaps she intended to thank him later, but he doubted it. More likely she would avoid him if possible, resenting the fact that it had been necessary to tell him even as much as she had in requesting the favor.

The rain seemed to have slacked up a little as he crossed the muddy street, but he would have gotten wet without his slicker. Just inside the restaurant he stopped to remove the dripping slicker and hung it on a peg near the door, glancing at Joe Deegan. Deegan sat on a stool at the counter talking to Jane Keller, who stood behind the counter with her arms folded, looking small and plain and somehow pathetic. It was all too obvious that she was in love with Joe Deegan, that he knew it and toyed with her for his own amusement, feeling nothing himself.

"Looks like you made it back," Deegan said. And there was a hint of malice in his easy grin. He squinted thoughtfully at Cobbett through the smoke of the cigarette that dropped from his thin lips. "Hear you lost another horse. Seems somebody shot that bay out from under you."

"Where did you hear that?" Cobbett asked idly, as he sat down at a table near the counter. "Barney Nash and his friends?"

Deegan looked smug as he drew on his cigarette. "Maybe it was one of them told me. I'm not sure where they heard it."

Cobbett glanced at Jane Keller's pale, freckled face. "You heard anything about it?"

She looked uncertainly at Joe Deegan and remained silent.

"I guess she only heard what I told her," Deegan said, grinning, clearly enjoying himself. "But it's all over town. Everybody knows about it."

"Well, it shouldn't be too hard to find out who started the story," Cobbett said calmly. "Couldn't be more than two or three people rode in from the west since the horse was shot—and one of them did it."

"That might be hard to prove," Deegan said. "Just because some-body was out that way and saw the horse—that's sort of jumping to conclusions, ain't it?"

Cobbett was silent for a moment, his eyes cold. He glanced at Jane Keller, then said to Deegan, "I believe there's a lady over at the hotel who wants to see you."

"A lady?" Joe Deegan said, his face suddenly blank. "Why would a lady want to see me?"

"I can't imagine," Cobbett said.

Deegan looked at him and grinned. "I guess she heard how hand-some I am. Whoever it is." He rose to his feet, picking his black hat up off the next stool and putting it on like he was in no hurry and only mildly curious. "I better go see what she wants," he said to Jane Keller, with an amused, half-malicious grin.

Though her face was pinched with a look of anguish, she smiled back at him and her eyes followed him as he left the restaurant. He gave Cobbett a little salute as he left, but said nothing to him.

Jane Keller looked through the window with tortured eyes, trying to see Deegan as he crossed the dark rainy street. Then she tore her eyes away from the window and looked unhappily at Cobbett. She seemed older than he had thought at first—too old and too plain to be thinking about Joe Deegan, when there were younger and prettier girls around.

Just as Ben Cobbett was too old to be thinking about Julie Tid-ings and Molly Hicks, when there were younger, more charming men like Joe Deegan around.

He thought wryly that perhaps he and the plain waitress, two old rejects, should team up. But neither was interested in the oth-er. They both wanted something they could not have, and seemed doomed to loneliness.

"What would you like, Mr. Corbett?" she asked with complete in-difference.

She even had his name wrong, he thought. She had got it right the first time, but then had heard someone else—probably Mac Mc-Cabe—call him Corbett and had decided she must have heard it wrong when Joe Deegan passed out the introductions. But Cobbett was not interested enough to correct her. He did not really care what she called him.

He glanced at the menu chalked on the blackboard behind her.

"How about the beefstew and some black coffee."

She went through a door behind the counter and soon returned with his supper on a tray. As she placed it before him she said, "That lady at the hotel? I guess it was the one who came in on the stage today?"

"I guess." Cobbett glanced at her, then went to work on the beefstew. "Deegan didn't know she was in town?"

Jane Keller dropped her glance. "I don't think so. If he did he didn't say anything about it."

And, Cobbett thought, Jane Keller had been very careful not to tell him.

"It was raining when the stage came in," Jane added. "I just caught a glimpse of her when she turned to say something to someone who didn't get out of the stage and she had a raincoat thrown over her head, but I could tell she had blond hair. It was that Tidings woman from New Hope, wasn't it?"

"I believe so."

"That's what I thought," Jane said with a note of bitterness in her tone. She looked through the rain-fogged window toward the hotel, then added, "She's married to Lot Tidings, a rancher over at New Hope, but that don't stop women like her. If they see a man they want they start running after him and they don't stop till they get him, and they don't care how much harm they do or who gets hurt."

Cobbett, busy with his eating, glanced at the plain little waitress in silence, mildly surprised at her pent-up bitterness.

"It's not Joe's fault," she added. "Who could blame him—a beautiful woman like that running after him. I just wish women like her and Molly Hicks would leave him alone. The same goes for Barney Nash and that wild bunch. Joe's really a nice boy, but it seems like all the wrong kind of people are trying to drag him down with them."

Cobbett continued eating in silence for a few moments, his attention seemingly on his food. When he spoke his tone was soft and sympathetic—unusual for him—but his words came closer to expressing his true feelings, his true opinion of Joe Deegan. "You don't think he's got the brains or the willpower to stay away from people like that and run his own life?"

"Joe likes to be friends with everyone, and that's his big weakness," she said. "People like Barney Nash and them try to get him to do bad things with them, and he does it just to keep from hurting their feelings. That's the only reason."

Cobbett gave her a pitying look, but said nothing more. He knew if would be a waste of breath. She reminded him of quite a few women he had known, mostly wives and mothers, who refused to believe anything bad about their men, in spite of the weight of evidence.

He was relieved, though a little surprised, when a man's voice called her into the kitchen. He had not known there was anyone back there.

He pushed his empty plate away and thoughtfully sipped his coffee, then laid some money on the table and rose. He slowly put on his slicker, leaving it unbuttoned, and took time to light a cigar before going back out into the rain. Cupping the cigar in his hand, he tramped through the mud and the rain to Duffy Shaw's saloon and pushed in through the swing doors. He put the cigar back between his teeth and walked to the bar, his cool gray eyes showing no change when he saw Archie Beebe standing at the bar with Barney Nash and the others. They were all here, including Chuck Moser, who gave Cobbett a startled look and then a sheepish grin. The others grinned also, but in a different way—smug, malicious grins that they might have copied from Joe Deegan.

"Heard somebody shot yore horse, Cobbett," Barney Nash said. "That's the second one, ain't it?"

"You know damn well it is," Cobbett said, motioning to the scowling Duffy Shaw for a drink. It seemed that Shaw, who owned the saloon, did his own bartending.

In the back bar mirror Cobbett saw Barney Nash and the others glance at one another and grin, but they seemed a little tense and on guard. They were wondering what he intended to do. The truth was, he did not know himself. After seeing Julie tidings again for that one brief moment in the hotel, petty grudges and stupid games seemed like a waste of time, not worth bothering about. There were other things a lot more important. He would probably never have any of those things himself, but that did not keep him from thinking about them.

Also, if he was going to get even, he would pick his own time, and it would not be tonight when they were all here together, expecting trouble and ready for it. He was not a coward, but he was not a fool either.

"If somebody shot my horse I reckon it would make me mad enough to do somethin' about it," Barney Nash said, glancing at Cobbett out of his mean little eyes.

Cobbett put down his drink and heard himself say in a quiet, hard tone, "What if the fellow who shot your horse was a lowdown yellow skunk who didn't have the guts to admit it?"

For just a moment Barney Nash's grin faded, but then it returned, broader on one side than on the other. "You wouldn't be tryin' to trick me, would you, Cobbett?" he asked.

"The one who tricked you was that grinning little worm of a man standing there beside you," Cobbett said. "He gets others to do his dirty work because he hasn't got the guts to do it himself. He's already got half a dozen men killed and he's still not satisfied. He'll get you killed too if you listen to him long enough."

"That sounds a lot like a threat."

"Call it a warning."

"Hell, Cobbett," Nash said, glancing down at his empty glass, "if I thought somebody killed my horse, I wouldn't give him no warnin'. I'd go after the son of a bitch."

"Sure you would," Cobbett said. "You'd wait for him behind a rock. Like you did this afternoon."

Nash grinned. "You sayin' that was me?"

"You were there. I heard your stupid laugh. But there was someone up there with you and I'm not sure which one of you fired the shot. Not that it really matters."

"He won't do anything without proof, even if he knows who it was," Archie Beebe sneered. "That's what comes of being a lawman for so long."

Tap Grodin bared his yellow teeth in a wolfish snarl and said, "Archie Beebe here says you're purty good with that gun you wear. You think you're good enough to beat Joe Deegan?"

"I think I'm good enough to beat you," Cobbett said quietly. "Deegan hasn't' asked me."

"You scared of him?" Grodin asked.

"You scared of me?" Cobbett replied.

"You crazy, Cobbett?" Barney Nash exclaimed, amazement on his bloated red face. "Even if you got Tap, the rest of us would fill you full of holes."

"Some of you might," Cobbett said, holding the cigar in his left hand. In the silence that followed he could hear the rain falling on the roof, and smell the bad whiskey and the damp sawdust on the floor. It was not much of a place to die, and he would have picked another time, but he was ready if they were.

"You boys be careful," Archie Beebe said, with a twisted smirk on his little face. "He's liable to kill all of you. Five men with five bullets."

"What makes you think I haven't added another bullet in my gun for you, Archie?" Cobbett asked. Beebe flushed and said nothing, and Cobbett looked at the others and said, "In case you're wondering why Beebe didn't include himself, I'll tell you. If anybody gets shot, it's not going to be Archie Beebe. When the fight gets started, you'll find him somewhere else."

There was a moment of silence. Then Duffy Shaw said in a hard voice, "You better go, Cobbett. And if you're smart, you won't come back."

Cobbett looked at the saloonkeeper's tough bulldog face and deep-set eyes, and he suspected that Shaw was more dangerous than any of the Nash gang. Maybe even more dangerous, in his way, than Joe Deegan.

"What's the hurry?" Barney Nash said. He ginned at Cobbett. "You aim to pin on that badge they been shinin' up for you, Cobbett?"

"Course he will," Archie Beebe said scornfully "He couldn't turn it down."

"You could be right, Beebe," Cobbett said. "When I see someone like you running around loose, it makes me want to pin on a badge and lock you up."

"What you planning to lock me up for this time?" Beebe asked.

"I'll think of something."

"I'll bet you will," Beebe said. Then he said to the others, "He killed my partner down in Indian Territory eight, nine years ago and got me thrown in jail just for runnin' a little whiskey to the Indians. Ever since then he's tried to keep me away from the places where he's the law. But I'm stickin' to him like a bur till I see him get what he deserves."

"Why don't you do the job yourself, Archie, instead of waiting for someone else to do it for you?" Cobbett asked, calmly smoking his cigar. He knew Beebe would not do anything.

"You'd like that, wouldn't you?" Beebe asked resentfully. "You'd like for me to draw on you, so you could kill me too. Well, it ain't gonna be that easy with me, Cobbett. I'll just wait. I got plenty of time, and I'll wait forever if I have to. Maybe there's something you didn't know, Cobbett. Whiskey Grogan was my brother. He changed his name because the law wanted him for killin' some niggers over in

Arkansas. He never did have much use for niggers or lawmen."

"I'm not surprised you waited this long to admit he was your brother," Cobbett said in a quiet, brutally indifferent tone. "He was an even lower form of scum than you."

Archie Beebe's red face twitched in anger, but he stared at the bar in silence, trying to get himself under control. He did not want to fight Ben Cobbett any more than he wanted to die, which would amount to the same thing if they used guns, or a good beating if it was fists.

"Why pick on the little fellow?" Barney Nash asked. "If you want to fight, we'll fight you."

"We?"

"I'll fight you by myself if you promise to fight fair."

"You'd lose," Cobbett said.

Barney Nash looked at him in surprise. "I don't mean guns, I mean fists."

"You'd still lose."

Barney Nash grinned and began removing his little derby and green coat.

"No fighting in here," Duffy Shaw said. "If you want to fight, take it outside."

"It's all right, Duffy," Barney Nash said. "I'll pay for the damages."

"With what?" Shaw asked. "You can't even pay for your liquor. Joe Deegan wins all your money playing poker, then you come in here asking for credit."

Barney Nash's face got red and he looked down at his empty glass. "The bastard cheats. I don't know how he does it, but he cheats. That's the only reason he wins all the time."

"He doesn't have to cheat," Shaw said bluntly. "You're as clumsy with cards as you are with your fists."

Nash stared at the saloonkeeper in surprise, almost in disbelief, and his face got even redder. "You lookin' for trouble too, Duffy?" he asked.

"None I can't handle," Shaw said, and turned his hard little eyes on Cobbett. "You still here?"

"You didn't see me leave, did you?"

The saloonkeeper reached for the bottle in front of Cobbett and put the cork back in it. "That one's on the house, but I can do without your business in the future, especially if you aim to take that marshal's job."

"I'll pay," Cobbett said, reaching in his pocket for some change. "And if I decide to take the marshal's job, I'll be coming in all along to make sure you're running a clean place."

Shaw placed his hands on the bar and stared hard at Cobbett. "Let me tell you something, mister. I've operated saloons in a dozen towns between here and St. Louis. In most of them towns they had a tough marshal, but none of them lasted very long. I've seen a lot of men like you come and go in my time."

"Sounds like you've done quite a bit of coming and going yourself," Cobbett grunted, rolling his cigar between his teeth. "What's a big operator like you doing in a town like this?"

"I was wondering the same about you."

"I was just passing through. But some of your friends seemed to want me to stay a while." Cobbett glanced at Barney Nash and the others out of the corner of his eye. "I may decide to oblige them."

"I don't think that would be a good idea," Duffy Shaw said. "Unless you change your attitude."

"The opinions of saloonkeepers don't interest me," Cobbett said. "If they keep in line I let them alone. If they don't, I usually throw them in jail or run them out of town."

Duffy Shaw's beady eyes glinted with hatred. "I wouldn't advise you to try either one with me," he said. "No one's ever done that and got away with it. Most of them marshals I mentioned were smart enough to leave me alone."

"Smart? That's not the word I'd use to describe them."

The saloonkeeper shrugged. "You can use any word you like," he said. Then he added, because he couldn't resist it, "The opinions of lawmen don't interest me. If they keep in line I leave them alone. If they don't, I usually run them out of town. Some left in a box."

It was suddenly so quiet in the saloon that the rain seemed to roar on the roof, and water dripped on a table with a loud persistent thud like a heart pounding. Ben Cobbett stood like stone, his weathered brown face expressionless.

Then he said in a soft, almost courteous tone, "You just made a bad mistake. Now I'm going to take that marshal's job."

"I'll be here when you're gone," Duffy Shaw told him. "But my guess is you'll never leave this town alive. This is your last town, Cobbett."

"It will be somebody's last town," Cobbett replied.

CHAPTER 11

When he was almost back to the hotel, Cobbett suddenly stopped and stood on the muddy street in the cold rain, looking at the shrouded dark hills west of town. His cigar had gone out but he did not bother to relight it. He removed it from his mouth and glanced at it in the dark. Without turning his head he asked, "You enjoy fooling around dark alleys on wet nights?"

The dark figure at the mouth of the alley chuckled. It was Joe Deegan. "I wanted to see if you'd notice me. You're pretty sharp, but if I was laying for you you'd be dead by now."

"Wrong," Cobbett said. "If you were laying for me, you'd be dead by now. I saw you go in there and if I hadn't known who it was I would have circled around behind you."

"But you knew I wouldn't ambush you, is that it?"

"Right. You think you could beat me to the draw, so you probably won't try to shoot me in the back."

"What do you think?" Deegan asked. "You saw me draw."

"Think you're the fastest gun in the world, don't you?" Cobbett asked, with the unseen ghost of a smile hovering near his lips.

"Deegan shrugged. "Who knows? They say that no matter how fast a man is, there's somebody faster. I don't buy that. There's somebody somewhere who's faster than anyone else."

"And you believe it's you."

"Could be."

"A lot of people have thought that. Most of them are dead now."

"I'm not," Deegan pointed out.

"I'm not either."

Deegan chuckled. "That's right, you ain't. But how long do you think you'll last, with all the enemies you've got?"

"You've got quite a few yourself. Maybe more than you know."

"If you mean Lot Tidings, I already know about him. But I don't let jealous husbands worry me."

Cobbett glanced down at his dead cigar through half-shut eyes, and dropped the cigar into the mud. "I gather you didn't worry very much about Roper Hicks either."

"Not enough to kill him, if that's what you mean," Deegan said in a different tone, one that was usually accompanied by narrowed eyes and slightly raised brows. "I think George Pasco shot him, but I ain't sure."

"You might tell her that. I understand she thinks old McCabe had him killed."

Deegan shrugged. "She can think whatever she pleases. I never try to change anyone's mind about anything. It don't do any good. Just causes hard feelings."

"I'm inclined to agree with you there."

After a moment Deegan asked, "You aim to take that marshal's job?"

"Everyone in town seems to think so," Cobbett grunted.

"It's that kind of town," Deegan said. "If one person *thinks* something, in five minutes everybody else *knows* it. As soon as Archie Beebe said he thought you were coming back to Rockville, the word spread through town and pretty soon there wasn't any doubt in anyone's mind about it. Hank Gilbert and some other's got together in old Snively's store and started talking about making you the marshal. They never said that was what they were up to, but everybody knew it anyway. But I think it was mainly that sawed-off barber's idea. He's always talking about law and order and saying something should be done about me and the Nash gang. One of these days I'm gonna have to go over there and give *him* a haircut. One that will last him a while."

"More like a scalping, you mean?"

"You've got the picture."

"You better get it done before I pin on that badge," Cobbett said.

"When I become marshal that sort of thing will have to stop."

"Don't count on it." Deegan came out of the dark shadows and Cobbett saw that he was wearing a raincoat that looked like Lot Tidings's mackintosh. He had his left hand in the pocket and so, probably, was his ivory-handled gun, or perhaps a smaller, hideout weapon. When he was almost to Cobbett, he turned and started down the street toward Duffy Shaw's saloon, repeating over his shoulder, "Don't count on it."

Cobbett stood in the rain looking after the young outlaw for a moment, then he went on to the hotel and climbed the stairs to his room. He removed his slicker and hung it on a nail in the wall, hanging his hat on the same nail. His corduroy coat and gunbelt he hung on the back of the straight chair, then poured water from the pitcher into the basin and washed his face. He ran a comb through his pale hair and looked at his bleak hard face in the bureau mirror. It was the face of a stranger, a man no one would ever know very well, not even Cobbett himself. He avoided thinking about himself and never wondered what made him the way he was. If he had thought about it, he would have concluded that it was because he had no wish to be like other men.

He wanted to strip and scrub himself raw, but he was expecting a knock on the door. So he sat down in the straight-backed chair and cleaned his guns while he waited, working quietly to keep from disturbing Julie Tidings in the next room. At the same time he tried not to think about her, for it was best to keep his mind off things he could not have. When he left Rockville he would leave alone, as always. He would not be running off with another man's wife. He knew himself better than that. There was also the matter of the woman preferring another man.

He had both guns cleaned and was reloading the .45 when the knock came. He quietly thumbed in the fifth cartridge, closed the loading gate and hid the gun in his lap under the rag he had used to clean it. "It's not locked," he said.

Hank Gilbert came in, looking at Cobbett in surprise. He smiled uncertainly. "A little careless, isn't it? Leaving your door unlocked?"

"I knew it would be you. Besides," he added, lifting the gun so that the rag slipped aside. It was not necessary to explain further.

The stout little barber looked reassured at sight of the gun. Cobbett had not let him down.

Cobbett rose to his feet, holstered the gun and transferred the gunbelt and his coat to the bedpost, pushing the only chair toward Gilbert. He himself sat down on the edge of the bed.

Gilbert shucked out of his slicker and accepted the chair, smiling at Cobbett. "How did you know it was me?"

Cobbett shrugged. "I knew someone would come. I figured it would be you."

Gilbert gave him a more serious look. "When you left I had a feeling you were going to New Hope to see the sheriff about a deputy's badge. I could have told you he wouldn't give you one. He's afraid to. Like everyone else, he's afraid of what Joe Deegan and the Nash gang will do. Every time anybody tries to do anything about them, they've suffered for it, in one way or another. But I don't have to tell you what I mean. When they heard you were coming back, Barney Nash and Tap Grodin rode out along the road a piece and when they came back they were joking about how they'd seen your horse get shot out from under you. Everybody knows it was them who did it."

Cobbett was silent for a moment, his face heating with anger. He was aware that Hank Gilbert was watching him closely to see how he would react to the news. "Which one of them had the rifle?" he asked.

"Tap Grodin. But he borrowed it from Dill Stringer. Stringer's the only one of that bunch who's got a rifle, as far as I know. They mainly depend on handguns."

"What would happen if Grodin was arrested?"

Hank Gilbert looked embarrassed. "You want the truth?"

"That's the only reason I asked."

"Nothing would happen," Gilbert said bitterly. "That jail is a joke. It wouldn't hold a man five minutes who wanted to get out. That's one reason Tobe Langley never bothered to arrest anyone. He knew he'd have to take the prisoner to New Hope and that he'd just be turned loose if it was any of the Nash gang."

"Why don't you build a new jail?"

The barber's dark face reddened and he sat looking at the floor in silence for a moment. He took off his hat and ran his fingers thoughtfully through his short curly black hair, which was peppered with gray. "The same reason," he said finally. "Everyone's scared. There was some talk about building a new jail once. All the townspeople were going to chip in to pay for it. But when Barney Nash and them heard about it, they went around bullying everyone and said they'd tear the jail down before we got it built. Everyone got scared and pretty soon there wasn't any more talk about building a new jail."

Cobbett heard a small sound in the next room and it occurred to him that Julie Tidings was probably listening to their talk and would repeat anything she heard to Joe Deegan. He started to warn Gilbert to keep his voice down, but decided against it. It was possible that she could not catch their words, although the walls were thin.

Gilbert studied him thoughtfully for a time. "I guess you know why I came to see you?"

Cobbett nodded bleakly. "You want me to take the marshal's job."

"You guessed it," Gilbert said, with an almost sheepish grin. "I know you said you weren't interested, but I thought you might have changed your mind after they shot that other horse you bought."

"I've been thinking about it," Cobbett admitted. "But after listening to what you've just said, I don't know what good it would do for me to take the job. You've got a jail that won't hold prisoners and a county sheriff that will turn them loose." Then he asked, "What about the circuit judge? Is he scared too?"

The look of bitter shame returned to Hank Gilbert's face. "Even more so than the sheriff. Besides that, I don't think he even cares what goes on in Rockville. It's like everyone would rather pretend this town doesn't even exist. Almost like them and the rustlers and troublemakers around here have come to a sort of understanding. As long as they just cause trouble around here and leave the rest of the county alone, no one will bother them."

Cobbett shook his head. "Then I don't know much I could do, or anyone else could do."

"There's got to be something someone can do," Hank Gilbert said stubbornly, a look of both anger and desperation in his face. He gave Cobbett an almost pleading look. "At least give it a try. You can quit after one day and I won't try to stop you. But at least give it a try."

Cobbett looked at the barber with cold anger in his gray eyes, and when he spoke there was anger in his tone as well, anger and resentment. "I'm just a stranger here. This is not my town. Why is everyone around here trying to get me to do their dirty work for them? Is it because I'm a stranger?"

"You're the only one who can do it. The only one who stands any chance against those men. We thought Tobe Langley would be such a man. But he never did anything until he tried to arrest Joe Deegan for killing the Pasco boys. You saw what happened then. He let Deegan buffalo him and run him out of town."

"What makes you think I won't let you down too?" Cobbett asked.

"I saw what you did to Barney Nash out there. Langley was a bigger, tougher-looking man than you, but he wouldn't have dared try anything like that. He didn't have the guts."

"I wouldn't want to tangle with Nash myself in a fair fight," Cobbett said.

"I can't say I blame you. It would be like trying to use your fists on the kicking end of a mean mule. But no one would expect you to fight him fair. I know I wouldn't. Any ordinary man would be a fool to tangle with that big bruiser in a fair fight. Not that he'd fight fair himself. I've seen him use every dirty trick in the book on a man half his size and then kick his ribs in after he was down. It was just a stranger passing through, minding his own business, like yourself. But Nash picked a fight with him in Duffy Shaw's saloon and followed him outside calling him names and daring him to do something about it. When the fellow started to get on his horse Nash pulled him off and went to work on him while the whole town watched, afraid to try to stop him. I don't think Joe Deegan was in town that day, but the others stood around grinning while Barney Nash beat that poor man nearly to death, then threw him across his saddle and gave the horse a slap on the rump and they stood there laughing and yelling dirty remarks as the horse galloped out of town, with that man managing somehow to keep from falling off. That's the sort of thing that goes on around here, and no one does anything about it because they're afraid of Barney Nash's fists and Joe Deegan's gun."

"What do you think I could do about it?"

"I don't know, but I think you'd do something, if you were the marshal. You wouldn't let them get away with things like that."

"Aren't you forgetting the fact that they've already shot two horses that belonged to me?" Cobbett asked. "I haven't done anything about that. They're laughing about it."

"That's exactly the sort of thing I've been talking about," Hank Gilbert said emphatically. "They do exactly as they please and then laugh about it, because they know everyone's afraid to do anything. But I don't think you're afraid and I don't believe for a minute that you intend to let them get away with that."

Cobbett shook his head. "There's not much I can do legally, and my hands would be tied even more if I were marshal. I know it was them, I guess by now everyone knows it was them, but I haven't got any proof and they'd deny it if they were ever brought to trial. Which doesn't seem very likely the way things are around here, does it?

From what you've said, it would be a waste of time to arrest them."

"I still think you could do something," the little barber said stubbornly. "Maybe you couldn't do anything about the rustling that goes on outside of town, but when they're in town you'd put a stop to some of the things they've been doing, like picking fights and shooting their guns at anything they want to use for a target. That's one thing in particular that we want stopped, before someone is killed by a stray bullet. And we don't want any more strangers beat half to death just because Barney Nash likes to show everyone how tough he is. It's getting so people are afraid to come to Rockville to buy supplies."

"Or get their hair cut?"

Gilbert nodded. "That too."

For a long moment Cobbett bleakly studied his hands. Then he drew in a deep breath and said in a weary tone, "I'll take the job on two conditions."

"Name them."

"I'll quit whenever I please, without any explanations."

"Agreed. What's the other condition?"

"I don't want any salary, but I want the town to pay all my expenses while I'm here. That includes hotel bills, meals, haircuts, ammunition—and horses."

Hank Gilbert blinked. "Horses?"

Cobbett nodded. "I want to be able to go for a ride when I take a notion and if anything happens to the horse I don't want to have to pay for it out of my pocket."

Gilbert thought for a moment. "It could end up costing us more than if we just paid you a straight salary."

Cobbett nodded shortly. "It could. But I don't intend for it to cost me anything. I don't want the job and I don't expect to be doing it for very long. But while I am doing it, I'm damned if it's going to cost me anything, unless it's my life."

"I don't know," Gilbert said slowly. "I'd have to talk to the others about it. I wanted them to come with me, in case anything came up that needed their say-so. But they thought it would be better if we weren't all seen together, which is just another way of saying they were worried about what the Nash gang might think about it."

"Sounds like they're going to be behind me all the way," Cobbett said dryly.

"*I'll* be behind you," Hank Gilbert told him. "I'm not much of a hand with a gun, but I'll do what I can if necessary, and I might be

able to help you out in other ways. But I'm afraid you won't be able
to count on much help from the others. They told me tonight that
was the reason they wanted to hire you, so they wouldn't have to risk
their own lives."

"No wonder the Nash gang likes it here," Cobbett said with a faint
smile.

The barber nodded absently, thinking of something else. "I have
an idea," he said. "The horses might not cost us anything. I'll discuss
it with the others. Why don't you go ahead and take this badge—I
brought it with me just in case—and we'll see how it goes."

CHAPTER 12

The jail, as Hank Gilbert had said, was a joke—just a plank room with an unbarred glass window at the back, through which a prisoner could easily escape. It was bare of furniture except for a lumpy mattress that Tobe Langley had apparently slept on. The small marshal's office in front was the other half of an abandoned two-room shack that had been converted, without effort or expense, into the marshal's office and jail. Except for the plain wooden desk and the swivel chair behind it, it was as bare as the jail room. There was no gun rack, nor any guns, and there was nothing in the desk except for a single pair of handcuffs in the top drawer. It was obvious that Tobe Langley had never done much paperwork.

Ben Cobbett did not intend to do a great deal himself during the short time he expected to be here. He had not come here looking for a home or a permanent job.

Before breakfast he swept the place out and with his bare hands knocked a cloud of dust from the mattress on the floor.

As he was about to leave the rear room that was the jail, he noticed something that brought a smile even to his bleak humorless face. There was a bolt on the door, but it was on the wrong side. It could be bolted only from the inside. A prisoner could lock himself in—or the marshal out, if he so desired—but the marshal could do neither from the outside.

The outside door to the marshal's office was the same. It could be bolted from the inside, but there was no way to fasten it from the outside. There was no lock on the door.

Cobbett closed the door and stood outside it for a moment sadly shaking his head as he ran his glance along the empty, muddy street. It had stopped raining again during the night and the rising sun was trying to shine through oddly shaped clouds in the east. One of the clouds resembled an Indian on a wild pony chasing huge buffalo along the crest of a dark ridge. Cobbett did not know what it meant, if anything. There were not many buffalo left for the Indians to chase, and most of the Indians were on reservations, eating government beef and not much liking it.

But when Cobbett looked again, the clouds had changed their shapes, so that they looked more like white men chasing cattle, and already vanishing themselves as the new day arrived. Though he was not superstitious, it made Cobbett uneasy as he walked back to the hotel, unconsciously turning up the collar of his coat against the damp chill.

When he entered the dining room the first person he saw was Julie Tidings. Instead of meeting his glance, she looked at his coat, as if to see if there was a badge pinned to it. That left little doubt in his mind that she had heard him and Hank Gilbert talking last night.

She did not speak to Cobbett, gave no sign that she remembered him. With the barest nod he went past her table and sat down at a table in the corner near the window where he could see out with little risk of being seen from the street. Anyone who looked in through the window would be looking at Julie Tidings anyway. But there was no one on the street yet, and no one in the dining room except for himself and Julie Tidings and the elderly waitress, who went back into the kitchen after bringing Cobbett his breakfast. He ate in silence, not looking at Julie Tidings, although he was aware of her covertly watching him.

After a few minutes she looked toward the kitchen door, then suddenly got up and came over to Cobbett's table, sitting down opposite him and saying in a low voice, "Excuse me. I forgot to thank you last night."

Cobbett lifted his glance and looked into her blue eyes. "It wasn't necessary," he said.

She dropped her glance for a moment and her soft, lightly tanned cheeks colored slightly. "I hate to bother you again," she said, "but I wonder if you cold tell me where Joe Deegan is. He came up to see me for a few minutes last night and then left. He said he was going to a saloon to tell his friends something and I thought he was going to come right back, but I haven't seen him since. The reason I'm worried is—well, I had my husband's raincoat and I let Joe borrow it. I thought he meant to bring it right back. I don't want anyone to see him wearing it. Those men he went to see last night know about us already." Her blush deepened and she again lowered her eyes for a moment. "I guess everyone else in Rockville does too, but I don't want them to see him wearing my husband's raincoat. Someone might tell him and I know it would make him furious. He probably wouldn't say much, but he'd find some way to make me pay for it."

Cobbett glanced at her and then ate in silence for a moment, his attention on his food. "Deegan tell you I was his friend?"

"Why, yes," she said, looking at him in surprise. "You are, aren't you?"

"No." Cobbett said quietly.

"Oh, brother," Julie Tidings murmured as if to herself. "I should have known ... the way he smiled when he said it. He said he thought you were going to become the new marshal. That also made me wonder—I mean, him being friends with a lawman."

Cobbett did not say anything.

Julie Tidings gave him a small, bitter smile. "I guess I've really made a fool out of myself, haven't I? Confiding in the last person I should have confided in. And I should have known better. I couldn't help overhearing some of what you and that man said last night—those walls are pretty thin—and from the way he talked, I should have realized you weren't the sort of man to understand why a married woman might have an affair with another man. But you were so quiet, I found myself smiling and I—I pictured you smiling too, to yourself I mean. I realize now how foolish that was. Looking at you now, I'm not even sure you can smile."

"I wasn't smiling last night," Cobbett said. "I didn't find what he said very amusing. But there's no reason for you to be concerned. I'm not in the habit of telling people what they know already."

Julie Tidings stiffened. Her face flooded with shame and anger. "I should have known everyone would find out. This town is full of gossips, just like New Hope."

"I'm afraid so," Cobbett agreed, glancing toward the kitchen.

Julie Tidings also glanced in that direction, then said softly, "I better get back to my table. If that old lady sees us sitting at the same table she'll tell everyone about that. If Joe Deegan gets the wrong idea, he'll kill you."

"Your husband might not like it either," Cobbett said dryly.

"You're just like all the rest," Julie Tidings murmured bitterly as she got up and moved away, stopping at her table only long enough to leave some money and get her bag.

Though he was far from indifferent to her charms, Cobbett did not watch her leave the dining room, but looked through the window as a group of horsemen, led my old Mac McCabe on a fine sorrel, trotted up the muddy street and halted directly in front of the hotel. Besides McCabe there were four riders and their faces were drawn and grim.

"Everybody out here!" old McCabe cried in his high-pitched voice. "I got something to say and I want everybody to hear it! That includes the trash in Duffy Shaw's saloon, if they're back by now from stealin' my cows!"

Leaving his breakfast unfinished, Cobbett got up and went out through the lobby to the veranda, where he stopped and stood silently watching. In the meantime McCabe and his men had turned their horses around so they could watch the front of Duffy Shaw's saloon, where Joe Deegan now appeared at the door, grinning and rubbing sleep from his eyes. A moment later Barney Nash appeared behind him, also knuckling his eyes and yawning. Other members of the gang seemed to be pushing and trying to get out past them, but not trying quite hard enough to succeed.

Mac McCabe pointed a long bony finger at them and cried, "There they are! Them's the ones what run off some more of my stock last night!" His high voice shook with righteous anger and he sounded more like a high-strung woman then the stout, tough old man he appeared to be, with his huge body and his craggy face set off by the great beak of a nose and big yellow teeth. He swung his head about to appeal to the townspeople who began to appear in doorways, but he spat at the street when he saw old Sheb Snively blinking sleepily at him, his mustaches twitching in dislike.

"What's all the fuss about?" Joe Deegan asked, grinning broadly. "Can't a man get no sleep after a hard night of boozing?"

"A hard night of stealin' cows, you mean!" McCabe corrected him. "And don't bother sayin' you and them others was in the saloon all night! It's happened before on rainy nights! You stay in town on purpose so you'll have a alibi and bed down in the saloon. But after everybody's asleep, you sneak out, get your horses and run off a bunch of my cows! You know by mornin' the tracks will be washed out, so you drive them into one of them canyons or draws at the south end of my range. After a hard rain there's enough water and grass for them to get by on for a few days, so you stop up the mouth of the canyon with brush and sneak back into town before day and just leave the cows there for a few days. You claim you was in town all night and old Mort's afraid to say anything and of course Duffy Shaw backs up your story. Then after a few days you go back and drive the cows off and sell them. Don't think I don't know how you boys operate!"

Joe Deegan's grin had grown into a chuckle. Far from being worried, he found the situation amusing. "What makes you think it was us, Mac? You see any of us doing it?"

"No, but when I do I aim to hang me some rustlers!" McCabe told him.

Deegan's smile faded for a moment and his blue eyes became frosty slits. Then he brought the smile back to his unlined baby face, but now there was something deadly in it. It was obvious that he could see Cobbett standing on the hotel porch, but he kept his bright narrow glance on Mac McCabe, except for a time or two when it flicked over McCabe's men. "You and who else?" he asked, barely loud enough for McCabe to hear him. "If you planned to start hanging rustlers, you shouldn't of let some of your men go. You should of hired more. You'll need them."

"You know why I let them go!" McCabe cried, trembling with anger. "You boys have run off so much of my stock I couldn't afford to keep them, especially through the winter. That bunch you got last night—we had them bunched up to drive to the railroad as soon as we could round up a few more to take with them, but you beat us to them! But this time you've gone too far! I've had enough!"

By the time the old man finished he was almost screaming his rage, and his men looked at him in alarm, afraid he would start a fight there and then and get them all killed. In a gunfight they would stand no chance against Joe Deegan and the Nash gang and they knew it.

Hank Gilbert stood in the doorway of his barbershop with a worried look on his dark face. "Hey, Mac," he called quietly. "Can I talk to you a minute?"

"Talk!" McCabe snapped.

Gilbert's glance shuttled toward the saloon. "It's sort of private."

McCabe's sharp old eye intercepted that quick look the barber shot at the saloon. "Well, I'm in a hurry," he said, "but I guess I can spare a minute."

He handed the reins to one of his men, swung down stiffly and plodded across the mud to the barbershop and ducked through the doorway. The door closed behind him. In the street his men shifted uncomfortably in their saddles and seemed afraid to look toward Duffy Shaw's saloon. Ben Cobbett's cold gray eyes went to Joe Deegan and Deegan grinned at him. Cobbett did not return the grin, but shifted his attention back to the barbershop as Mac McCabe came back out and returned to his horse, climbing into the saddle with some effort. He was a heavy old man, weighing a good two hundred and fifty pounds. As he rose into the saddle McCabe looked at Cobbett and showed his yellow teeth in a smile.

"I hear you're the new marshal," he said. "I was hopin' you'd take the job."

Cobbett shrugged, then said, "I was hoping I wouldn't. But I didn't seem to have much choice."

He heard one of the Nash gang laugh down at Duffy Shaw's saloon, and Mac McCabe said, "I sort of figgered it would come to that. Some people around here won't quit pushin' a man till his back's agin the wall and he ain't got no choice but to make a stand and fight back." He shifted his bitter eyes back to Joe Deegan and Barney Nash and raised his voice again. "I aim to comb all them canyons and draws till I find my cattle, and I better not find any of you boys with them!"

Deegan only shrugged, still grinning, and McCabe's glance returned to Cobbett. "You comin' with us, Cobbett?"

The old man had finally got his name right; Cobbett was flattered. But he shook his head. "Sounds like it may take a while. And my job's here in town."

"Well, you do what you got to do," McCabe told him, grim and unsmiling. "That's what I aim to do."

The old man started his horse and trotted slowly down the street, his men falling in behind him. As he passed Duffy Shaw's saloon, McCabe said to Joe Deegan, "I'm warnin' you for the last time—keep away from my stock and my daughter. I ain't gonna tell you again."

Deegan only shrugged, smiling and yawning indifferently, and McCabe and his men rode on out of town, turning south beyond the livery stable.

Cobbett glanced at Hank Gilbert in the doorway of the barbershop and Gilbert beckoned to him with a slight motion of his head. Cobbett stepped down off the hotel veranda and angled across the muddy street to the barbershop, aware that Joe Deegan, Barney Nash and the others were watching him from the entrance of Duffy Shaw's saloon. Hank Gilbert looked toward the saloon and then closed the door behind Cobbett, indicating the barber's chair.

"Have a seat. I'll give you a shave while we talk."

Cobbett hung up his hat and sat down in the chair facing the window. He kept his attention on Duffy Shaw's saloon while Gilbert fastened an apron around his neck and began to lather his face. Barney Nash went back into the saloon, but Joe Deegan strolled along the boardwalk and casually entered the hotel.

"I guess you're wondering what I wanted to see McCabe about?" Gilbert said, smiling.

"I'm not, but I imagine everyone else is, including Joe Deegan and his friends."

Gilbert shrugged, but he was no longer smiling. "I'm tired of wondering what they'll think every time I do anything. I'm tired of this whole town being afraid to breathe because of them." After a moment he added, "That's why we hired you."

Cobbett offered no comment. He had heard such remarks before, and knew it would do no good to tell Gilbert not to expect miracles.

"Anyway, what I wanted to see you about—I told McCabe what we were talking about last night, and he said you could use one of his horses anytime you need one."

"That's nice," Cobbett said. "When I need a horse all I have to do is walk out to his ranch and run one down."

"Oh, no," Gilbert said, "He's going to bring some into town and leave them at the stable where they'll be handy. What a lot of people don't know, that stable belongs to Mac, and he told me he was about ready to fire Mort Crumby and put someone there who'll do a better job and try to keep horses from getting stolen right under his nose. Mac feels sort of responsible for your horse being stolen, and he said if you lost one of his animals it wouldn't cost you anything."

"What does he expect in return?" Cobbett asked.

"I don't think he expects anything in return. He said it would be a small price to pay for having a man like you for marshal. And he said if the horses were stolen it wouldn't matter much in the long run, because sooner or later they'd probably be stolen anyway. He sort of grinned and said if them boys shot any of them, they'd just be robbing themselves of the money they might get out of them someday. Of course, I told him about them shooting that bay you bought from Mort, as well as your other horse."

"Of course."

Cobbett was watching the hotel entrance through the window. Joe Deegan still had not come back out.

"He would have soon known it anyway," Gilbert added, somewhat defensively. "And I felt he had a right to know the risk he'd be taking if he loaned you a horse."

"And I feel you might have mentioned it to me before you talked to him about it," Cobbett replied. "I don't want to feel indebted to a man I won't be able to help in return, especially under the circumstances."

"I don't think you should worry about that," Gilbert told him. "Mac knows that sooner or later you're bound to tangle with Barney Nash and them, the ones who've been stealing his cattle and horses, even if you never set foot outside of Rockville. That's what he's counting on. Anything you do against them will be in his favor. Mac knows that."

"I see," Cobbett grunted.

"But I don't think that's the reason he did it. If Mac likes you he'll do anything he can for you, and more than likely he'd feel insulted if you tried to return the favor. But he sure hasn't got much use for his enemies," Gilbert added with a faint smile.

Cobbett glanced through the window at Duffy Shaw's saloon. "Barney Nash and his friends spend a lot of time in town?"

"A big part of it, when they're not rustling stock. Sometimes it seems like they practically live in Duffy Shaw's saloon, and they're just about his only customers. Everyone else is afraid to go in there when they're there. They usually leave their horses at the stable like they owned it and never bother to pay for their keep. The stable loses money all the time. Mac only keeps it open as a benefit to the town. I imagine Mort has told them who it really belongs to, though he lets on to everyone else like it still belongs to him. He was going to have to close it down—that's why McCabe bought it and said he could go on running the place just like it was his and they'd say nothing about it really belonging to Mac. I didn't find out about it from Mac. Mort told me one day when he came in here about drunk. He must have forgot about telling me, because later on he was talking like he still owned the stable. I think he does own a few of the horses, but that's about all."

"Did he own the one he sold me?"

"I've been wondering about that," Gilbert said, scraping the last of the lather from Cobbett's face and reaching for a damp cloth with which to wipe his face. "I think he has sold horses that belonged to Mac and then told Mac they were stolen, but I'm not sure about the one he sold you. But if I were you I wouldn't trust him too far, especially in anything that involves the Nash bunch. He's more afraid of them than he is of you, because he knows they're a lot more likely to harm him, and he figures they'll still be here when you're gone."

"How many marshals have they run out of town?"

The question made Gilbert wince. "I was hoping you wouldn't ask," he said. "Every one we've had so far. The ones Joe Deegan doesn't scare away, Barney Nash does, him and the others. Tobe Langley lasted longer than the rest because he let them alone and usually kept out of sight when they were in town. When they were on the prod he used to bolt the office door on the inside and go out through the back window and hide in the sage till they quieted down or left town. By the way, what do you think of the marshal's office and jail?"

Cobbett looked up to see if the barber was smiling, and saw that he was. "Like you said, it's a joke. It's easy to see why Langley never bothered to arrest anyone. You can't fasten either of those doors from the outside and a prisoner could let himself out through the back window."

Gilbert looked embarrassed. "We started once to put locks on those doors, but we decided it wouldn't do any good. A prisoner who wanted out would just kick those old planks loose and go through the wall."

"So to keep from having to repair the wall, you left it where he could open the door and walk out or climb through the window, that it?"

"Something like that," Gilbert said, red-faced. He had his hand on a green bottle. "Face lotion?"

"No."

Gilbert put the bottle back on the shelf and unpinned the apron from around Cobbett's neck, shaking it off from habit although he hadn't cut Cobbett's hair and there was no loose hair on it. The stubby little barber had other things on his mind. "I'm going to try to get the others to pitch in with me and build a new jail," he said. "I don't believe they'd tear it down while you're here."

"They might after I'm gone," Cobbett said, rising from the barber's chair. He looked at his face in the mirror and saw that Gilbert had left a mustache on his upper lip. "You take a lot for granted," he said, giving the man a cold gray look.

"I saw the disappointment on your face the other morning after I shaved it off," Gilbert said. "You look better with a mustache. But I can shave it off when you come in tomorrow if you like. You can drop in every morning for a shave and I can keep you informed on all the latest gossip. People tell a barber things they might not tell a lawman." He smiled apologetically and ventured to add, "Especially one as unsociable as you."

"Maybe they just know it's unhealthy to tell a lawman anything," Cobbett grunted. "Joe Deegan and his pals might not like it."

CHAPTER 13

Cobbett started back across the street to the hotel, then changed his mind. Joe Deegan was still in the hotel, and with little doubt he was with Julie Tidings, in the room next to Cobbett's. When Cobbett thought of that he shifted his bleak glance to the false front of Duffy Shaw's saloon and turned in that direction.

Parting the swing doors, he stepped inside and looked about the dim barroom. There was no one at the bar, either behind it or in front of it, and he did not see Duffy Shaw, but there was a partly open door at the back and he could hear someone moving around beyond it. Barney Nash and his men had all returned to their blankets in a cleared area at the back of the saloon. Nash raised his head to peer at Cobbett and his bloated red face was oddly contorted. His head was bare and Cobbett noticed that his hair was thinning on top.

"What're you doin' here?" Nash asked irritably. "Can't a man get no sleep around here?"

"Rough night?" Cobbett asked, still looking idly about. He noticed a raincoat hanging on a nail in the wall. It was Lot Tidings's mackintosh and it had been ripped in several places and was spattered with dried mud.

Barney Nash scowled at him. "What's that supposed to mean?"

Duffy Shaw came out of the back room and looked at Cobbett with hard dislike in his eyes. His bulldog face had ridges and deep lines in it and was almost as gray as his thinning hair. "I thought I told you not to come back," he said. "Besides, I don't open till nine."

"Then what are they doing here?" Cobbett asked, nodding at Nash and the other men stretched out on the floor.

"They sleep here," Duffy Shaw said. "They're friends of mine."

Tap Grodin sat up on the floor and bared his yellow teeth in a wolfish snarl. His large dark eyes were bloodshot and a stubble of black beard covered the lower half of his face. "Don't tell him anything, Duffy," he said. "It ain't none of his business."

"I'm making it my business," Cobbett said, and pulled back his coat to show them the badge pinned to his shirt.

Barney Nash let out a snort of laughter. "They didn't waste any time pinnin' that badge on you, did they?"

The others sat up or raised their heads and smiled at Cobbett the way they would have smiled at a caged animal that they meant to torment.

Cobbett turned his cold eyes on Duffy Shaw, who had gone around behind the bar from habit but had no intention of serving Cobbett anything before nine, marshal or not. "What time do you close?" Cobbett asked.

"Hell, he ain't even open yet," Barney Nash exclaimed, and his friends laughed.

"Usually about one," Shaw said. "Why?"

"What time did you close last night?"

"You don't have to answer that, Duffy," Tap Grodin said.

"Were they all here when you closed?" Cobbett asked, ignoring Grodin.

"They were here all night playing cards," Duffy Shaw said. "That's why they're so sleepy this morning."

"I had a feeling you were going to say that," Cobbett said dryly. He again glanced about the saloon. "Where's Beebe?"

"I've got him doing some work in the back," Shaw said. Then he added deliberately, "I figger any enemy of yours is a friend of mine, so I give him a job helping me out enough to earn his keep and a little spending money."

"Generous of you," Cobbett said.

The saloonkeeper shook his head. "Not at all. I just don't like lawmen and he don't either. It'll be fun having him around."

"Well, it takes all kinds," Cobbett said. "Some people keep pet snakes." He nodded and turned to leave, then said as an afterthought, "I guess Joe Deegan was here all night too?"

Duffy Shaw slowly nodded. "That's right."

"That's what I figured," Cobbett said, looking at the torn muddy raincoat as he left the saloon.

Duffy Shaw saw the way he looked at the raincoat. The saloon-keeper waited, listening to the retreating sound of the new marshal's footsteps. Then he glared angrily at Barney Nash and the other four men lying on the saloon floor. "You dumb sons of bitches," he said. "Why don't you just tell him you stole them cows and be done with it?"

"Ain't nothin' he can do," Barney Nash said. "What happens outside of town ain't none of his business."

Archie Beebe came cautiously from the storeroom in back, where he had been listening. He looked toward the swing doors to make sure Cobbett had left, and then he said with a grin, "So they already made him marshal? I knew it wouldn't be long."

The dirty unshaven men stretched out on the saloon floor laughed when the funny looking little fellow said that. They were of the same mind. But Duffy Shaw's bushy gray brows knitted in a deeper frown. "I don't know why you're all so happy about it," he said. "We need him around here the way Custer needed Indians."

"If you want to get rid of him, I can tell you how to do it," Archie Beebe said. "We made things so hot for him in Miles City, he finally had to turn in his badge and leave."

Barney Nash sat up with an eager smile on his boated face. "How did you do it?"

"It wasn't hard," Archie Beebe said. "It was a lot of fun, in fact. But not much fun for Cobbett," he added, giggling.

"But what did you do?" Nash asked.

"All kinds of things," Archie Beebe said, his little face shining with fiendish mirth. "We never give him a minute's peace. We set up a system of signals, with somebody keeping a eye on him at all times or knowing right where he was. We'd wait till he went to bed or set down to eat and then somebody would shoot off a gun at the other end of town and be back in the saloon minding their own business by the time Cobbett got there."

The tired rustlers were all sitting up with interest, watching the little man with new appreciation. Barney Nash gave a shout of surprised laughter and Tap Grodin howled with savage glee. Even Duffy Shaw was watching the little man with his lips twisted in what might have been a smile.

Ben Cobbett stopped on the street, studying the deserted looking town with bleak eyes. The townspeople were keeping out of sight because they were expecting trouble, perhaps shooting and bloodshed. They did not want to get involved in it themselves, or to risk being cut down by a stray bullet. Let Cobbett handle it; that was what they had hired him for. And if he was killed, that would be unfortunate, but they would not lose much sleep over it. When a man pinned on a badge it was with the understanding that someone might be tempted to take a shot at it. It was an occupational hazard.

Joe Deegan came from the hotel and tramped along the boardwalk toward Cobbett, smiling cheerfully—almost too cheerfully. "Morning, Marshal," he said in a bantering tone, with a slight emphasis on "Marshal." "I was thinking about some breakfast."

Cobbett's glance touched Deegan and passed on, roving the empty street, the buildings along it. "I already had mine."

"How about some coffee then?" Deegan said, and then chuckled. "Jane Keller makes real good coffee. And I'll bet she's got a nice figure under that old dress. Slender women usually do, if they ain't too slender. Course I wouldn't know myself. Just guessing."

Cobbett turned his head and looked at the younger man with cold gray eyes. Deegan's charm, though treacherous, was hard to resist. Yet Cobbett knew he had to resist it.

"Deegan," he said bluntly, "we're not friends, you and I. Why don't we stop pretending we are."

The exaggerated look of disappointment that spread over Deegan's face was as false as the smile that had preceded it. In fact, the smile still gleamed in his blue eyes. Instead of being stung by Cobbett's rebuff, it amused him. He saw it as a new twist in the deadly game they were playing. "Suit yourself," he said with a shrug. "I just figgered we might as well be polite till we get ready to start blasting each other."

"I have what some consider a serious flaw in my character," Cobbett told him. "I'm not much of a diplomat. I can't be friendly with my enemies."

Again Deegan tried to look hurt and ended up chuckling instead. "I thought we were friends."

"I've heard what usually happens to your friends," Cobbett grunted. "It sort of makes me wonder what will happen to Barney Nash and those others if you ever decide you don't need them anymore."

Deegan's chuckle grew into a laugh, his white teeth flashing in the sunlight. "They're safe for the time being," he said. "Unless maybe it's Ned Ribble. Have you noticed how much like George Pasco he looks? Sort of makes you wonder, don't it? They must have had the same old man without knowing about it. They came from the same part of Arkansas, grew up on farms a few miles apart, so it could have happened. I reckon even back then women cheated on their husbands when they got a chance."

"You're going to get yourself in bad trouble one of these days, Deegan," Cobbett said quietly. "Some jealous husband will put a bullet in you, or hire someone else to do it."

Deegan laughed, shrugging his shoulders. "They'll have to get in line," he said. "And the way old McCabe talked this morning, they better hurry up, or they won't get a chance at me."

"Don't underestimate old McCabe," Cobbett warned him. "I got the impression he's about to do something desperate."

"There for a minute I thought the old fool was gonna draw on me," Deegan said, as if still a little surprised by the fact. "I was wondering what you'd do if he did."

Cobbett looked directly into Deegan's eyes and said, "I would have killed the one who was still alive when it was over."

Deegan looked at him carefully, as if to see if he was serious. "That would have been me," he said.

"That's what I figured," Cobbett replied.

Deegan began rolling a cigarette, watching Cobbett with narrowed eyes. He was no longer smiling. "What makes you think I would have stood there and let you do it?" he asked.

Cobbett did not answer that. Instead he said, "I intend to keep the peace in this town. Anyone who disturbs the peace or breaks the law will have to answer for it."

Deegan licked his cigarette and lit it, never taking his cold narrow glance off Cobbett. "What about the rustling?" he said. "What do you intend to do about that?" When Cobbett did not answer at once he added, "Ain't much you can do about it, is there? It's just like I told you the other day, even if they made you the marshal there still wouldn't be anything you could do about it. You ain't got any authority outside of town, and even if you did have, there wouldn't be anything you could do. Except maybe get yourself killed, like that old fool McCabe's gonna do if he keeps looking for trouble."

"I was just going to tell you the same thing."

Deegan shook his head and held a match to the end of his cigarette, a cold gleam in his pale eyes. "There ain't anything you can do," he said again. "There won't even be much you can do about what goes on here in town, right under your nose."

"Don't count on it," Cobbett told him.

Deegan did not bother to reply. He just bared his teeth in a taunting smile, then turned his back on Cobbett and tramped across the muddy street to the restaurant.

Cobbett stood staring at the restaurant even after Deegan had slammed the door behind him—almost as if he were slamming it in the face of the man he had invited to dine with him only a few minutes before.

Then Cobbett became aware of Hank Gilbert at the door of the barbershop making frantic motions to get his attention. But even as he gesticulated so urgently, Gilbert was beaming like a gossip or a news hound on the scent of a fresh scandal. Annoyed, Cobbett tramped across the drying mud and fixed the barber in a cold stare.

"What was that all about?" Gilbert asked.

"Listen," Cobbett said in the same quiet deadly tone he had used on Joe Deegan. "We better get one thing straight here at the start. I don't intend to come over here and report to you every time I—"

"Okay, okay," Gilbert said quickly, waving his hand. "Forget I asked. I just wanted to tell you, anytime you want a bath, I've got a nice tub in the little room right behind the barbershop and I usually keep plenty of hot water, just in case somebody in this country does decide to take a bath. You might rather take one over here than in the hotel washroom, with that old lady popping in and out with somebody's dirty laundry, like she didn't know anyone was there."

"They do laundry at the hotel?" Cobbett asked.

Gilbert nodded. "That's partly how they make ends meet over there. That and serving meals. Half of the time there's not more than two or three people staying at the hotel. But about that bath ...?"

"I thought I'd wait till the weather improves," Cobbett said dryly. "But for your information I took a bath in my room last night."

"I don't mean that kind of bath," Gilbert said, smiling to take the sting out of his words. "You've been on the trail for weeks and you can't get rid of it with a damp cloth. Maybe you don't notice it, but everyone else does."

"I'll take a bath when I get ready," Cobbett said flatly, "or never if it suits me."

"Suit yourself," Gilbert said, red-faced and smiling in embarrassment and apology. "I just wanted you to make a good impression."

"That's the least of my worries," Cobbett grunted. "Do you think I care what anyone in this town thinks about me? You may recall that I didn't exactly get down on my knees and beg for this job."

"You've made your point," Gilbert said. "It was the other way around. I practically got down on my knees and begged you to take the job. But you don't have to rub it in. The other townspeople weren't half as anxious to pin that badge on you as I was. I had to talk them into it as a matter of fact. They figured they'd just be bringing trouble down on themselves from the Nash gang. They didn't figure you'd last long and that bunch would just take it out on the town after you leave. I look for them to try to weasel out yet and persuade you to turn in that badge. All it will take is a few threats from Barney Nash and his men."

"They can have the badge back anytime they want it," Cobbett said. "Like I said before, I don't believe I'll be able to do much good here, the way things are."

"What about your horses that they shot?" Gilbert asked. "You want them to get away with that?"

"I could do as much about that without a badge as I can do with one," Cobbett said. "Maybe more, because without it I'd be less concerned about breaking the law myself—and that's the only way I'll ever be able to get even with them for that, by breaking the law myself."

"I was afraid of that," the barber said, his dark brown eyes somber and worried under the black brows.

"About that bath," Cobbett said after a moment. "As a matter of fact, I'd been thinking about taking a good hot bath and buying a few clothes. Mine are all dirty and about worn out. Why don't you go ahead and get that tub ready. I'll pick up a change of clothes at the store and then dive in."

Thirty minutes later Cobbett left the barbershop smoking a cigar, with his dirty clothes bundled up under his left arm. The marshal's badge was pinned to a new sheep-lined leather vest and the gray shirt and brown trousers he now wore were also new. The man in Mac McCabe's store had refused to let him pay for the clothes or he might have bought more while he was at it. As he had told Hank Gilbert, his old clothes were about worn out.

He crossed the street to the hotel carrying the old clothes and entered the lobby. As he approached the desk the clerk took in his new outfit with an approving eye, but his nose twitched in distaste when he noted that Cobbett still wore the same muddy boots which, though in good condition, were still muddy.

Pausing before the desk, Cobbett said, "I understand you do laundry here?"

The sallow-faced, weak-eyed clerk, who always seemed to be standing up behind the desk like a guard on duty, nodded his head. "Yes, we do. I started to tell you, but I wasn't sure ..." His voice trailed off. He watched almost in alarm as Cobbett piled the old clothes on top of the desk.

"Think they can do anything with these?" the marshal asked.

The clerk's nose twitched again as he looked down at the mud-splattered old clothes piled so unceremoniously on his neat desk. "I'm not sure about the coat. I'll have to ask Mrs. Gray. I don't guess it will hurt to wash it."

"It's been washed before."

"Then I don't guess there should be any problem," the clerk said, although the look of doubt and disapproval did not leave his eyes.

"I've got some more in my room," Cobbett said. "I'll go up and get them."

The clerk looked uneasy, but he did not say why.

Cobbett climbed the carpeted stairs to the second floor, and as he approached the door of his room he heard voices in the next room. Julie Tidings was saying in an angry high-pitched tone, "Just look at it! Mud all over it and torn like that! How am I going to explain that to him?"

"Tell him you went for a ride," Joe Deegan said in an easy, indifferent tone.

Julie Tidings's voice became even more angry and excited. "He won't believe it! He'll know I wouldn't ride in brush and thorns where I'd get it ripped this way!"

Then they fell silent as Cobbett, frowning in annoyance, inserted his key in the lock and opened his door. They remained silent while he gathered up the rest of his dirty clothes, but he heard Joe Deegan laugh quietly and say something in a low tone as he left the room and started back down the stairs.

At the desk he turned his key and the dirty clothes over to the clerk, who said, "They should be ready late this afternoon."

Cobbett barely nodded and walked on across the lobby, leaving the hotel. He went to the marshal's office and jail and remained there for the rest of the morning, sitting behind the desk with his muddy boots on top of it and watching the street through the window. He did not see Joe Deegan pass by on his way back to Duffy Shaw's saloon.

Several times during the morning he saw Sheb Snively come to the door of his store across the street and stare toward the marshal's office, his eyes blinking rapidly and his mustache twitching in anger. The window of the marshal's office had no curtain or blind and Snively could see the new marshal sitting there with his feet up on the desk, smoking a cigar and flicking the ash on the floor, just as Tobe Langley had done before him.

The word went out and shortly before noon Snively and three other angry townsmen descended on the barbershop. Snively, sputtering with indignation, called Hank Gilbert out to the boardwalk and pointed out the scandal. "Is this what we're paying him for?" the small old man screamed. "We were better off with Langley!"

Gilbert looked toward the marshal's office like one betrayed, his rather handsome dark face reddening with resentment when Cobbett continued to sit there with his muddy boots up on the desk, smoking his cigar. But the bandy-legged barber talked quietly and rapidly, with eloquent persuasive gestures, to calm old Snively down and reassure the others. All was well, he seemed to be saying. The new marshal had everything in hand. He knew his job and, for all his apparent indolence and indifference, was poised to strike the minute something happened. If anyone tried to disturb the peace, Cobbett would be on him like a hawk on a chicken. In the meantime, while things were quiet and peaceful—and just look how quiet and peaceful the whole town was—was it not better for the marshal to remain in his office and not provoke trouble?

Well, I dunno, old Snively seemed to say, darting a doubtful look at the marshal's office. Looks to me like we got another Toby Langley on our hands. I say get rid of him now, before he becomes attached to his soft job the way Langley did. That big rascal wouldn't even let us fire him. It took Joe Deegan to run him out of town—one of the very men we hired him to get rid of.

Cobbett crossed his muddy boots on the desk and flicked more ash from his cigar onto the floor. Pretty soon, he thought, everyone would want him to leave town except his enemies, who sort of thought it would be fun to have him around, as a fresh source of amusement. Things had been dull lately.

Hank Gilbert once more tried to mollify old Snively. The little storekeeper waved his arms impatiently. All right, all right. But I still say it's a mistake to keep him.

And having said something of the sort, old Snively marched rapidly off to the hotel, there to wait impatiently for them to start serving the noon meal, glancing at this watch every few seconds. The next time he would eat in the restaurant. The other three men remained on the boardwalk in front of the barbershop a few minutes quietly talking to Hank Gilbert, their eyes on the marshal's office. One of them was a tall fat man with a bloated red face, a handlebar mustache and a huge belly. The other two were nondescript townsmen. They soon strolled away, still talking, and Hank Gilbert went back into the barbershop, glancing over his shoulder at Cobbett's window.

Only then did Cobbett take his muddy boots down off the desk. He left the marshal's office and walked to the hotel, pitching his cigar into a puddle on the way. He found old Snively in the dining room, as expected, glancing at his watch, his mustache twitching in nervous impatience. He wanted to get back to his store. Someone might come while he was away and finding the door locked, go over to McCabe's store. Old Snively was too stingy to hire a clerk. Cobbett knew the type. The elderly white-haired waitress, flushed and beaming, was clucking about the small old man's table, setting food and coffee and water before him and trying to soothe his bad temper. It occurred to Cobbett that the waitress had probably been a beautiful woman once. She was still slender and shapely and her face was virtually unlined, young looking; only the white hair gave her away. She could have her hair dyed and easily pass for forty, although she was sixty or better.

She was more attractive even now, Cobbett thought, then Jane Keller, although not as attractive as Molly Hicks or Julie Tidings.

He automatically glanced about the dining room when he thought of Julie Tidings, although he knew she was not in the room. If she had been he would have seen her the moment he came through the door.

As he sat down at the table in the corner, old Snively darted a black look at him and began eating more rapidly. Ignoring the old man, Cobbett quietly gave his order and looked through the window at the street. When the smiling waitress brought his food he began eating, and at that moment he heard a shot from the direction of Duffy Shaw's saloon.

Though some distance off, and not wholly unexpected, the shot was loud and startling, and old Snively almost dropped his water glass and began coughing uncontrollably, while the waitress hurried after more water. Cobbett himself was engulfed by a feeling of sickness and rage that made his food seem tasteless and might even bring on a mild case of indigestion. He knew the shot had been fired deliberately for that purpose—that was why it bothered him—and he knew whose idea it had been. It was starting all over again, he thought bitterly, just like in Miles City. The stupid childish games calculated to make his job difficult and his life miserable. It would be even worse here, with men like the Nash gang eager to help Archie Beebe in any way that would make things unpleasant for Cobbett.

He did not go to investigate the shot. He knew that was just what they wanted him to do—leave his food and charge out of the hotel. By the time he got to the saloon they would all be inside minding their own business. So he kept eating as if nothing had happened, and old Snively stared at him in trembling indignation.

"I knew it!" the old man cried, throwing down his cloth napkin. "It's just a waste of time and money to hire a marshal! He sets there and don't do nothing, and they do whatever they please in Rockville, just like before!"

Chapter 14

The same thing happened again at suppertime, except that more shots were fired. They were getting bolder. There were several people besides Cobbett in the hotel dining room and they looked at him with raised brows. But they did not say anything and he continued eating in silence, his face drawn and a little gray. The townspeople saw the look on his face and mistook it for fear.

He could have told them it was something worse than fear. In the past he had sometimes felt the cold numbness of fear seeping through him like dampness into a cellar, but he had never let the fear get the upper hand. He had gone ahead and done what he had to do, with a kind of fatalistic calm, fully aware that he might be killed. But there was not much he could do about the feeling of anger and helpless frustration gnawing at his insides now. All he could do was suffer it in silence and wait for a chance to catch the perpetrators off guard, in the midst of their mischief. What he would to then he did not yet know. But he would do something. He would do something even if it was wrong.

The fat man Cobbett had seen earlier in the day, talking to Hank Gilbert, was in the dining room, occupying a table by himself at the corner of Cobbett's vision. He did not seem to be eating much for so big a man. Mostly he sat watching Cobbett. But when he looked at the big man Cobbett saw no sign of anger on his smooth round face or in his somber eyes. Instead there was a look of sympathetic understanding that aroused Cobbett's curiosity about the fat man.

The shooting continued until Cobbett left the hotel. Then he heard a familiar whistle and the shooting behind Duffy Shaw's saloon immediately stopped. Archie Beebe stepped out of an alley across the street from the saloon and strolled back across the drying mud to the saloon, innocently whistling a little tune. Cobbett did not see the ones who had done the shooting, but he heard them laughing as they entered the saloon by the back door.

He took a deep breath but it seemed that he drew more anger than air into his chest. He stood on the boardwalk in front of the hotel with the sunset flaming behind him and glared down the street toward the saloon. His jaw muscles swelled until they ached with the tension. His supper lay like a dead weight in his stomach.

He stepped off the boardwalk and headed down the street toward the saloon. He sensed that he was making a mistake, a bad mistake, but his anger propelled him anyway.

They were all in the saloon as he had known they would be, all standing at the bar with just poured drinks before them. Duffy Shaw was just recorking the bottle. They were celebrating and this round would be on the house, in honor of the occasion. They were all grinning, even Duffy Shaw, and Archie Beebe's tense little face twitched in silent glee. He did not look toward the swing doors as Cobbett came in, but was as aware of his entrance as a mouse is aware of the approach of a big silent cat. Beebe had no hole to duck into—but in a sense the saloon served the same purpose. He did not believe Cobbett would bother him here, in the presence of several hard tough men who were on his side. Also, like most criminals, Beebe felt protected by the very laws he violated. But as usual he had been careful to let others do the actual law-breaking while he merely kept watch from across the street and warned them when the law appeared in the form of his old enemy.

Barney Nash, standing just beyond Beebe, was the first to speak. "Hey, Cobbett," he said, pretending to be surprised to see the marshal, although his smug grin gave him away. "We were wonderin' where you was when all that shootin' was goin' on. Sounded like somebody tryin' to shoot up the town. You gonna arrest them?"

"Not this time," Cobbett said, his gray eyes so cold they glittered. "Except Beebe. He's the only one I saw."

Beebe darted an uneasy look at the marshal. His smile vanished and his twisted little face turned red. "What for?" he asked resentfully. "You know it wasn't me done that shooting!"

"When bank robbers get caught, the one who held the horses doesn't go free," Cobbett said. "And if he's the only one who gets caught, he has to face the music by himself." Cobbett fixed an icy stare on Archie Beebe. "Especially if robbing the bank was his idea."

"What's he talking about?" Tap Grodin asked. "We didn't rob no bank. There ain't even one in this town." Then he grinned. "If there was we'd rob it."

"Shut up," Dill Stringer muttered.

"I ain't scared of him," Grodin snarled.

"Let's go, Beebe," Cobbett said in a cold hard tone.

"Hold on a minute," Barney Nash said, setting his empty glass on the bar. "Archie never done nothin'. All he done was whistle. You can't arrest a man for whistlin'."

"Maybe you'd like to stop me?"

"I ain't goin' against yore gun, if that's what you mean," Nash said.

"That's what I mean," Cobbett snapped.

"You wouldn't talk that way if Joe Deegan was here," Tap Grodin said. "I'd like to see you draw on him."

"Behave yourself and you may live to see it," Cobbett told him. "Let's go Beebe. I'm not going to tell you again."

Trembling with silent fury, Beebe emptied his glass, stifled a cough as he set the glass down and wiped a hand across his mouth, then came timidly along the bar. He looked like a schoolboy who had misbehaved and was going up to receive his punishment.

"Where you gonna put him?" Barney Nash asked, grinning. "That jail wouldn't hold a fly."

"Maybe not," Cobbett said, plucking Beebe's gun from the holster and shoving it in his own belt. "But it will hold Beebe. He couldn't tear his way out of a paper sack."

Barney Nash guffawed, Archie Beebe's face got even redder, and Duffy Shaw said to Cobbett, "I think you're exceeding your authority. I believe that's the word lawyers use."

"I've exceeded it before," Cobbett said.

"He sure has!" Archie Beebe exclaimed, looking as if he might cry.

Cobbett grabbed the little man by the arm and shoved him toward the swing doors. "When scum like you can get away with breaking all the rules, I figure I've got a right to bend them a little."

He marched Beebe outside and along the boardwalk toward the

marshal's office, which was only two buildings down from the hotel. A little group of people had gathered on the hotel veranda to watch, including the fat man Cobbett had seen in the dining room and a middle-aged woman with graying dark hair that he had not seen before. When he was almost to the marshals' office he heard the woman say in an angry, grating voice, "Why is he arresting that poor little man? He wasn't the one who did all that shooting. He was over on the other side of the street when it was going on, like he got away from that crowd on purpose so everyone would know he didn't have any part in it. But the marshal is taking him to jail anyway. I guess he's afraid to arrest the ones who did the shooting, so he's taking it out on that poor boy. That's just the kind of stunt Tobe Langley would pull."

Archie Beebe stifled a snicker. Cobbett's jaw tightened and his hand tightened on Beebe's arm. He turned the little man and pushed him into the marshal's office, kicking the door shut behind him. The room was almost dark, but not too dark for him to see Beebe's face twitching in suppressed glee. It both surprised and delighted Beebe to see the town already turning against the tall marshal. That was icing on the cake—well worth getting arrested for, and he knew Cobbett could not hold him long.

Cobbett knew it too. He knew it had been a mistake to arrest Beebe. There was no charge he could bring against Beebe that would hold up in court, even if it were possible to bring him to trial. And in spite of what he had said in the saloon, he could not keep the little man in this old shack of a jail. The only way to do it would be to keep him tied hand and foot and the town would never stand for that, not unless he had done something really bad.

Cobbett would have to let him go, and in the eyes of the town that would be proof that he knew he had not been justified in arresting Beebe. And whatever Beebe did in the future would seem at least partly justified because Cobbett had arrested him for little or no reason.

The bitter taste of bile was strong in Cobbett's mouth, for he knew he had played right into Beebe's hands. The very same thing had happened before, in Miles city. Beebe had provoked Cobbett into making a fool of himself and turning many of the townspeople against him.

He grabbed a fistful of Beebe's shirt, jerked him up on his toes and said in a soft but savage tone, with his face only inches from Beebe's, "All right, Beebe. It looks like you've won another hand in your stupid game. But you better keep one thing in mind. I'm not a very good loser."

Cobbett's hard threatening face so close to his own and Cobbett's rough fist knotted in his shirt scared Beebe's smile away and set his teeth to chattering. Fear and hatred warred in his wild catlike eyes. He longed to spit in Cobbett's face, but was too cowardly and too clever to do so. There were safer ways to get even with Cobbett.

The plank door creaked open and the hard-faced woman from the hotel veranda stood there glaring in with frosty eyes. Behind her on the boardwalk stood four men who had followed her from the hotel. The fat man was not among them. "What's going on here?" the woman demanded in her harsh grating voice. "What are you doing to that boy?"

"Just giving him a little friendly advice," Cobbett said. "Who might you be?"

"That's none of your business," the woman said. "Release that poor boy. If you want to arrest someone, arrest Barney Nash or some of that crowd. They were the ones who did all that shooting."

"Did you see them do it?"

"No, I didn't see them," the woman said impatiently. "But everyone knows it was them."

"I don't doubt but what they did it," Cobbett said. "But Beebe put them up to it."

"Oh, that's nonsense!" the woman exclaimed. "They were shooting their guns all the time before he ever came here!"

Cobbett looked at Archie Beebe and saw his face twitching again. In the virtual darkness the woman would think the "poor boy" was trying not to cry. But Cobbett knew that Beebe was doing his best to hold back a howl of almost hysterical glee. Things were working out even better than Beebe could have hoped for.

"Go on, Beebe," Cobbett said. "Go back and plot some more mischief with your new friends."

Beebe turned at once and headed for the door, which he found blocked by the stout woman who had come to his defense. He took off his hat and bowed politely. "Thank you, ma'am," he said humbly. "It's a good thing you showed up when you did."

"I might not be around the next time," the woman said sternly. "You should stay away from men like that. Then no one would get the wrong idea."

"Yes, ma'am," Beebe said, meek and respectful. "But would you make him give back my gun, ma'am? A man never knows when he might need one in this country, and he ain't got no right to keep it."

"Well, of course he'll give back your gun," the woman said.

"Aggie," one of the men on the boardwalk said.

"You keep out of this," the woman said over her shoulder. "If you ain't got the guts to speak up, don't try to stop me." Then her frosty glance returned to Cobbett, and she made an imperious gesture. "Give him back his gun."

Cobbett, who seldom laughed, did so now, at the stout woman's domineering manner. The laugh took him by surprise and the woman went rigid with shocked indignation.

"What on earth are you laughing at?" she grated.

Cobbett shrugged. "Nothing." He drew Beebe's gun from his waistband and handed it to the little man, who stuck the gun in his holster and crowded out past the woman without another word to her or a glance at the silent men on the boardwalk as he headed back toward Duffy Shaw's saloon.

"It's pitch dark in here," the woman said in her scolding voice. "Why don't you put on a light?"

"There isn't one. Apparently Langley never used one."

"No, he didn't," the woman said. "This place was always dark at night. We never knew whether he'd gone to bed or was just sitting in here in the dark."

"I guess he could see more when the office was dark," Cobbett said. "Or perhaps he was afraid someone might take a shot at him through the window."

"He could have put a curtain on the window," the woman said. "A blind too for that matter. We paid him enough for doing nothing."

"Aggie," the same man said again. It was one of the men Cobbett had seen talking to Hank Gilbert at noon. "We should be going, Aggie."

"Not till I say what I came to say," the woman retorted angrily, her voice rising. "You men keep hiring marshals who never do anything but draw their pay and bleed this town and I'm sick of it. It looks like none of you are ever going to say anything about it so I'm going to." Then her voice lashed at Cobbett, "If you don't intend to do anything about that bunch, you might as well take off that badge right now and ride on!"

"What would you like for me to do?" Cobbett asked quietly.

"Run them out of town! If I was a man that's what I'd do!"

"How would you go about it?"

"I'd round up every able-bodied man in this town and arm them and then I'd give that bunch fair warning to get out of town or they'd be driven out!"

"That's exactly what should have been done a long time ago," Cobbett said. "But I got the impression that the able-bodied men in this town don't want any part of the Nash gang. That's the only reason they hired me. And they can fire me anytime. But as long as I'm doing this job, I'll do it my way."

"That's just what Tobe Langley said, and he never did anything!" the woman cried, turning to appeal to the men on the boardwalk. "Didn't I tell you we had another Tobe Langley on our hands?"

The same one, obviously her hen-pecked husband, spoke again in a quiet, patient tone. "You didn't have to tell us, Aggie. Sheb Snively's been saying it all day. You heard him say it yourself. Now try to remember you're a lady and quit shouting like a muleskinner."

"Oh, nonsense!" the woman said. "If you *gentleman* would start behaving more like men, maybe women could behave like ladies. But it's high time somebody did some shouting around here."

"I could post those men out of town," Cobbett said quietly. "But it wouldn't do any good unless this town was prepared for me to start shooting them on sight if they didn't leave."

The woman looked at him in a different way, and said in a quieter tone, "Are *you* prepared to go that far?"

"It doesn't matter," Cobbett said, "because the people of this town aren't ready for that yet. They may think they are, but when it gets started they would try to stop it. But then it would be too late to stop it."

"You do whatever you've got to do to get rid of those men," one of the men on the boardwalk said, his face unrecognizable in the fading light. "No one in this town will try to stop you. Maybe we haven't got the stomach for that kind of thing ourselves, but we won't interfere with you if you have."

After a long moment Ben Cobbett sighed. "All right," he said. "Go on back to your houses and lock your doors. Stay off the street and pretend you don't know what's going on. If you hear shooting, tell yourselves it's just the Nash gang letting off steam. Then when it's all over you can tell everyone you didn't know what was happening, that you didn't know anyone would be killed."

"Aggie," the woman's husband said. "We'd better go, Aggie."

The other men glanced uneasily toward Duffy Shaw's saloon and began drifting off in the other direction. The one left standing alone on the boardwalk darted a fearful look at the saloon and his voice became more urgent. "Aggie!"

"I see what you mean," the woman told Cobbett, with a scornful look over her shoulder at her husband. "Well, good luck. Maybe I was wrong about you. I guess we'll just have to wait and see, won't we?"

"Don't expect anything to happen right away," Cobbett told her.

"I don't," she said, already moving off with her husband, and sounding just as sarcastic as before. "I don't expect anything to happen anytime soon."

Cobbett sat down wearily behind the desk, leaving the door open, and a minute later the shadowy figure of a man appeared in the doorway. Cobbett could tell nothing about the man in the poor light except that he looked and smelled like a working cowhand.

"That you, Marshal?" the man asked.

"Right. What can I do for you?"

"I'm Cal Heffer," the man said. "Mr. McCabe sent me in with them horses you wanted. I left them at the stable."

"There's been a little misunderstanding," Cobbett said. "I told Hank Gilbert I wanted the town to supply me with horses while I'm marshal here. I didn't know he was going to ask McCabe to furnish the horses."

"Oh, that's all right," Heffer said, rolling a cigarette in the dark. He struck a match on the doorjamb and in its smoky yellow light Cobbett saw the narrow, clean-shaven face of a man still in his twenties, a tall young man with blue eyes and sandy hair, not unlike a thousand others of his breed. "Mac's more than glad to do it," he added. "I brought four, all geldings of course, and he said if them got stole or anything, we'd bring you some more."

"Tell him I'm obliged," Cobbett said. Then he asked, "Any luck finding those cows?"

Heffer shook his head, the tip of his cigarette glowing red in the dark. "They hadn't anyway when Mac sent me back to get the horses. I didn't figger we'd find them. There's about fifty square miles of canyons and rocks and mesas for them to hide in. That's some mighty rough country, and the Nash gang knows it a lot better than we do."

"That anywhere near their shack?"

"Naw. It's quite a piece south of there and more to the east, on the other side of the river. Not that it's much of a river, most of the time. It only looks like a river now because we've had so much rain lately. Most of the time this is mighty dry country with only a few waterholes, and it's even drier south of here. But after all this rain there'll be plenty of water for them cows for a while, like Mac said."

Heffer's cigarette glowed as he inhaled the smoke. "Oh, something else I wanted to mention about them horses. I waited till after dark on purpose and told Mort Crumby to keep quiet about them. But I also told him something else Mac said—that he was gonna have to let him go if he didn't quit stayin' drunk half the time and lettin' horses get stole right under his nose. That made him mad and he headed straight for Duffy Shaw's saloon to tell Barney Nash and them about the horses. He didn't say that was what he was gonna do, but I'd bet my saddle he's down there tellin' them right now. I figger Mac will let him go as soon as he can find someone to replace him, but that may not be soon enough to do you any good.

"But Mac said to tell you if they do steal them horses—all the horses in that stable are his by rights, and that includes the ones the Nash gang rides. I don't know if you've noticed it or not, but most of the horses they ride are still wearin' Mac's brand—that's how bold they are. But they know that if anyone says anything about it, all they have to do is say they rented the horses at the stable and Mort Crumby will back up their lies because he's scared of them and he don't care much anyhow since it ain't his stable now. So if they steal them horses I brought for you, Mac said you should use one of theirs when you need a horse, because they're really his horses anyway."

"What about the regular livery horses?" Cobbett asked. "Does Crumby own any of them?"

"Crumby don't own anything," Heffer said. "He sold everything he had to Mac. Mac told him if he could get a good price for any of the horses to go ahead and sell them. But Mort usually pockets the money and tells Mac the horses was stolen."

Cobbett nodded. "That's what I heard. I guess that horse he sold me belonged to McCabe."

"If he sold it to you it did," Heffer said. "Well, I got to get back to the ranch. But I think I'll get me a drink first."

"Better go to one of the other saloons."

"I aim to," Heffer said. "I don't aim to give Barney Nash any chance at me if I can help it. By this time he's usually drunk enough to be good and mean and lookin' for a fight. And Mac told me to stay away from that bunch and not get in no trouble while I'm by myself."

"Sounds like good advice," Cobbett said. "Thanks for bringing the horses."

"Good luck. You'll need it."

CHAPTER 15

Ben Cobbett remained seated behind the desk in the dark marshal's office for a minute after Cal Heffer had left. Then he got to his feet and checked his gun by feel and shoved it back into the holster. Leaving the office, he went down the street and pushed in through the swing doors of Duffy Shaw's saloon.

Mort Crumby stood at the bar with a glass of whiskey in his hand saying in a loud voice, "... then he sends one of his hands in with them horses for me to take care of and tells me not to say anything about it. Where does he want me to hide them, under my hat?"

Barney Nash and some of his men laughed, and Crumby, half smiling himself, bared his rotten teeth to say something else, then turned his gray-whiskered face toward Cobbett as the latter came in through the swing doors. The old man's face was flushed with drink and his eyes were bloodshot. In his filthy, baggy old clothes he looked about as seedy and disreputable as a man could look.

Tap Grodin snorted at sight of Cobbett and Dill Stringer spit on the floor. Ned Ribble and Chick Moser looked uneasy, but Barney Nash grinned like he was glad to see the marshal. He rubbed the back of a huge hand across his coarse bloated face and said, "Hey, Cobbett, I hear someone brought us some horses."

"If anything happens to those horses," Cobbett said flatly, "I intend to start using any horse I find in that stable. McCabe sent word it was all right with him and all those horses belong to him, including the ones you bastards ride."

Archie Beebe, all but hidden behind Barney Nash's bulk, spoke up then. "It don't include my pinto."

Cobbett glanced at the little man in the hazy back bar mirror and a wintry smile twisted his lips. "Don't worry, Beebe. I can tell your horse even in the dark, and I never had much use for paint horses. I can't think why, unless it's because you usually ride one."

Tap Grodin sneered. "I bet you won't take Joe Deegan's black, even if somebody does steal your horses."

"I doubt if he'll be playing any stupid games for a while," Cobbett said. "He's found a better way to pass the time."

There were snickers and guffaws.

Then Barney Nash said, "What do you need with a horse anyhow, Cobbett? I thought yore job was here in town."

Ignoring that, Cobbett looked at Mort Crumby, who was watching him uneasily. "It seems you sold me a horse that didn't belong to you," Cobbett said, walking up to the old man. "I want the money back. I'll turn it over to McCabe the next time I see him."

"Then what am I gonna buy hay and grain with?" Crumby asked hoarsely, his voice trembling with anger. "Now I got four more horses to feed and take care of because of you."

"Don't worry," Barney Nash said, grinning, his swollen red eyelids half closed. "You won't have them for long."

Cobbett glanced at Nash with cold eyes, then returned his attention to Mort Crumby.

"And anyway," Crumby added, "it ain't none of yore business. Mac thinks the stable takes in a lot more money than it does from renting out horses and taking care of other people's horses. If I didn't sell a few horses along, I wouldn't have no money to buy hay and grain with."

"Or whiskey," Cobbett added for him.

"I buy that out of what Mac pays me," Crumby said, his face reddening behind the dirty gray whiskers.

"He must pay you pretty well," Cobbett said, and there were more snickers from Nash's men. He held out his hand. "I want the fifty dollars I gave you for that horse. You can buy feed out of the money you've got out of other horses."

For a moment Crumby looked as if he would refuse. Then he reluctantly reached down into the pocket of his baggy pants and dug out a wad of greenbacks. Turning half away to keep Cobbett from seeing how much money he had, he found Barney Nash greedily eye-ing the money as he counted out the fifty dollars. Crumby thrust the fifty at Cobbett and stuck the rest back in his pocket.

"Yeah, he must pay you pretty well," Cobbett said again as he counted the money and pocketed it. "Either that or you're robbing him blind."

Barney Nash laughed and said to his men, "Looks like old Mort's a bigger crook then we are. You should see the wad of greenbacks he's got in his pocket."

"It ain't as much as you think," Crumby said in a worried tone. "Most of it's one-dollar bills."

"I didn't see no ones," Nash said. "All I saw was tens and twen-ties."

"McCabe said something else you boys should keep in mind," Cob-bett interrupted. "If you kill any more horses, you won't be hurting me. You'll just lose the money you could get out of them someday when you steal them."

"What makes you think we aim to wait that long?" Nash asked, with a smug grin, though his little eyes were mean and hard.

"Like I said," Cobbett told him, "if you do steal them, I'll just start using one of yours when I need a horse."

"Ours might not be here," Nash said.

"They also might not be here when *you* need them," Cobbett said. "You better keep that in mind too."

Barney Nash looked at his men and did not say anything. But evidently this was a possibility that had not occurred to him.

As he turned to leave the saloon, Cobbett glanced at Duffy Shaw and saw the hostility and dislike in every line of his bulldog face.

"Wait a minute, Cobbett," Barney Nash said. "I want to ask you somethin'. Somethin' I been wonderin' about. Last night you said if me and you had a fight, I'd lose. Even if it was a fair fight. What made you say that? I thought you was afraid to fight me."

"I never said I was afraid to. I said I didn't want to. There's a dif-ference."

Again Cobbett turned to leave, and again Nash stopped him. The big rustler was scowling now instead of grinning. His mood had de-generated; in the space of a few moments he had turned mean and dangerous. Perhaps it was the whiskey working on him. "Don't run off when I'm talking to you," he said. "Why don't we find out which one of us would lose? And if you want to fight dirty, two can play that game."

"Two can play the game you boys have been playing, too," Cobbett said.

"We can settle this right now," Nash said, pushing his empty glass away from him. "These boys won't bother you unless you hit me with yore gun or somethin'. Then I hope they break ever' bone in yore body."

"You're making a mistake," Cobbett said quietly.

"We'll see about that," Nash said, removing his green coat and laying it on the bar. He drew a revolver from his belt and put it on top of the coat. "I ain't armed, Cobbett, so you ain't got no excuse to pull a gun on me. If you had any guts you'd take it off and fight fair."

"I'll keep it in case your friends decide you need some help," Cobbett said.

Nash snorted at that. He shoved Mort Crumby out of his way and stepped forward, grinning with savage anticipation. "You better take a look in the mirror, Cobbett, and remember what yore face looks like, 'cause it won't ever look that way again. I aim to flatten yore nose and knock out all yore teeth and then kick in yore ribs. Then I aim to tie you on a horse and run you out of town."

"You won't do it with hot air," Cobbett told him.

"This is gonna be fun," Nash said and dived at Cobbett, his arms outspread to grab him in a bear hug. He ran into an unseen fist and heard a sickening crunch that he hoped was a busted knuckle but knew was a broken nose. That did not stop his bearlike rush and his great arms swept in to crush his foe, but closed on empty air. Cobbett had stepped aside and tripped him as he went by. Nash hit the floor with a loud grunt and came up with a roar or rage.

"You ain't fightin' fair again!" he howled, even as he brought up his boot to kick Cobbett below the belt.

But again Cobbett was too quick for him, stepping aside and kicking his other leg out from under him. There was not time to break his fall and this time the whole building shook when he crashed to the floor. And when he tried to get up there was a wrenching pain in his left knee and he felt certain his hip was broken as well. But he pushed himself up anyway and roared, "Stand still and fight fair, dammit!" And then his head jerked back as Cobbett punched him in the mouth, using his left hand. It was a surprisingly hard punch and Nash spit out part of a tooth. Then, deliberately, Cobbett kicked him in the ribs and Nash heard one of them crack as he bent over sideways and cried out in pain. It occurred to him that Cobbett was doing to him everything he had promised to do to Cobbett, and that galling thought was unbearable.

He backed off and roared at his men, who were gaping at him in disbelief, "Get him, you fools! You aim to just stand there and let him kill me?"

"Stay where you are," Cobbett warned them. "I'll put a bullet in anyone who moves or touches a gun. That includes you, Shaw."

The saloonkeeper shrugged. "It ain't my fight."

Cobbett was so surprised that he took his eyes off Barney Nash for a moment and looked at Shaw. Nash saw his chance and sprang at Cobbett, trying once more to get him in a bear hug. Cobbett leapt aside and grabbing Nash by an arm, rammed him head first into the bar. Nash bounced off the bar and flopped over on the floor, dazed.

Tap Grodin, his yellow teeth bared in a wolfish snarl and his hand gripping the butt of his holstered gun, stepped out away from the bar where he could see Cobbett and Nash more clearly past the others. Perhaps he was not even aware that his hand was on his gun. With his kind it was an instinctive, almost unthinking gesture when he felt himself or one of his friends in danger. But Cobbett had said what he would do if anyone moved—that is, made a threatening gesture—or touched a gun, and Grodin hand done both.

Without the slightest hesitation Cobbett whipped out his long-barreled .45 and fired. The gun exploded in his fist and the bullet, striking Grodin high in the right shoulder, spun him around. Grodin fell against the bar, dropping his own gun and grabbing the edge of the bar with his good hand to keep from falling all the way to the floor. He cried out when the bullet smashed into his shoulder and howled like an animal in pain as he hung there on the bar, his lips drawn back from his ugly teeth and a wild look in his dark eyes.

"I warned you!" Cobbett said in a quiet, savage tone. "The rest of you—unbuckle your gunbelts and toss them behind the bar."

Duffy Shaw started to protest about that, then took a closer look at Cobbett's cold hard face and changed his mind.

Dill Stringer, Ned Ribble and Chuck Moser also looked uneasily at Cobbett's face and then carefully unbuckled their gunbelts and tossed them behind the bar as they had been told to do.

"That goes for you too, Beebe," Cobbett snapped.

The little man had been staring at Tap Grodin and Barney Nash as if too numbed by what had happened to move. But Cobbett's voice, lashing at him like a whip, brought him out of his trance and he

quickly unbuckled his gunbelt and threw it behind the bar, fumbling
in his nervous haste.

Tap Grodin's eyes went to his own gun still lying on the floor
about five feet out from the bar. The throbbing pain in his shoulder
was driving him mad with hatred, hatred that was greater than his
fear. Maybe, while Cobbett had his attention on the others ... Tap
Grodin calculated his chances and flung himself away from the bar,
grabbing for the gun with his left hand.

He got hold of the butt of the gun and got his thumb on the hammer and began to bring the gun up, thrusting it out toward Cobbett.
A wild savage joy filled him and his lips twitched in a smile at the
thought of killing Cobbett, of shooting him down and then empty-
ing the gun into him. It was beginning to look like he was going to
make it, when a chunk of lead ripped through his body and spoiled
his aim. His gun went off but the bullet went over Cobbett's head
and splintered the ceiling, drawing an angry growl from Duffy Shaw
who never tolerated any wild shooting in his saloon. Another leak to
worry about when it rained.

Tap Grodin tried to draw back the hammer of his gun for a second shot, but he did not have the strength. The gun slipped from his
trembling hand and fell onto the floor. Then Cobbett was standing
over him, staring down at him with those cold gray eyes and contemptuously kicking the gun away.

"So you sons of bitches thought it was going to be fun having me
around," Cobbett said savagely. "How much fun is it now?"

Tap Grodin managed to raise his head off the floor to look up
at Cobbett. He strained and trembled with the effort and his black-
stubbled dark face was oddly contorted and his bad teeth were chattering, but his lips twitched in a smile. "Joe Deegan will kill you," he
whispered.

"Not for this he won't," Cobbett said. "You bastards are fools if
you think he cares whether you live or die."

But Tap Grodin died with the bitter smile—more like a wolfish
snarl—on his contorted face, died convinced that Joe Deegan would
kill Cobbett.

Duffy Shaw stood stiffly behind the bar watching Cobbett out of
the corners of his slitted deep-set eyes. His right hand was on the
sawed-off, double-barreled shotgun he kept under the bar. He felt
certain that if he killed Cobbett nothing would ever be done about
it. No one cared what went on in Rockville except the townspeople

themselves and they were afraid to do anything.

But then Cobbett, as if reading his thoughts, turned his head and snapped at him, "I want to see both of your hands flat on the bar. I won't tell you twice."

Duffy Shaw, scowling murderously at the marshal, slowly brought up his right hand, empty, and placed it palm down on the bar top beside his left hand.

"On second thought," Cobbett said, motioning with his gun, "come out from behind that bar. I want all of you to walk out ahead of me. I don't intend to get shot in the back as I leave here."

The saloonkeeper planted his feet stubbornly on the floor and stood behind the bar staring coldly back at the tall marshal.

Cobbett cocked his gun and yelled at him, "Move!"

Duffy Shaw reluctantly came around the front end of the bar and Cobbett motioned with his gun for the others to follow him outside. The marshal stood watching them coldly as they filed silently past him. When Archie Beebe went by, Cobbett reached out and patted his pockets and from one of them lifted out a small .41 caliber Colt revolver with a spur trigger.

"I was hoping you'd try to use this," Cobbett said, palming the pocket pistol.

"I figgered you was," Beebe said resentfully.

"If you want it back, you'll have to see that fat lady about it," Cobbett told him. "I never meant to keep that other gun and you knew it. But I'm going to keep this one to teach you a lesson."

Beebe followed the others on out through the swing doors, his red face twisted in bitter resentment. Cobbett remained in the saloon watching Barney Nash who lay on the floor feigning unconsciousness and watching for his chance at Cobbett. He meant to grab Cobbett's legs as the marshal went by and throw him down, then get on top of him and beat him to death.

"Get up," Cobbett said. "Get up or I'll finish kicking your ribs in."

Nash groaned as he struggled to his feet and stood hipshot, favoring one leg.

Cobbett motioned with his gun. "Get outside with the others."

"Hell, I can't walk," Nash said. "You crippled me, you bastard."

"Then crawl!" Cobbett said.

For a moment Nash glared at him through narrow bloodshot eyes. Then the big man turned and started limping toward the swing doors.

"I said crawl!" Cobbett snapped. "You already had your chance to walk. And I want to see a big grin on your face. I want everyone to see how happy you are. How much you enjoy having me around."

Nash kept walking as if he had not heard. He seemed anxious now to get outside with the others.

Cobbett stepped up quickly behind him and kicked his good leg out from under him. Nash's bad leg gave way under his weight and he fell heavily to the floor. Then, cussing under his breath, Nash crawled out through the batwing doors and halted on the boardwalk when he saw the others standing silently in the street watching him. Nash started to get to his feet and Cobbett said right behind him, "Keep crawling. I'll tell you when to get up."

Nash descended from the boardwalk as cautiously as a crippled steer at a river crossing but he more nearly resembled a huge bug as he crawled out across the ruts and puddles of the still muddy street toward his comrades.

Still on the boardwalk, Cobbett glanced along the street and saw several small groups of people standing in the shadows at the edge of the street and another small group watched from the hotel veranda. In that group he made out the stout woman and the huge fat man. Frowning in annoyance, he slipped Archie Beebe's little pistol into his pocket and stepped out into the street. He noticed the shabby old hostler, Mort Crumby, among the saloon crowd and he said to him, "Get on back to the stable and take care of those new horses. I want them all to have a good rubdown and plenty of feed and water."

"Yes sir," Crumby muttered and hurried off down the street, anxious to get away.

Cobbett indicated Duffy Shaw and the others. "I want the rest of you to stand right where you are till I'm off the street," he said in a soft deadly tone that carried threat enough without any additional words. Barney Nash started once more to get to his feet, but Cobbett said, "Not you, Nash. I'm not through with you yet. I want you to crawl up the street toward the hotel and I want to see a big smile on your face so everyone will know how much fun you're having."

Cobbett heard someone chuckle and he noticed Cal Heffer watching from the edge of the street. "I wish Mac could see this," Heffer said. "It would tickle him to death."

"Who said that?" Barney Nash asked, lifting his head to peer about. He saw Heffer and said, "You just wait till I get my hands on you."

"Crawl," Cobbett said and booted Nash in the rear.

Nash glared at his men and roared, "Do somethin'!"

"Ain't much we can do, Barney," Dill Stringer said. "He took our guns."

"Then use yore fists!" Nash cried hoarsely.

Stringer looked at Cobbett and did not say anything else. The others were silent also and no one made a move to do as Nash had ordered.

"I said crawl," Cobbett repeated, booting the big man again.

"I'll kill you for this, Cobbett," Nash said as he began crawling up the street.

"You'll have to be a lot better with a gun than you are with your fists," Cobbett told him.

"Joe Deegan does my gun work," Nash said. "You just wait till he finds out about this."

"That's where we're going now," Cobbett said. "To tell him."

As they went by the barbershop Cobbett saw Hank Gilbert standing at the door in his shirtsleeves. He was not sure but he thought he saw Gilbert shaking his head in disapproval. That did not much surprise Cobbett, but it served to remind him that he was all alone here as he had been elsewhere. The people of Rockville thought they wanted him to tame the wild ones, but to be effective his methods would have to be so brutal and merciless that the townspeople would be appalled. They would shake their heads, as Hank Gilbert was doing. They would even begin to feel some sympathy for the very men they had hired him to get rid of. It was an old story that he had seen repeated in too many towns.

"That's far enough," he said to Nash.

They had arrived before the hotel. Cobbett ignored the group of people on the veranda and looked up at the lamplit window of Julie Tidings's room on the second floor. "Hey, Deegan!" he called. "Come down and see how much fun it is to have me around! Barney Nash wants you to see how much fun he's having!"

"You're a fool, Cobbett," Nash said quietly. "He'll kill you."

Cobbett kept his attention on the hotel window and did not bother to reply. He was not surprised when Deegan opened the window and leaned out, grinning. He did not see Julie Tidings but he heard her say to herself when Deegan opened the window, "Oh no."

There was enough light from the hotel for Deegan to see Barney Nash on his hands and knees in the mud and Cobbett standing nearby with the gun in his hand. Deegan laughed and asked, "What you doin' down there, Barney?"

"Kill him, Joe!" Nash roared. "Kill the bastard!"

"No, no," Deegan said soothingly. "I wouldn't want to do that, Barney. It's too much fun having him around. Didn't I tell you things would liven up when he pinned on that badge?"

"Are you crazy?" Nash cried hoarsely. "He damn near broke my leg and he killed Tap Grodin!"

Deegan was silent for a moment. The light was behind him and Cobbett could not see his face clearly, but he sensed an ominous change in the young outlaw's attitude. But then Deegan shrugged and said carelessly, "Tap prob'ly had it coming. I've been expecting him to get himself killed for a long time. I thought a time or two I was gonna have to do it myself."

"Is that all you got to say?" Barney Nash cried. "Tap was yore friend and this bastard killed him!"

Joe Deegan's voice suddenly rose angrily, which was a surprise after his display of smiling amusement. "You ain't too bright, Barney. He's already got a gun in his hand. If I come down there, the first thing he'll do is put a bullet in you. Besides, I've got more important things to do right now."

"Oh, be quiet," Julie Tidings said, her voice just loud enough to be heard in the street below.

"She should be run out of town," the woman on the hotel veranda said, not bothering to keep her own voice down. "We don't need her kind around here."

"Aggie," the woman's husband said.

"Joe!" Barney Nash howled in angry desperation. "Damn you, Joe, don't let him do this to me in front of the whole town! He made me crawl all the way up here through the mud and my knee's swelled fit to bust! I got it twisted somehow when he kicked my leg out from under me, and I damn near broke my hip too when I fell!"

"Stop whining!" Joe Deegan said in disgust. "You're beginning to sound like a crybaby."

Just then there was a loud crash on the hotel veranda and Cobbett saw the big fat man lying on the porch floor.

"Oh, good Lord," the woman named Aggie said. "I bet he's had a heart attack. All this excitement was too much for his weak heart."

"What's going on down there?" Joe Deegan asked, leaning out the window.

"It's old Barford," Barney Nash said. "Looks like his heart give out."

"Let's try to get him inside," one of the men on the veranda said. "If we can carry him. I guess he'll weigh three or four hundred pounds."

Another man had knelt down and pressed his ear to the fat man's chest. After a moment he got back to his feet, brushing off his clothes. "Nothing we can do for him anyway. He's dead."

Barney Nash suddenly laughed. "Ain't he the one come out here for his health?"

"You filthy animal!" the woman cried. "It's your fault he's dead!"

"Don't blame me," Nash retorted. "It wasn't my idea crawlin' all the way up here. Yore fine upstandin' marshal made me do it."

The woman looked at Cobbett and said bitterly, "I hope you're proud of yourself. What did you bring that trash up here for anyway? You should keep that kind of trouble down there at the saloon where it belongs, instead of endangering the lives of decent folks."

Cobbett heard Joe Deegan laugh.

Tobe Langley had been watching the Hicks shack for over an hour from the top of a bleak rocky hill overlooking the shack. It was dark now, dark and cold and damp, and he shivered, feeling like an outcast, a lonesome old wolf that could no longer keep up with the pack. Molly Hicks had lit a lamp and he could see her moving back and forth past the window. He was satisfied now that she was alone in the shack.

He strode down the hill with the shotgun ready just in case. He knocked on the door and when she refused to open it, asking stupid questions, he kicked the door open and sent her sprawling. He was on her before she could recover and in a matter of moments he had her hands and feet tied. It was not until he moved away from her toward the window that she got a good look at him and saw who he was.

"So it's you!" she said, her lips twisted in scorn and loathing. "I might have know. That's all you're fit for, fighting women and people who can't fight back. You just wait till Joe Deegan gets here!"

"I intend to," he told her. "And it may be a pretty long wait, because he's shacked up in town with Lot Tidings's wife. So you might as well relax."

"I don't believe you!"

"What you believe ain't important," Tobe Langley said, looking out the window. "Just do like you're told and we'll get along just fine."

CHAPTER 16

It was quiet in Rockville for a few days. Barney Nash and his men remained in town but there was no loud coarse laughter from Duffy Shaw's saloon, where they stayed most of the time. There were no fistfights. No shots were fired. Everyone seemed to be waiting to see what would happen next.

Tap Grodin and the fat man with the weak heart, Sam Barford, were buried in the small graveyard at the edge of town on the same day. Grodin was buried unceremoniously early in the morning and Barford was buried later in the day, with most of the town in attendance at the brief graveside service. There was no minister in Rockville but someone read a few passages from the Bible and said the necessary words.

Cobbett did not go to the funeral. While it was going on, he moved his few belongings out of his hotel room and into the room behind the marshal's office that had been intended for, but never used as, a jail. His spare clothes he hung on nails in the wall that had evidently been used for that purpose by his predecessor, Tobe Langley. The lumpy mattress would suffice as a bed. Cobbett had often slept on the ground in his time and anything softer was comfortable enough for him. He did not expect to be here long in any case.

He had heard no sound in Julie Tidings's room next door as he gathered up his things. That Joe Deegan was in her room he well knew, but they were in the habit of keeping quiet when they heard him returning to his room and he had the feeling they were waiting for him to leave again. That was one reason he had decided to move out. He was making them uncomfortable and they were making him uncomfortable.

But there was another reason as well. It would be easier for him to come and go from the jail without disturbing anyone or anyone being able to keep track of his movements. If necessary he could leave by the back window and return the same way, as Tobe Langley had apparently done on occasion. There had once been a back door to the shack but planks had been nailed over it and Cobbett did not wish to attract attention by prying them off. He did not know why the back window had not been boarded up as well but there was no sign that it ever had been.

So he moved into his new quarters and waited, like the rest of the town, to see what would happen next.

The Nash gang, reduced by one member, seemed also to be waiting—waiting to see whether Mac McCabe and his men found the stolen cows or gave up looking for them, as they had done so often in the past. Cal Heffer had gone back to join the hunt and there had been no new word yet from the ranch. But unless the stolen herd had access to a permanent source of water, the rustlers would not be able to wait much longer. For the temporary streams and pools created by the rain would soon dry up, if they were not used up first. It had not rained since the night that the cattle were stolen and it did not look as if it would rain again any time soon. The sky remained clear and blue all day with only a few scattered white cloud puffs.

The mud of the street had hardened as it dried but it was soon tramped to fine powdery dust again. Life had to go on, for the living, and the townspeople could not remain indoors indefinitely despite the possibility of more violence.

They had shopping to do, errands to run. Only men like the Nash gang who had no work to do could afford to remain in a saloon twenty-four hours a day, playing cards and drinking and eating their meals at the free lunch counter and sleeping on the floor.

Undoubtedly they were getting bored and restless, and Cobbett knew that they had not forgotten about him. Not with Archie Beebe there to remind them. During the long hours they whiled away in the saloon they would be discussing pleasurable ways of getting even with him for killing Tap Grodin, nor was it likely that Barney Nash had forgot what Cobbett had done to him. While he licked his wounds he would be plotting his vengeance upon the man who had inflicted them and shamed him before the whole town.

Cobbett was surprised that they waited as long as they did. It must have gone against the grain for them to let him have a few days of peace and quiet, and he doubted if Archie Beebe let them have much peace during that time. For when the mischief began again it was in the form of familiar games that Beebe had invented and refined in Miles City and elsewhere. They were simple, even childish games, but they had the desired effect. Beebe had long since eliminated more complicated games that were apt to go awry in the hands of the sort of men who could be persuaded to pull such childish pranks.

Guns began popping again whenever Cobbett went to the hotel or the restaurant to eat, and by the time he got to the saloon, Nash and the others would be innocently playing cards, though Nash in particular was apt to give them away by grinning and cracking jokes, trying to see how far he could push Cobbett. Everyone in Rockville knew that Nash and his men were doing the shooting and no doubt some of the townspeople even saw them at it sometimes, but no one dared come forward and report it to the marshal. And it was virtually impossible for Cobbett to catch them at it, because someone, usually Archie Beebe, was posted on the other side of the street where he could watch the marshal's office and warn them if he saw Cobbett coming. Beebe felt himself immune to retaliation because Cobbett would not want the town to think he was overreacting and picking on a runt his size, who appeared for all the world to be minding his own business and just whistling a little tune to cheer himself up. The townspeople wanted the shooting stopped, but they did not want anyone else to die because of it.

The shooting began on the morning of the third day after Tap Grodin was killed and went on at intervals all that day and all the following night. No one in Rockville, including Cobbett, got much sleep. The guns banged again when he went to the hotel for breakfast, then fell silent after he returned to the marshal's office. After keeping the town awake all night, Barney Nash and his men had gone to sleep on the floor of Duffy Shaw's saloon, which Shaw obligingly kept closed until shortly before noon so they could catch up on their sleep. He promised to wake them in time to spoil Cobbett's lunch, sooner if he saw Cobbett sneaking across the street to the restaurant. The hotel dining room did not start serving lunch until twelve, and Shaw could keep an eye on the restaurant from the front window of his saloon.

Later on Archie Beebe, now sleeping like the others, would take up his position on the other side of the street where he could watch the front of the marshal's office without being seen himself until Cobbett came outside.

Shortly before noon Cobbett left the marshal's office and walked to the hotel. Once in the lobby he did not turn through the door into the dining room, but walked to the desk and said to the clerk, "I need to use your back door."

The clerk blinked in wonder. He glanced at the front door through which Cobbett had just entered. The sensible thing would have been for the marshal to go down the alleyway beside the hotel and not pester him at all. But he had learned that it was usually just as well not to ask questions; the answers only confused him further, and the less he knew, the better for his peace of mind. In as few words as possible he directed Cobbett to the back door.

Cobbett had arrived at the hotel a little early on purpose, thinking that Beebe would know they did not start serving lunch until twelve and would wait until then before the gave the signal. In the meantime, Cobbett had intended to move quickly through the hotel, out the back door and be waiting in the sage behind Duffy Shaw's saloon when Barney Nash and the others began firing their guns. But he had not allowed enough time for that or else Archie Beebe assumed that they would not keep the town marshal waiting in the dining room even though he was a little early. For as Cobbett stepped out through the back door of the hotel the shooting began and he saw Barney Nash, Dill Stringer and Chuck Moser behind the saloon with their smoking guns in their hands, firing into the air or at tin cans lying around, as the spirit moved them. He did not see Ned Ribble.

Nash and the other two saw Cobbett almost as soon as he stepped out the back door of the hotel. Caught in the act, they did not put away their guns immediately, but fired off a few more shots, assuming that it did not matter now and also wanting to show Cobbett that they were not afraid of him. They were all grinning, but more in embarrassment now then in amusement, and their faces were flushed and uneasy as the marshal started walking toward them, his own gun still in the holster.

For a moment they seemed on the point of turning their guns on Cobbett. But something about the set of his face or the look in his cold gray eyes made them change their minds. They put their guns away and entered the saloon by the back door.

Knowing he would find the back door bolted when he got there, Cobbett turned through an alley and got to the street just in time to see Archie Beebe slinking back across the street to the saloon. Either Beebe had guessed that something had gone wrong or someone in the saloon had signaled to him. He walked with his eyes on the ground, only raising them once to dart a quick worried glance at Cobbett. He quickened his pace a little, trying to reach the saloon before Cobbett did. But his legs were short and Cobbett's were long, and as it happened Cobbett got there only a step or two behind him and lifted Beebe's gun out of the holster as he followed him through the swing doors.

Ned Ribble sat by himself at a table, staring at an empty glass. He did not raise his glance when Cobbett came in right behind Archie Beebe. The other three were lined up at the bar, fortifying themselves with whiskey. Barney Nash and Chuck Moser were still grinning like little boys caught in someone's watermelon patch, but Dill Stringer's face was like a death mask.

Cobbett silently reached out with his left hand, caught Archie Beebe by the belt to stop him and then almost gently pushed him to one side out of the line of fire. To the other three Cobbett said, "Back off from the bar about two steps."

They looked at him and saw that he was holding Beebe's short-barreled .45 carelessly in his hand, pointed in their general direction. The gun was not cocked but his thumb rested lightly on the hammer. Their own guns were in their holsters and empty for all they knew. They had not counted the shots they had fired out behind the saloon or thought to reload afterwards.

"You ain't mad, are you, Cobbett?" Barney Nash asked with a tense grin. Usually he was the one standing closest to the front entrance of the saloon, but on this occasion he was the one closest to the back door, whether by accident or design Cobbett did not know.

"Just do like I said," Cobbett told him.

The three men looked at one another and after a moment they silently took a couple of steps back from the bar.

"Now I want all of you to lean forward and put your hands on the edge of the bar," Cobbett said.

Again they reluctantly obeyed.

"Beebe," Cobbett said without bothering to look at the little man, "get their guns."

Beebe looked resentfully at him, but then he silently went up to the three men leaning against the bar and pulled their guns out of the holsters. Then he turned and looked questioningly at Cobbett.

Cobbett nodded at a table. "Put them on that table."

Beebe put the guns on the table.

Then Cobbett said to him, "Now pick up one of them and hit Chuck Moser on the head with it."

Both Beebe and Moser looked at Cobbett in surprise and alarm, and the other two looked at him uneasily, perhaps sensing that the same was in store for them.

Duffy Shaw spoke up from behind the bar. "You can't make him do that."

Cobbett kept his eyes on Nash and the others as he said to the saloonkeeper, "One more word out of you and you will get the same."

The saloonkeeper opened his mouth to protest, then closed it without another word.

"Beebe," Cobbett said.

Archie Beebe looked at him with his face flushed with bitter resentment and hatred. Beebe knew that Cobbett was making him do this for a reason, and the reason was to get his new friends sore at him. If he laid them out with the barrel of a gun, they would blame him for it, even though Cobbett had ordered him to do it. They would also remember, as they fingered the lumps on their heads, that it was Beebe who had got them in trouble. In the future it would be harder, if not impossible, to get them to do anything else of the kind, knowing what sort of punishment to expect if they were caught.

Beebe looked down at the gun he was holding in his hand. It was Dill Stringer's heavy Dragoon Colt, converted to use centerfire cartridges, and even a light tap with it would hurt a man pretty bad. He did not know why he had selected that gun, the biggest and heaviest of the three, and he was alarmed by the thought that they would probably blame him for that also. Such a weapon, used like a club, might easily crack a man's skull. Yes, they would be down on him all right, no question about it.

He suddenly looked up at Cobbett and asked, "Why are you doing this?" He hoped Cobbett would admit his real reason, so they would know what his game was.

But Cobbett did not oblige him. "There's no jail in this town that will hold anyone. So from now on when you put them up to something like this, you're going to have to give them a little lump on the head. It's going to be that way from now on, if you keep following me around. I don't know why I didn't think of it sooner. I've got a feeling it's going to get harder and harder for you to find anyone stupid enough to do your dirty work for you. Before you tap those boys on the head, you might like to tell them what happened to some of the people you got to do your dirty work back in Miles City."

Archie Beebe did not want to do that. Some of those boys had become permanent residents of Miles City, for the simple reason that they had been buried in the graveyard there.

He understood what Cobbett was up to. The longer he waited about hitting these men on the head, the more they would learn that he did not want them to know. The marshal had neatly trapped him; now he had no choice but to lay these men out cold and make them good and mad at him.

He drew in a deep breath that sounded like a sob and stepped up behind Chuck Moser, who was looking around at him in silent alarm, somewhat resembling a huge insect of some kind that was too scared or too stupid to move. But when the heavy gun rose and chopped down at his head, Moser instinctively tried to duck and the gun only struck him a glancing blow on the side of the head. That however was enough to make him lose his balance and as he fell his head hit the edge of the bar and he sprawled unconscious on the floor.

Dill Stringer, leaning forward with his hands braced on the bar, looked down at the unconscious man with an expression of vague worry in his eyes, but he did not say anything.

"Now Stringer," Cobbett said to Beebe.

Beebe laid Stringer out beside Chuck Moser. Then the little man looked worriedly at Barney Nash, who had his huge head turned watching him with a look in his slitted eyes that Beebe did not like.

Beebe started to back away and as he did so, Barney Nash gave an angry grunt, shoved himself away from the bar and whirling lashed out with his big fist and caught Archie Beebe squarely between the eyes, knocking him out cold. Beebe collapsed on the floor near the two men he had laid out with the gun barrel, and Barney Nash turned his mean little eyes toward Cobbett.

Cobbett was smiling a very cold smile. His glance traveled across the room to the worried face of Ned Ribble, rested there a moment and then traveled back across the room and stopped on Duffy Shaw's angry bulldog face. "You've got a choice," he said. "You can take Beebe's place with the gun, or you can take Nash's place against the bar. Which will it be?"

The saloonkeeper's mouth fell open and he exclaimed angrily,

"You call that a choice?"

Cobbett shrugged. "It's the only one you've got."

Duffy Shaw looked at Barney Nash, and Barney Nash looked back at him.

"You try hittin' me with a gun, Duffy, and I'll lay you out too," Barney said. "My head's still sore where Cobbett hit me the other day with is gun."

Duffy Shaw looked at Cobbett. "You wouldn't try anything like this if Joe Deegan was here," he said.

"You starting that too?" Cobbett asked in annoyance. "You boys don't seem to understand. Joe Deegan doesn't give a damn about any of you. If he was here he'd laugh. He'd enjoy watching it."

Duffy Shaw uncomfortably rubbed his jutting chin as he thought about that. Seeing him, Barney Nash's hand went to his own chin. Both were silent, not liking the thought of tangling with each other, for they were both tough strong men. Shaw, though getting on in years, was still in good condition, and the veteran of many barroom brawls in which he had participated. He had frequently doubled as bouncer in his own saloons.

"What happens if we just refuse to do it?" Shaw asked.

"Then I lay you both out."

They did not much like that thought either.

"What if I said we wouldn't do no more shootin' while you're marshal here?" Barney Nash asked.

"I wouldn't believe you."

Barney Nash took off his little derby and rubbed his head where it was still sore from the clout Cobbett had given him with his gun. His eyes narrowed and glinted with hatred. "What if I said I'd kill you if you hit me again with yore gun?" he asked.

Cobbett shook his head. "I wouldn't believe that either. Better men have tried."

Barney Nash thought about that for a minute. He put his little derby back on, completing the incongruous effect of his gaudy attire. "What did you mean when you said maybe Beebe should tell us what happened to them fellers who helped him in Miles City?"

"Several of them are dead. He didn't want to tell you that. The reason should be obvious even to a knucklehead like you."

The big man's face reddened in anger as he looked down at the unconscious Beebe. "The little bastard!" he said, and suddenly gave Beebe a good kick in the ribs.

"Why not save it till he wakes up," Cobbett suggested. "It will hurt more then."

"I didn't think of that," Nash said. "If you won't knock me out, I'll knock him out again when he wakes up."

Cobbett glanced at the unconscious Beebe and smiled. "It's a deal."

CHAPTER 17

Ben Cobbett once more headed for the hotel, where he ate a leisurely meal. There were several townspeople in the dining room and they watched him anxiously, merely picking at their food, tensed for the eruption of more gunfire, an unsettling racket that the marshal seemed to bring with him when he came to the hotel to eat. They resented him for bringing this new affliction down upon them, ruining their meals. But this time the town was strangely quiet and they watched him with puzzled eyes while he ate, seemingly relaxed and in no hurry, his hard face expressionless as usual. But inside he was smiling. He felt better than he had felt in days.

Yet he knew this was not the end of it. Archie Beebe would be more corroded with hate now than ever, and more determined to get even with Cobbett. The same could be said of Barney Nash and Dill Stringer, both hardened, dangerous men. Chuck Moser would do whatever the others wanted to do, for he was that type. Ned Ribble— Cobbett did not yet know about Ribble.

The elderly white-haired waitress was going around with the heavy coffeepot, refilling everyone's cup, smiling and quietly friendly. She had the grace and charm of a lady, and her face had a glow that made her beautiful in spite of her years. She was happy because she liked everyone and everyone liked her, including Cobbett, who was nevertheless puzzled by her obvious fondness for people who seemed in no way likable—old Snively for example, that absurd irascible little man with his blinking suspicious eyes and twitching mustache. She was conciliatory and even apologetic when old Snively was rude and snappish and if he said anything halfway pleasant her face lit up like a candle, with a soft warm glow. It was beyond Cobbett's comprehension, completely foreign to his own nature and experience. He would have either ignored the old man or put him in his place with a few blunt words, job or no job.

When she came to refill his cup, her hand rested lightly on his arm for a moment to get his attention and when he looked up at her she smiled and said softly, "Anytime you need any more clothes washed, just bring them. It's not a bit of trouble."

Then she moved away and Cobbett sniffed uneasily. Sure enough, he could smell the stale sweaty odor of his clothes and his own unwashed carcass. He had not changed his clothes now in four or five days and before that they had gathered dust on the shelf for he did not know how long. For a surprised moment he sat there with a look of wry amusement on his hard face. Was that sweet old lady trying to tell him something?

Leaving the hotel, Cobbett picked up a change of clothes at the jail and then crossed the street to the barbershop.

Hank Gilbert was just finishing a sandwich. He usually ate his meals in the barbershop in order to save money, business being slow. "Decided to take a chance?" he asked, smiling.

"I don't think there's any danger for a while," Cobbett said, as he sank into the barber's chair.

Gilbert laughed quietly. "I don't think so either. I saw that little guy hanging around the mouth of one of those alleys, but he didn't seem to be watching for you or anything. Maybe they threw him out of the saloon or he snuck out to be by himself. Looked to me like he was crying."

"Uh-oh," Cobbett said. "That's a bad sign. The last time he was seen crying he borrowed some money and hired a man to kill me."

The barber looked carefully at Cobbett's poker face to see if he was joking. "No fooling?"

"No fooling."

"What happened?"

"The man was a bad shot. Beebe couldn't borrow enough money to hire a good one."

"I see," Gilbert said softly. "You want me to leave the mustache?"

"Uh-huh."

"I got plenty of hot water if you need a bath."

"Everyone seems to think I do," Cobbett said dryly.

"I noticed you brought a change of clothes."

While he was in the barber's chair, Cobbett saw Joe Deegan leave the hotel and walk down the street to Duffy Shaw's saloon. Deegan was wearing a black broadcloth suit, a white shirt and a black string tie, all bought in Snively's store. He did not look toward the barbershop although, with little doubt, he had seen Cobbett enter the barbershop from the window of Julie Tiding's room.

In the saloon, Deegan ordered a drink and did not immediately respond to Barney Nash's angry bellow: "It's about time you showed up! We got a herd to move!"

"Them cows should have been moved yesterday," Deegan said, after sipping his drink for a moment. "The water in them holes is prob'ly gone my now. If we all leave town, Cobbett will figger that's where we're headed, to pick up those cows. But if two of you go and the rest of us stay here, he won't think much about it. Ned and Chuck can handle them cows all right anyhow. You and Dill stay here and raise a little hell to keep Cobbett's attention on you and if he asks where Chuck and Ned are, tell him they went back to the shack."

"Where you gonna be?" Nash asked.

"I'll be around."

"I reckon I know where you'll be," Nash growled. "I can't blame you much either. But I'm beginnin' to wonder if we can count on you for anything or not. I never thought you'd let Cobbett pull the kind of stuff he's been tryin' to pull around here."

Joe Deegan's eyebrows lifted slightly and there was a cold deadly look in his eyes. But his voice remained soft and quiet. "Don't worry about Cobbett. Just let him think he's got us all buffaloed, including me. It will be a lot more fun to kill him when the time comes."

Deegan remained in the saloon only a few minutes and then walked back up the street to the hotel while Cobbett was still seated in the barber's chair getting the stubble scraped from his face. Again Deegan, passing by on the other side of the street, avoided looking toward the barbershop or the marshal's office. He was neither smiling nor frowning now; his face was as expressionless as the face of the man watching him through the window of the barbershop.

Later Cobbett, feeling refreshed after soaking in Gilbert's tub and putting on clean clothes, strolled down the street smoking a thin cigar. He went past Duffy Shaw's saloon, went on to the livery stable at the end of the street to check on the horses Mac McCabe had provided for his use.

Mort Crumby emerged from the stable as Cobbett stepped up to the corral. "I hope you're proud of yourself," the old man said in a bitter trembling voice, holding his bearded chin. "Barney Nash saw me give you that fifty dollars in the saloon and later he come down here and wanted to borrow the rest of it. I knew if I didn't let him have it he'd take it and maybe beat me up besides. But he won't ever pay me back. That money's just gone, every cent I had in the world."

"How much did he get?" Cobbett asked.

"Nearly five hundred dollars!"

"I thought you said you didn't have much?"

"What did you expect me to say around that scum?" Crumby asked.

"You want to file a complaint?"

"What good would that do? Even if you made him give the money back, he'd come after it again the minute you leave town and he'd make me wish I'd never said anything. From what I hear, you ain't gonna be here long, is that right?"

"Could be," Cobbett said. "Well, you shouldn't feel too bad about it. You stole if from McCabe."

"What do you mean I stole it from McCabe?" the old hostler asked resentfully.

"You know what I mean. He's losing money on this stable while you get fat. You rent out horses or sell them and tell him the horses were stolen or the money went for expenses. If there was a jail here that would hold anyone, I'd put you in it."

"You mean you'd lock me up and let Barney Nash go free?"

"No, I'd put him in there with you and let you and him fight it out. It's the best way to handle thieves who fall out."

"I ain't no thief," Crumby said in a complaining tone. "Mac give me that money for the stable."

"Like hell. You drank that up a long time ago."

"I don't drank much," Crumby whined, rubbing his mouth with his left hand, the other instinctively going to the flask he kept in his back pocket.

Cobbett grunted and turned his attention to the horses in the corral. One of them, a sorrel, caught his eye. It was the shade of sorrel, almost brown, that westerners usually called a chestnut sorrel. The other three horses Cal Heffer had brought, two bays and a line-back dun, were all fine looking animals. But Cobbett had become partial to sorrels because he had owned a very good one for several years—the one Barney Nash and his friends had killed just to annoy him and to show him they could do it and get away with it. Every time he thought about that, Cobbett was gripped by a sudden cold rage that it took him a few moments to bring under control.

He turned and walked past the old hostler who, seeing the frosty look in his gray eyes, instinctively retreated into the stable. Cobbett barely noticed him. He walked back up the street with his eyes straight ahead.

Archie Beebe had posted himself at the mouth of the alley beside Duffy Shaw's saloon, to wait there for Cobbett and demand his guns back—this time Cobbett had kept his pearl-handled .45, a gun Archie Beebe loved better than his own mother. The gun was thrust in the marshal's waistband for the whole town to see, like a gesture of contempt, a deliberate insult. The sight made Archie Beebe tremble. He had rehearsed a little speech, muttering the words with his hand over his mouth, in case anyone was watching him. But with the other hand he made angry gestures, giving himself away. What right did the marshal have to turn his friends against him like that and take his guns? What had he ever done to deserve such treatment? Hadn't he always been very careful not to break any laws that anyone could lock him up for?

Cobbett was almost abreast him now and Beebe was getting set to scream the words at him in anger. But the look in Cobbett's eyes frightened him and he backed away, as Mort Crumby had done. He backed into the alley, tripped on something and fell, then scrambled to his feet and ran down the alley, looking back, his heart pounding with frantic fear that Cobbett would give chase. But Cobbett, after scaring him half to death, went on up the street as if unaware of his existence. That, to Beebe, was the ultimate insult, the final blow to his pride.

This, he told himself as he ran off down the alley, sobbing now in his bitter shame and frustration, was the last straw. Cobbett had made him look ridiculous once too often and this time he would have to pay for it, just as soon as Beebe could get his hands on another gun and catch the tall marshal off guard for a moment. It no longer mattered what happened to Beebe afterwards—Cobbett had to die.

But even as he was thinking it did not matter, Archie Beebe saw himself sobbing brokenly, throwing himself upon the mercy of the court, pleading temporary insanity like that fellow had done over in England, and maybe getting off with a very light sentence at worst. If a man was clever enough he could make the laws work to his own advantage. Sometimes it even seemed that laws had been created as a refuge for criminals, to protect them from rougher, quicker forms of justice.

And that suited Archie Beebe to a T. Just the thought of it turned his bitter sobbing into hysterical glee. He would put a bullet in Cobbett, ride like hell to New Hope and turn himself in. That fat sheriff over there would undoubtedly be pleased to hear that he had killed Cobbett, a man who had insulted him in public. The sheriff would say a few words to the circuit judge on Beebe's behalf and Beebe would be a free man in no time. Archie did not know why he had not thought of it sooner.

A little before dark, Cobbett got the sorrel from the livery stable and rode out of town heading west along the stage road. Since no one believed that he was leaving town for good, it was assumed that he was just going for a ride, perhaps trying out one of the horses Cal Heffer had brought.

Only minutes later, Chuck Moser and Ned Ribble got their own horses from the stable and headed south along the river road, Moser chuckling at their good luck. But Ned Ribble was worried—more about Joe Deegan than about Cobbett. He kept remembering the way Deegan had looked at him in the saloon. Just a casual look that might have meant nothing at all—and that was just what worried Ribble, for that was not the way Joe Deegan normally looked at you. He either smiled at you or his cold blue eyes narrowed in a frown.

He knows, Ribble thought. He knows George and Dave were my half-brothers. It was even possible that one of them had told Deegan before they fell out over Molly Hicks, although neither of them had ever mentioned it to Ned if they knew about it. They must have known; everyone else back home had known about it. Ned had looked so much like their father that it had been something of a local joke, and Joe Deegan had certainly not overlooked his resemblance to the two brothers or the fact that they had come west at the same time.

Ribble did not know why he had not stuck with George and Dave when they had split with Deegan and the others. Perhaps he had been afraid to do so, afraid Joe Deegan would kill him too. There had never been much doubt in his mind that Deegan would kill George and

Dave. The only surprise had been that it had not happened sooner.

If Deegan believed that Ned intended to avenge the two dead men somehow, then Ned Ribble was as good as dead already. Deegan would find some excuse to force him into a fight, or just shoot him down without any warning whatever, as had been the case when Deegan had killed Roper Hicks.

Ribble suddenly broke out in a cold sweat, thinking, My God, he knows I know about that. I'd almost forgot. That and this other too— my goose is cooked.

It was almost full dark when the rider suddenly appeared from nowhere, halting his horse in the road before them, blocking their way. Ribble's first wild thought was that it was Joe Deegan and that Deegan meant to kill him here and now. But then he realized that it was the tall marshal. Cobbett had outsmarted them. He had figured that if he left town, some of them would head for the stolen herd, and instead of continuing west he had circled around to head them off.

Ned Ribble was so relieved that it was not Joe Deegan that he almost smiled. But Chuck Moser did an unexpected thing. He wheeled his horse and spurred back toward town, at the same time jerking out his gun and throwing a wild shot back at the marshal. An instant later Cobbett's own gun roared and Chuck Moser swayed in the saddle but grabbed the horn and galloped on up the road.

Cobbett rode forward holstering his gun and said, "I want you to take me to those cows, Ribble. And then I want you to get out of the country—for your own good."

Ribble had the odd feeling that Cobbett had read his mind, and if the marshal had detected his growing dissatisfaction and uneasiness, others must have noticed it as well. He turned in the saddle and looked back toward Rockville, then asked, "You think they'll come after us?"

"I hope not, for their sake," Cobbett said in a quiet but ringing tone which suggested that he was about at the end of his patience and his restraint.

Ned Ribble drew a deep breath. "All right," he said heavily. "I'll show you where them cows are, but there's something I want to do first. Something I should have done a long time ago."

"What's that?" Cobbett asked, sounding a little suspicious.

"Go by the Hicks shack and tell Molly who killed her husband," Ribble said. "It's time she knew the truth." A moment later he added, "It was Joe Deegan, but I figger by now he's got her believing it was

George and Dave Pasco, so she won't blame him for killing them."

Chuck Moser galloped his horse all the way back to Rockville, his bloody right shoulder stiff against the throbbing pain, his right arm tight against his side. He brought the horse to a skidding halt in a cloud of dust at the rack before Duffy Shaw's saloon and, dropping the reins and grabbing the horn with his left hand, he swung to the ground. A sharper pain stabbed through his shoulder when his boots hit the ground and a whimper escaped through his clenched teeth. Not bothering to tie his mount, he wedged the swing doors open with his good shoulder and staggered to the bar, gasping, "Gimme a drink, Duffy. I'm bleedin' to death."

Barney Nash and Dill Stringer stood further down the bar, sharing a bottle. They gaped at Moser in surprise. He had lost his hat and his gun and his jacket was covered with blood on the right side.

"What happened?" Nash roared, for he was in a mean, dangerous mood.

"Somebody shot me," Moser gasped, reaching for the glass with his trembling left hand. "I think it was Cobbett."

Barney Nash's narrow eyes glinted with hatred at the mention of Cobbett's name. "Where's Ribble?" he asked.

"I don't know," Chuck Moser groaned, his lips pulling back from his teeth in pain as Duffy Shaw, without a word, sloshed whiskey from the bottle onto his wounded shoulder. It was like sloshing coal oil on a fire; the pain blazed up in Chuck's shoulder. With his left hand he jerked the bottle out of Duffy's hand to keep him from doing that again, and then refilled his already empty glass, spilling some of the whiskey. He started to drink directly from the bottle, but the scowling saloonkeeper grabbed the bottle away from him.

"What do you mean you don't know?" Barney Nash asked. "You was with him."

"I lit out after Cobbett shot me," Moser said, using the left sleeve of his coat to wipe off some of the whiskey he had spilled down his chin. "Why ain't there no doc in this town? A man gets hurt around here, he's in bad trouble."

"He'll make Ned take him to where them cows are," Dill Stringer said suddenly.

Barney Nash's mouth fell open in alarm and he snarled, "Go tell Joe Deegan to get hisself down here."

Dill Stringer finished his drink at a gulp and wiped his mouth with his hand as he headed for the swing doors. Chuck Moser staggered over to a table and slumped in a chair, holding his hurt shoulder and groaning as he rocked back and forth. Barney Nash and Duffy Shaw silently ignored him as they waited for Joe Deegan. But when Dill Stringer returned, he was alone.

"Where the hell's Deegan?" Nash cried.

Stringer shook his head. "He wouldn't come."

"What do you mean he wouldn't come?"

Stringer walked slowly to the bar and poured himself a drink from the nearly empty bottle before answering. "He was in her room, but he come out in the hall and said for us just to act like nothing had happened. He said if McCabe gets his cows back, we can steal them again when they start driving them to the railroad."

"I hadn't thought of that," Nash said, scowling at his ugly, heavy face in the back-bar mirror. "But I still don't like it. Cobbett's got away with too much stuff since he come here. And that barber Hank Gilbert—he's been eggin' him on and even tryin' to help him, the sawed-off little runt." Nash stood thinking darkly about that for a moment, his bloodshot eyes narrowed in a frown. Then he finished his drink and said, "Come on, let's go teach that little bastard a lesson."

The barbershop was still open but there was no one in it except for Hank Gilbert himself. He was relaxed in the barber's chair, reading an old newspaper. He glanced up in surprise when he saw Nash and Stringer come in, and a look of worry came into his dark eyes when he noticed the wooden expression on Stringer's face and the gleam of hatred in Nash's eyes.

He started to get up out of the barber's chair but Nash, with a bearlike sweep of his heavy arm, knocked him back down in it and pinned him there while Stringer turned to pull the blinds. Then they both went to work on him and the small barber, trapped in his chair, had little chance to defend himself. He was a strong little man and fought desperately and silently, though he knew this was the end for him. They had not come here just to maim him, they fully intended to kill him. That was apparent from the numbing brutality of Nash's blows and the attempt of Dill Stringer, standing behind the chair with a hand in his hair, to pull his head against the chair back until his neck broke. Finally Stringer lifted him up in the chair until he could bend his head back over the top of the chair back, and Nash, seeing his chance, put all his brutal strength into one mighty swing of his huge fist at the barber's exposed chin. There was a sickening snap of bone breaking in Hank Gilbert's throat and that was the last sound he ever heard. The last thing he could make out in the suddenly fading light was a bearlike figure looming over him. The bearlike figure was Barney Nash.

Nash, seeing that the barber was dead, stepped back and rubbed his sore knuckles. "Let's get out of here," he said.

Dill Stringer had noticed the gold watch chain across the front of the barber's vest and he took time to get the watch and chain before he followed Nash out of the barbershop.

Ben Cobbett would have preferred to ride on past the Hicks shack, which he saw was dark. But Ned Ribble turned his horse off the rutted road into the yard, and Cobbett did not try to stop him. What happened next took him completely by surprise.

From the dark window of the shack a shotgun roared and the charge of buckshot blasted Ned Ribble out of his saddle.

Cobbett sensed, rather than saw, the twin muzzles of the shotgun shift toward him, and he instinctively jerked out his long-barreled .45 and thumbed a quick shot at the window. Even as the gun bucked in his fist, Cobbett heard his bullet shatter a pane of glass and the man cried out and fell back from the window with a crashing thud.

CHAPTER 18

An instant after the heavy body of the man crashed to the floor, Cobbett bent low in the saddle and galloped his horse straight at the shack. While the horse was still in motion, swerving toward the corner of the shack, Cobbett leapt to the ground and kicked the door open. He plunged into the dark room swinging the barrel of his gun in a savage arc, but there seemed to be no one within the reach of his arm.

Then he heard someone struggling over in the corner and making muffled exclamations. As his eyes adjusted to the darkness he saw the woman sitting in the corner with her hands and feet tied and a gag in her mouth. Closer by, in front of the broken window, lay the still body of the man who had blown Ned Ribble off his horse.

Cobbett turned suddenly and went back out into the cold windy night, ignoring the muffled protests of the woman. He walked quickly to where Ribble lay on the hard ground and knelt beside the chunky rustler. Ribble was still conscious, but just barely.

In what must have seemed a harsh and callous tone, Cobbett asked, "The cows, Ribble? Where are they?"

The dying man tried to lift his head and said weakly, "Box canyon ... Dead Man Gulch." That was all. His head fell back to the ground and he was dead.

Cobbett stood up and went back into the shack. He made sure the man on the floor was dead and only then holstered his gun and turned his attention to the woman. He struck a match, saw a kerosene lamp and lit it, then untied the woman and removed the gag from her mouth.

"You sure took your time," she said, rubbing her swollen ankles and then her wrists.

Cobbett did not answer. He was staring at the dead man, surprised to see that it was Tobe Langley.

"That bastard's been here for three days and nights waiting for Joe Deegan," Molly Hicks said bitterly. "Where is he anyway?"

"In town when I left," Cobbett said, still staring at the dead Langley. His tight lips twisted in bitterness at the realization that he had come close to getting killed by a man who was laying for Joe Deegan, and because of Deegan he himself had killed a man he had no wish to kill. The baby-faced killer would be tickled pink about this.

"Is it true what that bastard said?" Molly Hicks asked, her voice shaking with anger.

"I don't know which bastard you mean or what he said."

Molly Hicks was silent for a moment, her face flooded with shame and bitterness, biting her lips, blinking back tears. "He said Joe was in town with some woman. Julie Tidings. He said Joe stayed with her when he went to Salt Lake, and her husband paid him some money to kill Joe because of it."

Cobbett turned and watched the woman in silence for a moment, his jaw hard with anger. "I thought it was fairly common knowledge by now," he grunted.

"Then it's true," she said bitterly. "I knew better than to trust that bastard."

"If he was laying for Deegan, why did he kill Ned Ribble?" Cobbett asked. "Those two don't look much alike even in the dark."

"He figgered it was some of Joe's friends and he was afraid they'd try to kill him or tell Joe he was here." Then she looked curiously at Cobbett. "What are you doing riding with Ned Ribble?"

"He was taking me to where they hid those cows," Cobbett said. "He wanted to stop by here and tell you it was Joe Deegan who killed your husband."

Her eyes widened in surprise. "I don't believe you!"

Cobbett shrugged. "I didn't figure you would. I didn't figure you'd believe Ribble either. He got himself killed for nothing."

"Joe told me is was George Pasco," Molly Hicks said, as if trying to believe it.

Cobbett glanced at her in silence, and then changed the subject. "You have any idea where your father is?"

She shook her head, looking away. "He hardly ever comes here."

"I've got to find him," Cobbett said. "Unless you want to show me where they hid those cows."

"Me!" Molly Hicks exclaimed. "I don't know where those cows are. I ain't seen Joe or any of the others since the night ..."

She broke off and Cobbett finished for her, "The night they stole those cows." After a moment he added, "I can see why you don't want to do it. Joe Deegan might not like it."

"If I knew where those cows are," she said, "I'd tell you. But I don't know where they took them this time."

"Do you know where Dead Man Gulch is?"

She shook her head, her glance shifting away from his, and he had the feeling she was lying when she said, "No, I've never been there." She might be mad at Deegan at the moment, but when the chips were down she would not betray him to a stranger with a tin star pinned to his vest.

Cobbett sighed and walked to the door. There he paused and turned, watching her with hard eyes. "If Nash and Stringer come by here, tell them I've developed a personal interest in those cows and I'd be mighty disappointed if they tried to get them back."

"Wait a minute," Molly Hicks said. "You ain't going to leave *him* here, are you?" She nodded at the dead Tobe Langley.

"If I have time I'll come back later and bury him," Cobbett said. "But I want to find McCabe first."

"Wait a minute," Molly Hicks said again, getting unsteadily to her feet. "I'm going to tell Joe Deegan what you said about him killing my husband. I'm going to get the truth out of him if I can. I've always sort of wondered if he did it, but I didn't want to believe it was him. But whether it's true or not he's going to be mad about you telling me, so you better keep out of his way. He's killed men for less than that."

"I know," Cobbett said. "That's why I told you."

He went on out, found his horse and rode on south. He had not gone far when he saw Mac McCabe and his men coming up the road at a gallop.

"We heard shootin'," McCabe cried. "Sounded like it come from Molly's place. Everything all right up there?"

"It is now," Cobbett said. "But Ned Ribble and Tobe Langley need burying."

"Cobbett?" the rancher said in surprise, peering at the tall marshal. "What you doin' out here?"

"I was trying to find you," Cobbett said. "Ribble said those cows were in a box canyon near Dead Man Gulch, as best I could make it out."

"I'll be danged! So the varmint talked before he died, did he? Dead Man Gulch! Now why didn't we think of that? That box canyon off Dead Man is a perfect place for them cows. They used it before, I think. You sure my daughter's all right?"

"She seemed to be. You might look in on her when you get a chance."

"Well, I shore am obliged to you, Cobbett," the huge rancher said, with a catch in his voice. "Anything I can do for you, just let me know."

"There is one thing you could do," Cobbett said.

"What's that?"

"Send someone to New Hope in a day or two to pick up your horse."

"But the horse is yours!" McCabe said. "All four of them if you want them."

Cobbett would have gladly bought the sorrel, but he knew McCabe would not accept any money for it. So he said, "I was thinking about taking the stage from New Hope to the railroad and then go by train."

"I was hoping you'd stay a while," McCabe said, regret plain in his voice.

"I sort of thought about it a time or two," Cobbett said, not quite truthfully. "But the people of Rockville have decided they don't want me for their marshal."

"Don't that beat all," McCabe said. "Them fools don't know when they're well off."

"Well, I better get back to town," Cobbett said. "I'm a little out of my jurisdiction."

McCabe cackled. "Yeah, that's what I thought." Then he sobered. "Well, if Molly's all right, I guess me and the boys better go get them cows, before them varmints try to beat us to them."

"Don't let them get away from you this time," Cobbett told him, reining the sorrel around.

"We don't aim to," McCabe told him. "I'm obliged to you, Cobbett, for everything. And I'd feel a lot better if you'd just keep that sorrel.

I had a feelin' you'd like him, any man would. And if you don't take him, them rascals is just sure to steal him before long."

Cobbett hesitated. "I can't take him as a gift, but I might buy him from you, if the price is right."

"How does five dollars sound?"

Cobbett started to shake his head and say it was much too cheap. But he saw that the old rancher was holding himself tense, hoping Cobbett would accept the offer. It meant a lot to McCabe; he wanted Cobbett to have the horse.

"That sounds about right," Cobbett decided.

On his way back to town, Cobbett remembered that he had promised Molly Hicks to come back and bury the dead men. He would have preferred to ride on by her shack without stopping. The less he saw of her, the easier it would be to forget her. But he was a man who kept his promises when humanly possible, and did what had to be done. Seeing to the burial of Langley and Ribble was his responsibility and he would not shirk it.

It would not have surprised him to find her already gone or on the point of leaving for town to have things out with Joe Deegan. But lamplight still glowed through the broken window of the shack and she came to the door when she heard his horse turn off the road into the yard.

She raised her hands to comb her long red hair back with her fingers and he saw the outline of her deep breasts silhouetted in the lamplight. "Did you find Mac?" she asked.

Cobbett nodded in the dark as he stepped down from his creaking saddle. "I met them not far down the road. They heard the shots and were coming to see if you were all right."

Molly Hicks thought about that for a moment as she continued to run her fingers through her hair. When she spoke again it seemed to Cobbett that her voice sounded softer and more womanly somehow. "Have they gone after the cows?"

"Yes," he said, glancing about the yard. "Have you got a pick or a shovel?"

"Around behind the house, leaning against the wall."

He went around to the rear of the shack to get the pick and shovel, then with Molly's help, carried Langley's body outside.

"I didn't think to ask you," he said. "Is it all right to bury them here?"

She shrugged. "I don't guess it matters. But let's get them out of the yard and over in the edge of the brush so I won't see the graves every time I come outside."

She helped him carry the two dead men out of the yard, but then she went back inside and he did not see her again until he had finished burying the two dead men and carried the pick and shovel around to the back of the shack. Returning to the front yard, he got back in the saddle and only then did she open the door.

"Are you going back to town now?" she asked.

"Yes."

"I thought about riding in with you," she said, "but I don't guess it would do any good. That bastard expects me to wait here until he takes a notion to ride out and see me. But when I need him he's shacked up with another woman." Then she asked, "Do you think Ned Ribble told the truth about him killing my husband?"

"I don't think he just made it up. He was too scared of Deegan to make up a lie like that about him."

"That bastard," Molly Hicks said quietly and bitterly. "He killed my husband just to get him out of the way, so I'd be here by myself when he took a notion to ride by. But I'm just as much to blame as he is. I think I've known all along that he did it just so he could see me more often. I just wouldn't admit it to myself." Then she looked at Cobbett and said, "I guess you think I'm pretty awful."

He shrugged. "It doesn't matter what I think. What you think is what you've got to live with."

Molly Hicks stood there in the doorway, indifferent to the cold wind, and seemed to be listening to his words even after he had quit speaking. After nearly half a minute she said, "If you see Joe Deegan, tell him not to bother coming here again. It won't do him any good." Then she stepped back inside and closed the door.

Cobbett rode on toward Rockville, a little saddened by the thought that he might never see her again. He had only seen her two or three times and she did not really mean anything to him. It was just that she was a beautiful, desirable woman and he was a lonely man, conscious of getting older and running out of opportunities.

When he got back to Rockville, the town seemed too quiet. He had the feeling that everyone was indoors and not making a sound because they were expecting trouble. Mort Crumby remained out of sight in the dark hayloft and Cobbett took care of the horse himself. Minutes later, as he went up the deserted street past Duffy Shaw's saloon, the silence seemed to throb in his ears. Going on, he saw that a light still burned in the barbershop, but the blinds were drawn. That struck him as odd, and his eyes narrowed in puzzlement. He could not remember seeing the barber's blinds drawn day or night. But he supposed that Gilbert had become uneasy because he knew that his public support of Cobbett made Cobbett's enemies want to destroy him too.

Cobbett turned toward the marshal's office and stepped up to the door. Then he suddenly froze with his hand raised to push open the door. The door was open a few inches. Of course, the wind might have blown it open. But Cobbett had a strong feeling that someone was in the office waiting with a cocked gun for him to open the door. Probably Beebe. Cobbett suddenly remembered that he had left Beebe's guns, still loaded, in the top drawer of the desk.

He stepped aside and put his back against the wall to the left of the door, looking across the street at the barbershop. He fished for a cigar and put it in his mouth, but did not light it. "Beebe," he said, "if you're in there you better come out before I get mad."

There was no sound from the dark office. Just then a gust of wind blew dust along the street and the door of the barbershop creaked open. He expected to see Hank Gilbert come out and call to him, either to warn him that Beebe was in the office or to tell him he wasn't, which now seemed likely. But Gilbert did not appear at the door of the barbershop. Cobbett saw him sitting in the barber's chair as if asleep, except that his head hung over to one side at an unnatural angle.

Cobbett forgot all about Archie Beebe. He dropped the unlighted cigar and crossed the street in long strides, stepped in through the open door of the barbershop and saw that Hank Gilbert's eyes were open and sightless in death. His neck had been broken and his face was a bloody pulp, battered almost beyond recognition.

Cobbett drew in a deep breath and turned on his heel, leaving the barbershop. He went down the street in long strides, heading for Duffy Shaw's saloon. As he went in through the swing doors he loosened his gun in the holster.

Dill Stringer stood at the bar, Duffy Shaw behind it. Barney Nash was over at the free lunch table fixing himself a thick sandwich. There was no one else in the saloon.

Barney Nash turned, his little eyes widening in alarm at sight of Cobbett. Dill Stringer looked at him, but showed no particular expression.

Cobbett's cold eyes stabbed at the scowling saloonkeeper. "I guess they've been here all night."

The saloonkeeper's scowl deepened. "That's right."

Cobbett did not bother to reply. His attention had returned to Barney Nash and Dill Stringer. He suddenly noticed the gold watch chain dangling from Stringer's coat. He saw the little clasp knife on the chain, and knew the chain and the watch in Stringer's pocket had been taken from Hank Gilbert, perhaps after the barber was dead.

Dill Stringer saw Cobbett looking at the watch chain, he saw the icy glitter of hatred in Cobbett's gray eyes, and knowing he had nothing to lose, he suddenly went for his gun.

Cobbett whipped out his own gun and fired before Stringer's gun ever left the holster. His bullet spun Stringer half around and Stringer hung on the bar for a moment before sliding down it to the floor, dying as he fell.

Barney Nash was still turned sideways, his heavy chin almost resting on his shoulder as he watched Cobbett with a look of fear and hatred mingled in his narrow eyes. His hand had gone inside his green coat to grip the butt of the double-action Colt stuck in his waistband, but his hand froze there and his eyes froze on the smoking gun in Cobbett's hand. Cobbett had cocked the gun again immediately after firing at Stringer and the muzzle now gaped at Barney Nash. Yet the gun itself did not frighten Nash as much as the deadly look in Cobbett's eyes.

Cobbett drew in a deep breath and his whole body seemed to expand with hatred, with a cold rage. All the bones in his rugged face seemed to stand out against the leathery skin. "Nash," he said, "you've lived too long." And he took up the slack on the trigger, the gun exploding in his fist.

Barney Nash's heavy dark face turned strangely pale, then congested with red as his heart started pumping wildly to keep him alive. For a moment he stood hunched over with the thick sandwich crushed in his huge fist, staring at Cobbett in disbelief. Then he suddenly crashed to the floor, taking the free lunch counter down with him.

There was a look of disbelief on Duffy Shaw's bulldog face also. His beady eyes, widened in alarm, darted from the dead men to the gun in Cobbett's hand. He seemed afraid that Cobbett would turn the gun on him.

And for a moment Cobbett seemed tempted to do just that. Then he deliberately holstered his gun and said, "It looks like you're going to need some new customers."

Duffy Shaw again glanced at the two dead men. It looked that way to him too. Tap Grodin, Barney Nash and Dill Stringer were all dead, and although he did not yet know that Ned Ribble was dead, he doubted if Ribble would be back. Chuck Moser had headed for New Hope to find a doctor and probably would not come back either, even if he did not bleed to death on the way. That left only Joe Deegan of the old bunch, and Archie Beebe had stayed out of the saloon after being knocked down by Nash.

Duffy Shaw knew he was finished in Rockville, but he had no intention of admitting that to the man who had ruined him. Instead he repeated something he had said before, "I'll still be here when you're gone."

"Don't count on it," Cobbett told him. "No one will be afraid of you without that crowd to back you up. My guess is the people of this town will run you out before you attract any more flies, and if they don't, Mac McCabe will."

The saloonkeeper shrugged. He knew this was not the time to argue. He also knew that Cobbett was right.

Cobbett left the saloon and went along the windy, deserted street to the marshal's office, his bleak eyes on the barbershop. Hank Gilbert was dead because he had wanted to make the town safe for decent, law-abiding people, and because he had been willing to stand up for what he believed in. He was the only one in the town who had supported Cobbett and he was dead because of it. In killing the men who had murdered him, Cobbett had done what he felt he had to do, for he had known that nothing would be done about them unless he did it himself.

Yet he knew that in taking the law into his own hands he had forfeited his right to wear a badge, and he would never wear one again. Once inside the dark office he unpinned the badge and put it in the top drawer of the desk. It was then that he discovered Archie Beebe's guns were gone. He had almost forgotten about Beebe, and that sort of carelessness might cost him his life. For he knew Beebe had not forgotten about him, nor abandoned his plans for revenge.

CHAPTER 19

Cobbett slept for a few hours on the lumpy mattress in the room behind the marshal's office. He was awakened by a pounding on the front door. He opened his eyes and blinked at the daylight coming through the back window. He had overslept. Sitting up he ran a hand through his pale hair, knuckled the dregs of sleep from his red-rimmed gray eyes, put on his hat and pulled on his boots and belted on his gun as he got to his feet. Going through the marshal's office, he opened the front door and found Joe Deegan in his new black suit, wearing his ivory-handled gun and staring back at Cobbett through icy blue eyes.

"You went too far last night," Deegan said in a soft deadly tone. "Now I got to round up another outfit and I ain't in the mood."

Cobbett's eyes went past Deegan to the barbershop across the street, where a small group of townsmen had gathered, talking quietly. Someone had "discovered" the body of Hank Gilbert. Cobbett felt certain the townspeople had known about Gilbert's brutal murder even before he himself had, but they had been afraid to leave their houses while it was still dark. That was why he had not bothered to inform anyone about it last night, and he had been too tired to dig another grave himself. In any case, the townspeople could give Gilbert the sort of funeral he deserved, and they would want to pay their respects, once they found the courage. Everyone had liked the friendly little barber.

Cobbett's cold glance returned to Joe Deegan's handsome baby face. "You won't need another outfit," he said. "You're finished in this town."

"We'll see about that," Joe Deegan replied. "You're the one who's finished. They've already give you your walking papers. Everyone's just waiting for you to leave so things can go on like before. They liked it better the way it was before you came here, and it will be that way again after you leave. Except you ain't leaving."

"No?"

Deegan shook his head. "I've got a little trip to make, but I won't be gone long. Don't run off before I get back."

"If you're thinking about riding out to the Hicks place, don't waste your time," Cobbett said deliberately. "Molly Hicks asked me to tell you not to come back."

"So you told her about me and Julie Tidings," Deegan said in a soft, bitter tone. "I never figgered you for a gossip." Then his blue eyes got even colder, if that was possible. "What were you doing out there anyway?"

"Looking for rustlers," Cobbett said dryly. "I understand they hang out around there a lot. Or did."

"Rustling ain't no concern of yours," Deegan snapped. "I already told you that."

"You also told me I couldn't do anything about it," Cobbett grunted.

"You can't. Not legally."

Cobbett sighed. "Since when are you concerned about what's legal?"

"I ain't," Deegan said. "But I figgered you were."

"Not anymore. I unpinned that badge last night. I won't need it for you."

"You'll need a lot more than a badge to hide behind," Deegan told him.

"We can settle that right now," Cobbett said. "There's no point in putting it off."

But Deegan turned away. He was not ready yet. "I'm going to ride out and talk to Molly first. You better try to enjoy yourself while I'm gone, because if you're still here when I get back, I'll kill you."

"I'll be here."

Deegan only nodded and went down the street toward the livery stable to get his horse. Cobbett noticed that he did not stop at Duffy Shaw's saloon for a drink, which would not have surprised the ex-marshal. But apparently Deegan did not feel the need of anything to steady his nerves.

Archie Beebe crept out of the narrow alley beside the marshal's office, where he had been hiding and listening. His little red face was twisted in a malicious grin that did not entirely hide his bitter hatred for Cobbett. "I was beginning to think I was going to have to kill you myself," he said. "But now it looks like I won't have to. You don't stand a chance against Joe Deegan. He's faster than anyone I ever saw. He's even faster than Whiskey was."

"Whiskey's dead," Cobbett pointed out, his eyes still following Joe Deegan down the street. "If he was so fast, why did he try to dry-gulch me?"

"Whiskey didn't believe in taking chances," Archie Beebe said with pride. "He was that much like me."

Cobbett glanced at the little man with withering contempt in his eyes, not bothering to reply. The look in his eyes expressed his opinion of Archie Beebe better than words ever could.

Beebe's face reddened with resentment when he saw that look. "I went in there last night and got my guns," he said, his weak voice trembling in fear and anger. "They're mine and you didn't have no right to keep them."

"I was just trying to save your life, Beebe. Those guns will just get you killed."

"Hah!" Beebe said. "It ain't me you're worried about. It's yourself."

Cobbett did not answer. He had noticed three townsmen, among them old Sheb Snively, coming across the street from the barbershop. When Beebe saw them he turned and crept back down the alley.

Snively had appointed himself spokesman for the trio. He wiped his damp blinking eyes. His little mustache twitched in his grief and outrage. But Cobbett had seen him almost as upset over an underdone steak, and he stared back at him now without any sympathy.

"Hank Gilbert they beat him to death last night," Snively said in his curiously accented voice. He waved his arms excitedly. "It's got to stop! Something must be done about those bad men!"

"Something's already been done about them," Cobbett grunted. "They're all dead except Joe Deegan."

"Yes, but he is still alive!" Snively exclaimed, again waving his arms. "And we heard what he said to you about getting a new gang together!"

"You've got mighty good ears for an old man," Cobbett observed.

Snively impatiently waved that aside. He had no time for small talk. "It will be just like before! He will get a new gang together and they will run this town just like they owned it! Just like it was before! Hank Gilbert was right! Too late we see it, but he was right all along! We want you to stay on here as our marshal, and we will pay you for it as much as we can. How much will you take, your bottom offer?"

"Sorry," Cobbett said, cool and distant. "I'm not interested. I've got other plans."

One of the other townsmen spoke up, a man whose name Cobbett still did not know, although he had seen him several times before, usually at a distance. "Is it because you want more than we can pay you," the man asked, "or because you're afraid of Joe Deegan?"

Cobbett looked at the man with cold eyes and deliberately lit a cigar before answering. It was in his mind that none of these men, nor anyone else in Rockville, had seen fit to invite him into their homes. To them he was just a rough, violent man who made his living with a gun, not much better than those he kept in line. To them he was at best a necessary evil, and they wanted as little personal contact with him as possible. They were here now only because a greater evil threatened, one they did not know how to cope with themselves. A job too rough and dirty for their soft clean hands.

"You're wasting your time," Cobbett said with sudden impatience. "I'll be leaving sometime today. You'll find that badge in the top drawer of the desk, when you find someone else to pin it on."

He stepped back into the office without giving them time to reply and shut the door in their faces.

As they headed back across the street, he heard old Snively say in a tone of disgust and outrage, "He's scared of Joe Deegan like everyone else! He'll sneak out of town while he's gone, the way Tobe Langley did! That's why Deegan left! He knew Cobbett would jump at the chance to get away!"

Cobbett himself suspected that Deegan had ridden out of town to avoid the risk of an awkward meeting with Julie Tiding's husband, who was due on the morning stage from the east. It was even possible that Julie Tidings herself had persuaded him to leave town for a while. It would look better if her lover was not around when her husband arrived.

Cobbett unhurriedly packed his saddlebags and rolled his blankets, then waited in the marshal's office, sitting in the chair behind the desk, smoking a cigar, while the town watched the front of the marshal's office and wondered why he did not leave.

Around ten the stage went by the marshal's office and stopped in front of the hotel just up the street. A short time later Lot Tidings opened the door of the marshal's office and came in, closing the door behind him. He looked at Cobbett uncertainly out of his pale bleak eyes. His stiff gray hat and new Prince Albert were flecked with the dust of travel.

"I just heard the news," he said quietly, something like amazement coming into his eyes. "It sounds like you've been busy. But now there's talk you plan to leave town, with Joe Deegan still alive. I don't know if I mentioned it or not, but he's the most important one. There wasn't much point in killing the others, unless you get him too. He'll just form a new gang and go on stealing stock and doing what he's always done. I understand he's already talking about it."

Cobbett continued to smoke his cigar in silence, his gray eyes colder than before. But whether it was because he was thinking about Joe Deegan, or Lot Tidings, the latter could not tell.

"I talked to the governor," Tidings added, rubbing his mouth with his left hand and watching Cobbett carefully with his bleak eyes. "He's a cautious man and he didn't want to put anything in writing. But he assured me privately that you have nothing to worry about. In the unlikely event you're ever brought to trial for anything that happens here, you can count on a full pardon as soon as it can be arranged."

Cobbett felt his face heating with anger. He felt certain that Tidings had not even seen the governor. After he killed Joe Deegan, Tidings would not care what happened to him.

"You didn't go to Salt Lake to see the governor," he said flatly. "You went there to find out if your wife saw Joe Deegan while she was there. And you want Deegan killed for the same reason, not because he's been stealing cows."

Tidings looked embarrassed. Not angry or offended, just embarrassed and a little sheepish. "You can't really blame me for not bringing my wife into something like this, can you?" he asked reasonably.

"She's already in it."

Tidings sighed, nodded sadly. "My wife, I'm afraid, is no lady. She got involved with a married man when she was only sixteen. I knew about it, but I married her anyway and brought her out here, thinking that would be the end of it. Now she's started seeing Joe Deegan. I'm not sure just how long it's been going on. For quite a while, I guess. But I intend to put a stop to it. If you won't do it, then I'll have to find someone else. As a matter of fact, I had a feeling you might not want to do it, so I already made a little deal with someone else. But apparently he failed, because he didn't meet me here as planned, and Joe Deegan is still alive, it seems."

"If you're referring to Tobe Langley, he's dead all right. He killed the wrong man and tried to kill me too. He didn't know it was me and I shot back before I knew who he was."

A look bordering on distaste flickered across Tiding's face and was gone. "I had a feeling he'd botch the job, and maybe shoot off his mouth besides. Afterwards I regretted saying anything to him about it."

Cobbett did not say anything and Tidings looked at his watch. "I've got to hurry or the stage will leave without me. My offer still goes. Now you can understand why it means nothing to me to have the others dead, but I'll still pay five thousand dollars for Deegan."

Cobbett shook his head. "If I kill Joe Deegan, it won't be for money."

"You think about it," Tidings told him. "Think about all the things you can buy, all the things you can do, with five thousand dollars."

"I already thought about it," Cobbett said. "I don't want any of those things that bad."

"Well, if you change your mind, the offer still goes," Tidings said, already at the door. "And I don't care about your personal reasons for killing him. It will be enough for me to know he's dead, and I'll take your word for it. Just come to New Hope and pick up your money. You think about it."

Tidings went out then without waiting for Cobbett to reply. Cobbett saw him go past the window, turning up his collar against the cold wind. A few minutes later, still seated behind the desk, Cobbett heard the stage pull out for New Hope.

He sighed, thinking about Julie Tidings leaving on the stage, to all outward appearances a proper lady, and a very beautiful one at that.

He got to his feet, remembering that he had eaten no breakfast. He was not really hungry, but he had a long ride ahead of him before the next decent meal, and it never paid to begin a long journey on an empty stomach. You never knew what might come up. Leaving the marshal's office, he crossed the deserted street to the restaurant, where he found Jane Keller wringing her hands. She gazed at him in horror and disbelief.

"You must hurry!" she exclaimed. "He'll soon be back!"

"Who's that?" Cobbett asked idly, as he pulled back a chair and sat down.

"You know who! Joe Deegan! He'll kill you!"

"That shouldn't bother you too much," Cobbett said dryly. "He's killed men before."

"I know, but—this time I have a bad feeling!" she said, still wringing her work-roughened hands, a look of pleading and desperation in her freckled, careworn face. "Please go before he gets back! Maybe he isn't any good, and he don't care much about me. But I—I love him, a lot more than those others ever will! And I don't want anything else to happen!"

"Maybe there isn't anything to worry about," Cobbett said in a strangely casual, indifferent tone, glancing at the menu on the small blackboard. "Everyone seems to think he'll win."

"Then why don't you leave?" she asked in amazement.

"Habit, I guess," Cobbett said. "I always like to finish what I start. Could I get something to eat and some coffee? I wouldn't want to keep Deegan waiting, if he gets back before I finish."

As it turned out, Cobbett was just leaving the restaurant when he saw Deegan riding back into town on his fine black horse. Cobbett angled across the street and stopped in front of the marshal's office and stood there with his eyes slitted as if half asleep, dozing in the morning sun. Deegan, seeing him, got off the black horse and wrapped the reins around the nearest rail, then came on afoot, watching Cobbett with a look of murderous hatred in his icy blue eyes. Deegan had not liked what Molly Hicks had told him and it was obvious that he blamed Cobbett for spoiling his visit, among other things.

Halting in the street thirty feet away, the baby-faced killer said in the softest, deadliest tone of voice, "I said I'd kill you if you were still here. I guess you didn't believe me."

Cobbett moved his left shoulder in a brief shrug. "I figured you'd try."

A scornful smile twisted Joe Deegan's lips, and then his gun was suddenly in his hand. The townspeople, watching tensely from windows and doorways, all had their eyes riveted on Deegan, and yet they did not see him draw. There was only the suggestion of a blur, too swift for the eye to follow, and then they saw the gun in his hand and heard the explosion and only then did they look toward Cobbett, expecting to see him drop dead with a bullet through his heart. That was what invariably happened to men reckless enough to draw on

Joe Deegan.

But something was different this time and they blinked in puzzlement, unable to comprehend why Cobbett was still on his feet, with a smoking gun in his hand. A moment later, to their growing astonishment and disbelief, Joe Deegan fell slowly forward on his face, still clutching his unfired gun. The roar they had heard had come from Cobbett's gun, not Deegan's.

Cobbett stood motionless for a moment looking at Deegan's prone lifeless body. Then he holstered his gun, entered the marshal's office and came back out with his saddlebags, blanket roll and Winchester. Ignoring the awe-struck crowd already forming around the motionless body of Joe Deegan, he walked down the street to the livery stable and presently came back along the street on the rangy sorrel. He rode past the staring townspeople as if they were not there, but his bleak gray eyes paused briefly on Jane Keller, who stood at the door of the restaurant, trembling in the cold wind, a look of numbed horror on her plain face. He started to touch his hat, but she was not looking at him, she was looking at the worthless but charming young man he had killed.

So Cobbett rode on out of Rockville without saying goodbye to anyone, and a short time later Archie Beebe got his pinto from the stable and followed him. The others were all dead, but Archie Beebe had survived as usual. He could not die, he told himself, not while Ben Cobbett was still alive.

CHAPTER 20

Archie Beebe followed the tracks of Cobbett's horse all the way to New Hope, arriving there shortly after dark. He checked into the New Hope Hotel, signing his name in the register immediately below that of Ben Cobbett, making a mental note of Cobbett's room number which the clerk had written in after Cobbett's name.

Mr. and Mrs. Lot Tidings had also taken a room in the hotel, it seemed. Passing the door to the dining room, Archie Beebe had seen Mr. Lot Tidings dining alone. Presumably Mrs. Tidings had remained in their room. Pleading a headache, as likely as not, but probably just wanting to avoid the stares of other diners who would be eagerly awaiting the latest gossip about her. Archie Beebe had a plan that he thought might work, but he would have to be very careful or it might backfire on him.

He hurried upstairs with his thin blanket roll, hoping to see Julie Tidings alone before her husband returned from the dining room. He knocked on her door, quietly but insistently. After a moment she opened the door and stood there pale and shaken, as if expecting the worst. Her blond hair needed combing and her blue eyes were sort of red as if she had been crying.

Beebe swept off his hat and bowed low, raised back up and said, "Afraid I got some bad news for you, ma'am. I just rid all the way from Rockville to tell you. Joe Deegan was a close friend of mine and I know he'd want me to tell you."

Her hand clutched at her white throat. "Is he—?"

Archie Beebe bobbed his head, darted an uneasy look both ways along the hall. "I wonder if I could come in for a minute so we can talk more private, ma'am? There's something else I got to tell you and it's for your ears only. I'm afraid I'm running a big risk just to tell you."

She gave him a puzzled look, then stepped back from the door. "Yes, please do come in."

Beebe again glanced up and down the hall, then stepped into her room and closed the door softly behind him. For a moment he stood with his back to the door listening.

"What did you want to tell me?" Julie Tidings asked, watching him now with a trace of doubt in her eyes. She had regained her poise and her composure. Rising to the occasion like a true lady, Beebe thought cynically. Her lover might be dead, but her own life had to go on.

"I don't know if I should tell you or not, ma'am," Beebe said, awkwardly fumbling with his old hat, his cynicism hidden behind a show of meek respect.

"Tell me what?" she asked impatiently.

"Well, it's like this, ma'am. I heard your husband trying to hire Ben Cobbett to kill Joe, and not long after you left on the stage, he done just that. So you figger it out."

Julie Tidings swayed and grabbed the bedpost for support. For a moment she looked like she would faint. Then she got hold of herself and stood biting her lips bitterly, silently fighting back the tears.

"Was I you, ma'am," Archie Beebe said, watching her with a cunning half smile, "I just might take it into my head to hire someone to kill Ben Cobbett."

At that moment he heard someone go down the hall toward the head of the stairs, and his heart started pounding at the thought that it might be Cobbett.

In fact, it was Cobbett, and he heard Beebe suggesting to Julie Tidings that she hire someone to kill him.

Cobbett went on down the hall to the stairs and descended them, an idea forming in his own mind. Entering the dining room, he gave his order and attacked his food when it came, pretending not to see Lot Tidings across the room.

Tidings had finished his food and was sipping a second cup of coffee. After glancing about the nearly empty dining room for a few minutes, Tidings got up and brought his coffee cup over to Cobbett's table and sat down opposite him. "I didn't expect to see you so soon," Tidings said softly, studying Cobbett's long poker face. "Is Joe Deegan—?"

At Cobbett's not, Tidings began to smile, the first time Cobbett had seen him smile.

"I'm not sure your worries are over though," Cobbett added casually, his attention still on his steak and potatoes. "One of Deegan's friends seems inclined to take his place. That Archie Beebe fellow."

"That little runt!" Tidings exclaimed.

Cobbett nodded. "He's up there with her now."

"You're kidding!" Tidings said in a tone of disbelief.

Cobbett shrugged. "Go see for yourself."

"I think I might just do that," Tidings said and started to rise from his chair. "This has gone far enough! Here in the hotel, right under my nose!"

"That sort of thing happens all the time, from what I hear," Cobbett said.

"Well, it's not going to happen to me all the time," Tidings said. Then he bent closer to Cobbett and lowered his voice, almost whispering, "Take care of that little bastard for me and I'll add another thousand to the five I already promised you for Deegan."

Cobbett shook his head. He was thinking that since Tidings had tried to trick him into doing his dirty work for him, he might as well do the same thing to Tidings.

"I keep telling you I never did that to Deegan for money," he said. "I had my own reasons. And I don't intend to take care of Archie Beebe for you. If you want him killed, you'll have to do it yourself. No one would blame you for doing it, but if I did it, it would be simple cold-blooded murder and they'd hang me."

Tidings watched him for a moment in bleak disappointment. Then his pale greenish eyes suddenly blinked. "Say that again."

Cobbett looked at him curiously. "I said they'd likely hang me if I did it."

"No, I don't mean that," Tidings said. He again bent closer and said softly, "You know a lot about the law, Cobbett. What do you think would happen if I went up there right now and shot that little bastard while he's in the room with her?"

"In this country? Your fat friend the sheriff probably wouldn't even arrest you." Cobbett glanced about the dining room. "Where is he anyway?"

"Out of town on some business or other," Tidings said, his mind on something else. He suddenly got to his feet. "Excuse me."

Cobbett watched the older man leave the room and head for the stairs. A few minutes later he heard a shot on the second floor. That, he thought, takes care of Archie Beebe.

Thank you for reading
A Few Dead Men
by Van Holt.

We hope you enjoyed this story. If so, please leave a review about
your experience on Amazon so others may discover Van Holt.

You may also enjoy another story about some famous gunfighters
called *The Antrim Guns*

Excerpt from
Six-Gun Serenade
by Van Holt

Jed Baker reined in when the roan gelding pricked his ears toward the
clump of brush and trees a hundred yards away. Outwardly relaxed, Baker
slowly rolled and lit a cigarette while his gray eyes studied the brush from
under the brim of his battered hat. His clothes were worn and dusty but
the walnut-butted Colt .44 in the tied-down holster looked as if it had just
come from the factory. Its mate was tucked in his waistband under his coat.
Baker kept his hands well away from both guns.

As he shook the match out, a calm strong voice called, "Come on in, Jed.
It's all right." And a tall man in a black hat and coat emerged from the brush
on a sleek black horse and halted to wait for him.

Recognizing the picturesque figure, Baker rode forward and returned
the other's nod.

Bill Hicken showed strong white teeth in a smile, idly twisting the corner of his tawny mustache. "Hello, Jed. Didn't recognize you at first. Reckon
my eyes ain't as sharp as they were. I ain't seen you since Lawrence. What
have you been doing all these years?"

"Drifting, mostly."

Without seeing to Hicken's pale blue eyes took in Baker's travel-stained
clothes and scuffed boots. The new guns did not escape his notice. Hicken
himself still wore the pair of double-action Starrs he had carried during the
war, but they had been converted to use .44 centerfire cartridges and he
wore them now in polished black holsters thonged to his legs.

As the result of his skill with those guns and his willingness to demonstrate it when necessary, Bill Hicken had become a famous man in the seven years since the war. He had killed five men in one bloody shootout in which Hicken had nearly lost his life, having received several bullet wounds. There had been several other well-publicized fights. Jed Baker, while shunning notoriety himself, had often heard about the blond gunfighter whom he had ridden with during the early years of the war.

They rod on along the trail side by side, Hicken remarking casually that there was a town not far ahead.

"I don't blame you for pulling out after Lawrence," he added. "That was a bad business. I left Quantrill's band not long after that myself. I was so disgusted I switched sides as a matter of fact. Did some spying for the Union."

"So I heard."

Hicken shrugged his broad shoulders. "Not many people know I rode with Quantrill. I imagine you've kept pretty quiet about riding with him yourself."

"I've never bragged about it," Baker admitted.

"You ever run into any of the old bunch?" Hicken asked curiously.

Baker shook his head. "But I've never been back to Missouri. Or Kansas either. Not east Kansas anyway."

"Those boys are scattered everywhere, the ones who're still alive," Hicken said. "Some went to Texas, some to California and the mining camps of Montana and Idaho, and some became outlaws. I guess you know I killed George Fry when I was marshal of Abilene?"

"Yes, I heard about it."

"Blackie Fry has sworn to kill me. By himself he don't worry me. But if it comes to a fight Zeke Mayall and the Leeker boys will help him."

"There's only five of them," Baker said. "Maybe you'll get lucky again, the way you did when you shot it out with the Midkiff bunch." His lips were twisted in a wry smile. He had never really believed that story.

"I hope I don't get that lucky again anytime soon," Hicken said. "I nearly died from the lead they put in me, and some of it is still in me. That old sawbones never did find it all, or else he was afraid to go in after it."

Baker's bleak gray eyes studied the barren rocky hills ahead. He rubbed the chestnut stubble on his jaw and asked, "You got any idea where Blackie Fry and his pals are now?"

Hicken shook his head. "I heard they were looking for me. But they must not be looking very hard. I'm not hard to find."

The name of the town ahead was Westbrook. A short time later Jed Baker and Bill Hicken rode down its one dusty street, lined with frame shacks and adobe huts. It was midafternoon and the street was almost deserted. They left their horses at the only livery stable and checked into the only hotel.

Baker did not see Hicken again until that evening when he entered the Ace High Saloon. The blond gunfighter was having a drink at the Barney Antrim and asked Baker to join him. Hicken was wearing a new white shirt under his black frock coat, and new pearl-gray trousers. His hair had been trimmed, his strong bronzed face shaved clean except for the mustache, and his black boots had been shined.

Baker had also bathed and shaved and was wearing a second-hand brown corduroy suit that he had bought for a dollar and a gray wool shirt that he had bought for a quarter.

Hicken nodded toward a back door. "I've been invited to sit in at a private poker game. You care to join us?"

"No, I guess not."

"Well, maybe I'll see you later. How long you plan to be in Westbrook?"

"I'll be leaving in the morning."

Hicken thoughtfully twisted his tawny mustache. "This game may last most of the night. If I don't see you again before you leave, maybe I'll run into you again before too long."

"I hope so."

Hicken nodded and went toward the back room, touching his hatbrim to a very pretty dark-haired girl who appeared to be no more than eighteen. She smiled at him and then turned Herman Spink bold eyes to Jed Baker.

After a moment she came over to stand beside him and said, "Hello, handsome. Like to buy me a drink?

Baker had only a few dollars left in his pocket, but he shrugged and said, "Why not."

The girl turned to the bartender. "The usual, Sam Mullen." Then she again regarded Baker with her clear greenish eyes. Perhaps they were blue-green. In the dim light it was hard to tell, and Baker, though not as indifferent to her beauty as he appeared, managed not to stare at her.

Her face was smooth and rather small, her lips thin but lovely, her teeth white and even. Her slender girlish figure was set off by some very womanly curves. She seemed very sure of herself, and relaxed and happy. But her smile was becoming a little strained and she seemed to resent Baker's quiet reserve.

She drank a little of the clear liquid that the bartender had put in her glass. Baker felt sure it was water. But that was all right with him. He had seen many saloon girls her age or even younger drinking beer and whiskey and it always saddened him.

"I'm Molly," she said.

"Baker."

"Is that all, just Baker?"

"Jed Baker."

She again regarded him with her clear, bold eyes. "You seem to know Bill Hicken. He's a very famous man. How is it I never heard of you?"

"Because I'm not famous, I guess."

"That makes sense," she agreed. "Where did you know Bill Hicken?"

"In Missouri and Kansas, a long time ago."

"What brinks you and Bill to New Mexico?"

"I'm just passing through. I couldn't say about Hicken."

Baker suspected that the girl was merely making conversation because it was part of her job to be friendly with customers. When four dusty cowhands came in she smiled brightly at them and left Baker without a word, going to greet the cowhands whom she apparently knew. When Baker left the saloon a few minutes later, she was sitting at a table with the cowhands and did not even glance up as Baker went past on his way out. But one of the cowhands stared at him with hostile dark eyes.

Baker was thoughtful as he walked back to the hotel. He had a feeling that he had seen the dark-eyed cowhand before somewhere, but could not place him.

He went up to his room and stretched out on the bed in the dark without taking off his clothes. He was tired from riding but not sleepy. Staring up into the darkness, he saw the girl's smooth white face and shapely figure. It had been a long time since he had seen a girl who had affected him as she had. There was something about her, something wild and reckless behind her quiet composure... and perhaps her figure had something to do with it.

But there was no point in thinking about her. He would be gone tomorrow morning and would probably never see her again.

Later, as he was getting sleepy, he suddenly remembered where he had seen the lean dark cowhand before, or rather his picture. It had been on a wanted poster tacked to a tree in Colorado. His name was Paul Curtin and he was wanted for murder and horse stealing. He had shot a man in a fight over a saloon girl and on leaving had grabbed the first horse he came to for a quick escape.

Baker heard footsteps outside his door and then a knock. He tensed and then relaxed when Bill Hicken's quiet voice said, "It's me, Jed. Can I see you a minute?"

Baker got up from the bed, struck a match to light the lamp, then opened the door. Hicken came in, blinking his pale blue eyes at the light. Then he grinned at Baker. He seemed slightly intoxicated.

"Those cowpunchers followed me out of the saloon, Jed. The dark handsome one said tell you to stay away from his girl. I think he wanted to tell me the same thing, but he was a mite careful what he said because of my reputation. If he only knew. You're probably better with a gun than I am. You used to be, anyway."

"He hasn't got anything to worry about. His girl asked me to buy her a drink because that's her job, and then she forgot all about me when he came in. And I'm leaving in the morning."

"If you leave they'll think it's because you're scared."

Baker shrugged. "That doesn't bother me."

Hicken thoughtfully twisted his mustache. "That dark one—I've got a feeling I've seen his face somewhere before."

"I had the same feeling, and a few minutes ago I remembered where it was. It was on a wanted poster in Colorado. He shot a man in a fight over another girl, or maybe it was the same one for all I know."

"That's Molly's quite a looker, ain't she?" Hicken said, his eyes a little dreamy. "But Mac Curry sees red if anyone even glances at her."

"Is that the name he's using? It was Paul Curtin on that wanted poster."

"It's Mac Curry now. He and those other three work on a ranch near here. But I was told in confidence that they're suspected of rustling and horse stealing. You better watch out for them, Jed. Sounds like a bad bunch. They probably won't bother me, but they haven't heard of you and may try to pick a fight with you."

"They'd better do it tonight," Baker said. "I'll be leaving about sunup."

The preceding was from the western novel
Six-Gun Serenade

To keep reading, click or go here:
http://amzn.to/164cS7t

Excerpt from
The Gundown Trail
by Van Holt

The brown and empty plains rolled on and on to a far horizon where the faded earth touched a faded sky. About all a man could see was distance.

And that was about all Ben Hite wanted to see.

He had not always been like that. Once he had been young and foolish and his head had been filled with hopeless dreams. But all that, he hoped, was behind him.

He was still young in years—not quite thirty—but old in experience. Not that he had ever done much that was worth remembering, and most of the people he had known were better forgotten. A very few of them had been his friends, once. They were more easily forgotten than his enemies. Most of them.

Now he rode alone, with the bleak eyes of a man who had come to prefer loneliness but knew he could not avoid others forever. He needed supplies, he longed for a bath and a shave, fresh clothes, his horse needed a rest. He would have to stop in the next town. Towns meant people, and people meant trouble. Wherever a few of them gathered together, there was sure to be friction and strife that too often led to violence and bloodshed.

That was a strange thing about people. They could not get along without one another, and they certainly could not get along with one another. The older Ben Hite got, the more it puzzled him. He could no more understand their persistent and often tragic tendency to flock together than they could understand his aloofness.

He searched the plains with a trace of worry in his gray eyes, and meanwhile searched his memory. This was not his first trip through Texas, but Texas was a big place, and he was not familiar with this part of it. If the plains looked familiar, it was because he had become used to their monotony.

Far off to the southwest there was a smudge on the horizon, a huddle of buildings. Not large enough for a town. A ranch, or perhaps a stage stop. Hite would have preferred a town, for in a town he was more likely to find what he needed, and less likely to intrude on anyone's privacy or disturb anyone's peace of mind.

He seemed to have a talent for disturbing people, though it was the last thing he wanted to do. They sensed in him something wild and lonely and deadly, though it was well hidden behind a hard weathered face that made him look older than his years. Even before they noticed the tied-down gun, they knew he had killed men, and would kill more if he had to.

But there was a lot they did not know, a lot they would never know. The past was not something he cared to talk about.

It was late fall, and the sun felt good on his back. By the time he reached the place, the sun had moved around to shine in his face, but his eyes were hidden in the shadow of his hatbrim. As he dismounted and tied his roan gelding to the hitchrail, he glanced at a sorrel that he judged had been standing there for some time. The sorrel returned Hite's interest.

The sign above the door said COODER'S. He had heard about the place. It was a stage stop, store and saloon, all in one large room, with two small sleeping rooms and the owner's private quarters at the back. The other buildings Hite had seen were a couple of sheds, and there was a pole corral.

Inside he found, instead of the usual long plank table to be found at stage stations, several small tables, and sitting at one of them was a strikingly beautiful young woman with a lot of blond hair and large blue eyes.

It had been a long time since Hite had shown more than a passing interest in any woman, but he could not help staring at this one. It was a moment before he noticed the man sitting with her—a man a few years younger than Hite, with a handsome face set off by heavy sideburns, a carefully trimmed mustache, and arrogant dark eyes that glared at Hite with resentment and scorn. He had seen Hite looking at the woman and did not like it.

An older man with large haunted eyes stood uneasily behind the plank bar near the door. Hite turned that way.

"Beer," he said. "And I need a sack of grub. Here's a list." He laid it on the bar as the old man set a glass of foaming beer before him. He had planned to eat here, but now decided against it. The handsome fellow with the dark sideburns had all the earmarks of trouble.

The old man, whom Hite took to be Cooder, glanced silently at the list, then left the bar and headed for the store counter on the other side of the large room and closer to the rear.

Hite guessed that the woman was waiting for the next stage. She wore a brown traveling dress tailored to set off her slender, full-breasted figure to best advantage. She was still in her early twenties, and her face was smooth and flawless, but in some way she seemed a lot older than that. Her sky-blue eyes were clouded with unpleasant thoughts, and her lips were twisted with scorn and resentment, as if mirroring the young man's expression.

Hite had the sudden notion that he had seen her somewhere before, or someone who looked a lot like her, and he took a closer look at her.

"What you starin' at, mister?" the young man asked.

"Not at you," Hite replied, and turned his attention back to Cooder as the old man returned and put the gunnysack of grub on the bar. Hite laid a gold piece on the bar and pocketed his change, then prepared to finish his beer, handling the tall mug with his left hand.

"Maybe he's seen me somewhere before," the young woman said in a sardonic tone, and Hite shot her a quick glance.

"This lady's sittin' here with me, mister," the young man said. "And I'm tired of you starin' at her."

"If I offended the lady," Hite said, "I apologize."

"I don't like your looks, mister," the young man said.

Hite felt cold inside. He could have turned and walked out, and there was a good chance that the young man would not have shot him in the back. Not in front of Cooder and the girl. But Ben Hite could not turn his back on trouble, although he had turned his back on almost everything else.

"I don't like horse thieves," he said and saw the young man stiffen without looking directly at him. The girl seemed more amused than surprised, but she was now sitting back in her chair, watching Hite with interest.

"You callin' me a horse thief, mister?" the young man asked.

"No," Hite said. "I'm just saying that sorrel out there was stolen from me about a month ago."

"You're lyin'! I bought that horse!"

"I'm sure you've got a bill of sale?"

"I've got one all right," the young man said. "But I ain't showin' it to you. I ain't showin' you nothin'."

"Then I guess I'm calling you a horse thief," Hite said.

Many known horse thieves could not stand to be called one. The young man's face flooded with rage and he jumped to his feet, knocking his chair over as he grabbed for his gun.

Hite turned and drew in one movement, swinging his long-barreled Colt .44 around. The gun bucked and roared in his fist.

The young man fell back over his chair, his boots shooting into the air as he crashed to the floor, a bullet through his heart.

The young woman shoved back in her chair and got to her feet, moving away from the table. But she still seemed more amused than frightened. She had seen men shot before. Violence was no stranger to her. Hite had her placed now.

"I saw your picture once," he said. "Or a painting."

She sighed, her lips twisting in a weary smile. "You and everybody else," she said. "Someday I'm going to burn that saloon down, or hire someone to do it. But I don't guess it would do any good. That painting's the first thing Pete would grab."

"Can't say I blame him," Hite said, holstering his gun and reaching for the grub sack. He nodded at the dead man. "He a friend of yours?"

"No, but that didn't stop him," she said. "It usually doesn't stop his kind. I was sitting here minding my own business and he came in and sat down. There for a minute I was afraid he'd seen that painting too, but I guess not. If he had, I'm sure he would have told me about it. He told me everything else." She gave Hite a long thoughtful glance. "Mister, I don't know if you're aware of it or not, but you just killed Toby Musser, Barney Musser's kid brother."

"Then I killed the right man," Hite said, heading for the door. "I heard he was the one who stole my horse."

"They'll come after you," she said, "Barney Musser and his whole gang."

Barney Musser's gang—five or six tough violent men who did as they pleased and laughed at the law. Some said they stole from the rich and gave to the poor, but in reality they stole from almost everyone and wasted the money on whiskey, women and gambling.

As he stepped outside into the bright sunlight, Hite wished he had asked the girl if she knew where they were. But he did not want her to think he was too worried about them.

He tied the grub sack behind his saddle, then stripped the saddle from the sorrel and left it on the ground. As he rode away leading the sorrel he looked back and saw the blond-haired girl at the door watching him.

This was the first time Hite had showed any surprise, but it was unlikely that she saw it in the brief moment before he turned his attention ahead. Like most women of her kind, she had long since lost interest in men, and had not even tried to hide her bored indifference in Hite's presence. So he could think of no reason why she had come out unless it was to see which way he went, and the only reason for her to do that would be so she could tell someone. That someone, he suspected, was Barney Musser.

Had she lied, then, about knowing Toby Musser? But come to think about it she had not denied knowing him, had only denied being his friend. Perhaps she had known him, and perhaps she knew Barney and the others. If so, she would describe Hite to them.

As it turned out it did not matter. Fate had played tricks on Hite before and seemed about to play another.

He had left the stage road and headed out across the trackless prairie to avoid meeting anyone. But he had not gone a mile when five riders topped the rise ahead and came directly toward him. Somehow he knew who they were even before they got close enough for him to recognize them from wanted posters he had seen here and there. He did not change his even pace or his course except to angle a little to the right so he would pass them on that side, and he drew the sorrel up close on the off side of the roan, hoping they would not recognize the led horse.

He drew to a stop when they reined in before him. The obvious leader of the group looked like an older, stronger, tougher version of Toby Musser, minus the fancy mustache.

"Howdy," he said, flashing a toothy grin. "You just come from Cooder's?" When Hite silently nodded, he asked, "You see a handsome young feller on a sorrel about like the one you're leadin'?"

Before Hite could reply, one of the others—a big man with a tangled growth of whiskers—said, "Hell, Barney, that is Toby's sorrel."

Barney Musser's grin faded. His dark eyes glared at Hite with sudden suspicion and hatred. He reined his horse sideways to get a good look at the sleek rangy sorrel. Then he said, "Mister, that's my brother's horse!"

Hite shook his head, keeping a tight grip on the sorrel's reins with his right hand, but also keeping that hand close to his holstered gun. He remembered that he had not replaced the empty shell in the gun, which left only four loads in it. There was a Winchester carbine under his right leg, but by the time he got it out of the scabbard he would be dead.

"The horse is mine," he said, "and I've got a bill of sale to prove it."

"Never mind that," Barney Musser said angrily. "What about my brother?"

"You'll find him back at Cooder's."

Something in his tone brought a sharper glance from the outlaw leader. "What do you mean by that?"

"Your brother's dead," Hite answered quietly, watching them through bleak slitted eyes.

Barney Musser stiffened in the saddle as if he had been pierced through with a Comanche lance. A look of pain and grief and rage contorted his strong dark face.

"Kill the bastard," one of the others muttered, and Hite's narrowed eyes shifted just enough to see that it was Sim Gattey, a bony-faced man in his twenties, with a look of casual and callous arrogance about him.

The others stared at Hite in hard-eyed silence. Big shaggy-haired Rance Duffett, the one who had recognized the horse. Red-bearded, pale-eyes George Hogate. Wall-eyed Pink Mayhew.

With a sudden savage cry Barney Musser went for his gun, only to find himself staring into the muzzle of Hite's .44. None of them had seen him drop the sorrel's reins and draw the gun. Rance Duffett's eyes were wide with surprise. Barney Musser's face flooded with almost unbearable rage. For a long moment his hand gripped the butt of his half-drawn gun. Then with a bitter curse he shoved the gun back down in the holster. None of the others had attempted to draw, though their hands were near their guns.

"Your brother got what he deserved," Hite said. "He stole my horse and went for his gun when he couldn't bluff his was out of it."

Barney Musser's face twisted with grief and hatred. "You killed my brother over a damn horse," he said.

"They hang horse thieves in this country, and there's a good reason for it," Hite said. "But I killed your brother because he tried to kill me."

"You better kill me too, while you've got the chance," the outlaw said. "If you don't, we'll be comin' after you."

"I figured you would," Hite said in a bleak weary tone. "I reckon the Yarber boys and Tucker Looman will want to get in on the fun, when they find out about it. But you better tell them it won't be any fun. The next time I draw a gun I intend to use it."

"The Yarber boys are our cousins, Toby's and mine," Barney said. "But more like brothers than cousins. They all thought the world of Toby, and so did Tucker Looman. They've got them a little ranch now, but when they hear about this they wouldn't stay out of it if I asked them to."

"Well, I guess if they're old enough to kill, they're old enough to die," Hite said. "That goes for the rest of you. It can stop here, or you can come after me and some more of you will die. It's up to you." He pointed at Barney Musser with his left forefinger. "If I see anybody touch a gun when you boys ride off, I'll shoot you first."

A muscle twitched in the outlaw's jaw. Without replying he jerked his horse's head up and rode past Hite. The others hesitated for only a moment before following him.

"If you know any prayers," Rance Duffett said as he lifted the reins, "you better say 'em."

Hite did not reply. He turned in the saddle to watch them ride off. When they were out of pistol range he holstered the Colt and slid the Winchester out of the scabbard. George Hogate turned his pale green eyes to look back, and Sim Gattey turned his sly evil face also. But none of them reached for a gun.

Hite watched until they disappeared over the first rise. Then he put the roan into a lope across the bleached prairie grass, leading the sorrel.

The preceding was from the western novel
The Gundown Trail

To keep reading, click or go here:
http://amzn.to/1g1jDNs

More hellbound gunslinging westerns by Van Holt:

A Few Dead Men
Coming Soon

Blood in the Hills
http://amzn.to/16jWNvB

Curly Bill and Ringo
http://amzn.to/Z6AhSH

Dead Man's Trail
http://amzn.to/ZcPJ47

Death in Black Holsters
http://amzn.to/1aHxGcv

Dynamite Riders
http://amzn.to/ZyhHmg

Hellbound Express
http://amzn.to/11i3NcY

Hunt the Killers Down
http://amzn.to/Z7UHjD

Riding for Revenge
http://amzn.to/13gLILz

Rubeck's Raiders
http://amzn.to/14CDxwU

Shiloh Stark
http://amzn.to/12ZJxcV

Shoot to Kill
http://amzn.to/18zA1qm

Six-Gun Solution
http://amzn.to/10t3H3N

Six-Gun Serenade
http://amzn.to/13BoWCL

Son of a Gunfighter
http://amzn.to/17QAzSp

The Antrim Guns
http://amzn.to/132I7jr

The Bounty Hunters
http://amzn.to/10gJQ6C

The Bushwhackers
http://amzn.to/13ln4JO

The Fortune Hunters
http://amzn.to/11i3VsO

The Gundowners
(formerly So, Long Stranger)
http://amzn.to/16c0I2J

The Gundown Trail
http://amzn.to/1g1jDNs

The Last of the Fighting Farrells
http://amzn.to/Z6AyVI

The Long Trail
http://amzn.to/137P9c8

The Man Called Bowdry
http://amzn.to/14LjpJa

The Stranger From Hell
http://amzn.to/12qVVqd

The Vultures
http://amzn.to/12bjeGl

Wild Country
http://amzn.to/147xUDq

Wild Desert Rose
http://amzn.to/XH7Y27

Brought to you by Three Knolls Publishing
Independent Publishing in the Digital

Agewww.3knollspub.com

About the Author:

Van Holt wrote his first western when he was in high school and sent it to a literary agent, who soon returned it, saying it was too long but he would try to sell it if Holt would cut out 16,000 words. Young Holt couldn't bear to cut out any of his perfect western, so he threw it away and started writing another one.

A draft notice interrupted his plans to become the next Zane Grey or Louis L'Amour. A tour of duty as an MP stationed in South Korea was pretty much the usual MP stuff except for the time he nabbed a North Korean spy and had to talk the dimwitted desk sergeant out of letting the guy go. A briefcase stuffed with drawings of U.S. aircraft and the like only caused the overstuffed lifer behind the counter to rub his fat face, blink his bewildered eyes, and start eating a big candy bar to console himself. Imagine Van Holt's surprise a few days later when he heard that same dumb sergeant telling a group of new admirers how he himself had caught the famous spy one day when he was on his way to the mess hall.

Holt says there hasn't been too much excitement since he got out of the army, unless you count the time he was attacked by two mean young punks and shot one of them in the big toe. Holt believes what we need is punk control, not gun control.

After traveling all over the West and Southwest in an aging Pontiac, Van Holt got tired of traveling the day he rolled into Tucson and he has been there ever since, still dreaming of becoming the next Zane Grey or Louis L'Amour when he grows up. Or maybe the next great mystery writer. He likes to write mysteries when he's not too busy writing westerns or eating Twinkies.

CPSIA information can be obtained at www.ICGtesting.com
Printed in the USA
LVOW12s2215080114

368618LV00001B/378/P